Angel MINE

KAY MAREE

Table of Contents

Angel Mine

All rights reserved

Copyright © 2017 by Kay Maree

Cover Design © Designed With Grace -
http://www.designedwgrace.com/
Cover Images © Adobe Stock & Deposit Photos
Editing – Susan Horsnell & Word Writer Pro

Social Links

Facebook:

https://www.facebook.com/kay.maree.334

Twitter:

https://twitter.com/MisKay85

Goodreads:

https://www.goodreads.com/book/show/34528910-angel-mine?ac=1&from_search=true

Goodreads Author Page:

https://www.goodreads.com/user/show/65394903-kay-maree

About the Author

I live in Newcastle, on the New South Wales coast of Australia with my husband and three beautiful children.

Between being a taxi for my children, and working full-time, I somehow find the time to write. It's something I love with a passion and with the encouragement of my very supportive husband, I have accomplished one of my dreams – releasing my first novel.

I hope you fall in love with my characters as much as I have.

I love reading and getting lost in a good book when I manage to snatch five minutes to myself.

Kay Maree

Dedication

I dedicate this to all the wonderful people in my life - my husband and three beautiful children, Mum, Dad, my two sisters and my Mother-In-Law.

To my amazing husband, you have stuck with me through all my highs and lows, you have stood by me and encouraged me to keep moving forward no matter how hard, no matter the sleepless nights and I can never thank you enough.

To my three beautiful children, you guys are my world and I would move heaven and earth to make sure you know you can do anything, be anything you want xx

To my Mum and Dad, thank you for always supporting me, being proud of me no matter what I have chosen to do in life. You guys have shown me every day of my life what true love and strength really are. No matter the mistakes I have made, I wouldn't be the woman I am today without you guys xx

To my beautiful friends, Philippa, Tiffany and Silvia. Thank you, you girls put up with so much of my crazy, and take me for who I am no matter what, you girls have shown me what true friendship really means. Love you Girls xx

Susan, my beautiful friend and editor you took a chance on me and I can never thank you enough for everything you have done. You truly are a beautiful person inside and out with such a kind heart.

Prologue

"Mommy help ..... Ow!" Evie sobs and attempts to reach out to me.

"Darren! Please don't hurt her, I'll do anything you want. *Please,* don't hurt her" I beg him, hoping he is listening to me because all I can hear is Evie screaming in pain after being thrown to the floor while trying to help me.

"You *will* do what I say or I'll take her away and you will never see her again. DO. YOU. UNDERSTAND. ME? Darren growls and spit hits my face.

My stomach roils at the stench of alcohol on his breath. He yanks my head back twisting my hair, and I try not to cry out in pain.

I give a slight nod, the best I can with him wrenching my head back, hoping like hell I can get to her soon.

"And just remember, *I* own her….." Darren thrusts his arm toward Evie, then jerks my head back harder pulling a squeal from my mouth. "…..just like I own you, and I can do whatever the fuck I want."

"Yes, I know, I'm sorry. *Please* let me go to her, *please* Darren. She's hurt and needs help. *Please* let me go to her." I'm begging him, while trying to hold back my tears.

Darren suddenly releases me, shoving me to the floor like I'm no better than scum off his shoes. He nods his permission and watches me crawl over to Evie. She's laying on her side on the floor, sobbing her little heart out. I attempt to draw in a deep breath to calm my nerves, but it hurts, everything hurts.

I gather Evie in my arms cradling her to my chest while I check her over the best I can. Thank god she has no serious injuries but for a tiny bump on her head. As I cradle her into my chest, I rub small soothing circles over her back. The front door slams shut, the sudden loud noise causes me to flinch and hold Evie closer. I exhale with a groan and allow my tears to fall.

This needs to stop! I can't let this Monster keep doing this. I have to find a way to escape.

"Sweet pea everything is going to be ok. I promise, I'm going to protect you, if it's the last thing I do" I coo to Evie as I rock her back and forth. "Mommy will fix this." I murmur soft words into Evie's little ear to soothe her the best I can. "I love you baby girl and no matter what it takes I *will* save us both"

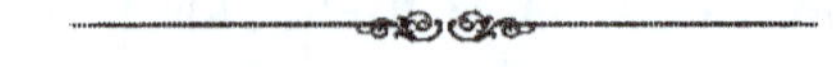

The following morning, Darren is up and gone before 8am. Now is my chance. I grab the mobile phone my best friend, Kat sent to me. It's a burner and can't be traced, she had been worried the last couple of times I had spoken to her. I made sure I kept it well hidden from Darren.

I send her a quick text letting her know we probably have about a two-hour window. Then, I grab the bags I stuffed under Evie's bed the previous night while Darren was out. I make a quick sweep with my eyes, making sure everything is in order before I run down the stairs to grab Evie. Just as we are making our way down the hallway toward the front door I hear keys rattling in the lock. I freeze, every nerve in my body going on alert. I squeeze Evie's hand a little bit harder. I feel the blood drain from my face, my heartbeat pulsates in my ears and all I can think is …… this is not going to end well.

With our bags in one hand, and holding Evie's hand in the other, I'm frozen in place. As panic and fear gallop through my veins. I attempt to slow my breathing, I'm terrified, knowing this time we may not make it out alive. My fight or flight instincts kicks in and I look toward the back of the house, wondering if we could make it in time.

The front door flies open before I have a chance to react. I can't breathe, I can't move. Then, I see Kat standing there and she's yelling at me to hurry up. I blow out the breath I didn't realize I was holding, and notice Evie does the same thing.

Kat's screech snaps me back to the present. "BROOKLYN!!!" It's enough to get me moving "Come on girl, we don't have much time, we need to leave right now!"

"You scared the crap out of me…" I rush through the door. "I thought… I thought it was Darren coming home."

"Oh shit, I forgot to tell you I had a key cut just in case I ever needed to get to you fast. Sorry, Dollface."

"I'm just so glad it was you."

"We really have to leave. Like now!!" Kate glances at her watch.

"Put Evie in her car seat, then let's get the hell out of this place."

One

Brooklyn

2 months later.....

I'm standing in my living room talking to Matt, a pharmaceutical rep like Darren. They travel around together, covering similar territory. I notice what started as a slight headache was morphing into a migraine. I excuse myself and head to the kitchen to grab some Aspirin before finding quiet to let the pain killer work before it was too late.

I quietly slipped upstairs to our room to lay down to allow the Aspirin to take effect. A few moments later Darren quietly slips into our room. He looks good tonight in his tux and gelled back hair.

Ok, maybe just a bit too much gel, but that's Darren. He always goes over the top with things like this party, it was supposed to be a small gathering but turned out to be triple the number of people I expected. Oh well, whatever makes him happy. My eyes finally lift to his face and I notice he's not smiling. His eyes are narrowed and fierce, I go on high alert immediately.

Did I forget to do something? I mentally do a check list, but before I can come up with something I may have forgotten, Darren whispers menacingly, "What do you think you are doing?"

My eyes widen, I don't understand his accusatory tone of voice. He's speaking like I was purposely doing something wrong. I open my mouth to try to explain "I was getting a headache and thought I should lay down..." Before I can finish what I'm saying, he is hovering over me like I'm his prey. He grabs me roughly, dragging me up by the hair. My hands go directly to my head to try and stop some of the pain radiating through my head as I feel my hair coming out by the roots

"Ow! Darren, you're hurting me please, stop!"

"You stupid Bitch." He smacks me across the face. Hard.

I am absolutely stunned. I don't know how I'll be able to calm him down. Normally, he would never behave this way while we had company. His usual modus operandi is to give me a shove or snarl nasty words, corner me to let me know punishment is coming when no one else is around.

"You think you can flirt with Matt and get away with it, you slut! I knew it was only a matter of time before I caught you trying to open your legs for someone else."

"Darren, I don't know what you're talking about I would never...."

"Shut your lying mouth." Darren hisses through clenched teeth as he hits me again across the face. *"Stop crying, your tears mean nothing to me."*

I attempt to pull myself together and try not to anger him further, but it's hard when he still has one hand tangled in my hair and the other holding me roughly by the chin. I can't move my head and his hold is painful.

"Why do you always find a way to ruin my plans? You always try and make everything about you. Do you know how fucking selfish and self-centred you are? Let me tell you once and for all, the world does not revolve around Brooklyn Mackenzie. How dare you try and take the focus off me and my party!" His face is close to mine and I smell the alcohol on his breath.

"Do you know how much trouble I have gone to for this night? I have been planning this for months and now you have ruined it. Always trying to make everything about you and what you need WELL, WHAT ABOUT ME AND WHAT I NEED HUH? EVER THINK OF THAT YOU STUPID BITCH!!" This time he doesn't hold back as he yells in my face.

"I'm sorry I didn't mean to....

Another slap cuts me off and he throws me back to the bed, he bends down and hisses through his teeth, "You don't fucking move do you understand me?"

I nod but don't say a word, too scared I may say the wrong thing and anger him further.

Darren turns and stomps to our bedroom door. Before he leaves he says over his shoulder, "You're going to show me how sorry you are when this party finishes and you're going to enjoy every minute of it, understand me?"

He doesn't give me a chance to reply before slamming our bedroom door. I roll over and hug my knees to my chest, bring my hand up to my burning face and cry into my pillow.

I wake with a gasp struggling to breathe, my heart thumps out a military tattoo against my ribs. I close my eyes and focus on steadying my breathing. I fight back the fresh images of when Darren first started hitting me. My nightmare was so vivid, so real, I feel like the abuse has just happened. After wiping beads of sweat from my face, I reach over with a shaking hand for the glass of water on the nightstand. The time on the clock flashes 6.35am. Taking a gulp of water, I feel the cool liquid running down my throat, easing my stomach. I may have escaped the *monster* but he still haunts my dreams.

I'm jolted from my thoughts by the sound of giggling drifting to me from downstairs, it brings a smile to my face. We're safe, it could have been a lot worse. *But, for how long?* A nagging voice in the back of my mind insists on knowing. I shake my head, not ready to think about possible danger right now. I rise from my bed and prepare for the day.

As I pad down the stairs heading toward the kitchen in my new home, running my hand along the wood carved banister, I take in my new surroundings and remember the first day Evie and I turned up at Kats. We had next to nothing, but for a couple of bags.

Kat has lived in Newcastle, on the New South Wales coast of Australia, going on six years now. She moved to the area after buying a small coffee shop.

When Evie and I first arrived, she introduced me to a lovely older couple in their late seventies - Mr. and Mrs. Peterson. Mrs. Peterson, or Gwen as she keeps telling me to call her, helps Kat at her cafe now and then. Harry (Mr. Peterson) and she have been retired for quite some time now, but they get bored and are eager to help.

Thanks to this generous couple, who own a pair of villas, Evie and I have this new home. They suggested we live in one and they live in the other. The properties are nice inside considering the outside isn't much to look at. It's fine by me, what do they say — *don't judge a book, or in this case a villa, by its cover?*

There are three floors with two bedrooms, two bathrooms, two living rooms and two flights of stairs. The kitchen and laundry are on the bottom level. Gorgeous blue gum floorboards are throughout each level; walls are cream painted with intricate patterns molded throughout the ceilings. It's beautiful, to say the least, mixed with old and modern, it just feels warm and cozy. There is even a little courtyard out back I thought was cement, but Harry said it was actually tar.

As Gwen was showing me around the house and pointing out several features, I realized there was a lot of history here. I was fascinated by what Harry had explained - the captains of ships use to call all the houses along this street, *Boatman Row*. He further explained, the properties are Heritage listed, which means whoever owns these houses cannot change the outside. Hence why they look the way they do on the outside but they are allowed to be updated inside.

Most have either attics or basements, but as some are deemed unsafe, they have been closed off. We have an attic in ours but apparently, it isn't safe so has been closed off. This fact doesn't bother me as I don't like small, confined spaces and it gives me one less area I have to clean.

To Evie and me, our new home is beautiful and gave us the new start we so desperately needed. We are grateful and lucky to have Gwen and Harry in our lives.

⁕

I round the corner into the kitchen and find Evie sitting at the breakfast bench with Aunty Kat eating toast and telling jokes, I can't help but laugh. When I do, two sets of eyes swing my way. I cross the kitchen and flip a switch on the kettle turning it on and give Evie what I hope is a megawatt smile I'm not really feeling. I'm still trying to shake off the nightmare, but I don't want her to think I'm sad anymore.

"Morning sweet pea, I hope you had sweet dreams." I bend forward and kiss her forehead.

"Oh Mommy, I had the best dream ever. I was just telling Aunty Kat, I was flying on the back of a unicorn, way up high in the sky through clouds and rainbows. Oh, Mommy, it was the best dream." Evie sighs dreamily.

"Oh my gosh, that sounds so amazing." This time when I smile, it's genuine. I love how her little mind works. For a five-year-old, her imagination is off the charts and never ceases to amaze me, I love watching her play and talk, she is so expressive. She makes me happy and I know I'm blessed to see that smile every day of my life. *I own her just like I own you and I can take her away just like that.* I shake my head to purge Darren's voice. These nightmares are starting to shake me up more each time I have one, and it doesn't help that all day every day, I feel like I'm being watched.

Stop it right now, Brooklyn! You're being paranoid because it's only been 2 months, it's still too fresh. We're fine, we're safe, but for how long? Knock it off! Give yourself time to settle and you will see YOU ARE SAFE! Plaster a smile on your face and make your coffee. Everything is fine.

"Hey, earth to Brooklyn, hello." Kat waves her hand in front of my face to get my attention.

I jump as I'm snatched back to the present. "I'm fine, everything is fine. I'm not going crazy! What were we saying? Oh, yeah that's right rainbows, unicorns, and coffee. Yes, coffee. I need coffee." I drag my fingers through my hair as I quickly turn away "Kat would you like some?" I ask over my shoulder.

"I'm good Dollface. Are you sure you only need coffee? Maybe you need something stronger like, I don't know, Vodka maybe?" I turn around to find Kat is trying to keep a straight face.

When I glance at Evie, my little girl bursts into laughter. "Mommy you are so funny. Aunty Kat, Mommy is so funny."

"Oh yea, Babydoll your Mommy is so funny and crazy too. Maybe we should buy her some *Fruit Loops* when we shop for groceries. What do you think?" Kat nudges Evie trying to hold back her own laughter.

Evie starts nodding and laughing so hard, tears are leaking from her little eyes. I can't hold it back anymore and I start laughing. "Let me have my coffee and then we can head off."

"Mommy, remember I'm spending the day with Gwen while you're at work with Aunty Kat."

"I remember." I smile and sip at my coffee thinking of how Evie is growing up so fast, I can't keep up.

"Sweet pea, why don't you go and brush your teeth and grab your things then we'll head on over."

"Ok Mommy, be back soon." She jumps down from her chair and runs up the stairs.

I turn back to Kat and smile, thinking about how lucky I am to have these two in my life. Kat stands and rounds the bench. She gives me a hug and whispers, everything will work out eventually and to give it a little more time, and to drink more coffee. After the coffee comment, we share a laugh as we pull away.

"Ok Dollface, when Babydoll returns, we better leave and get to work. And, just so you know, we sell coffee there too. I kind of know the owner so I can get it free for us." Kat winks which generates another laugh and smile from me.

I mumble, "smartass," under my breath as I stride away to grab my purse.

Kat laughs again and she has that kind of laugh that causes everybody else to laugh.

My thoughts drift to my friend. Kat is petite at only 5'3" tall, she has gorgeous red hair, crystal blue eyes and an hour glass figure which could bring any man to his knees. She really doesn't understand how beautiful she is, inside and out. She's always dressed up like a rockabilly 50's pinup girl and don't get me started on that mouth of hers, she is worse than a sailor, but she is my best friend, my life saver, and I know we will always have each other's backs.

Two

Brooklyn

After settling Evie with Gwen and Harry we head off to work. Kat's coffee shop is about fifteen minutes away and is called *Coffee Kat*. When she first bought the place, I asked her why she gave it that name. She said, "It's unique, just like me." I couldn't have agreed more.

It's a small café, but it gets pretty busy, enough to keep her running all day. It has a cozy vintage feel; exposed brick walls give it warmth. Old style booths with brown leather seats and wooden tables are along one side of the café. Above them, on the wall, are old photos of soldiers and pinup girls. Separate wooden tables and chairs are dotted through the rest of the room and soft mood lighting drifts down from the ceiling. Grey Ironbark floorboards add to the rustic atmosphere. Shelving displays old Retro coffee tins and bottles. The serving counter is complete with a Retro coffee machine, cash register, and a glass display case at the opposite end. Music from the fifties is played throughout the day. It's an inviting and warm place which reminds me so much of Kat.

As soon as we open the doors it's pretty much non-stop with the before work crowds grabbing their beverage of choice before heading for their place of employment. The first few days when I started working with Kat, I was a little thrown off by everything, but I eventually got the hang of it and now we have a system. She prepares the orders and I smile and play nice with the customers. Kat says, "pretending to be a nice person all the time gets exhausting." Her theatrics always crack me up and I roll my eyes at how her mind works. Our agreement makes her happy so I'm happy unless we get a jerk, then Kat comes out to play, those moments are the funniest. She tells them in no uncertain terms, if they don't like it then they can get the hell out. It's always hard in those situations trying to keep a straight face.

After being rushed off our feet for the past two hours, we can finally relax a little and start on restocking the cakes and slices in the glass dessert cabinet, getting ready for our lunch time rush. As I'm placing the last tray in the cabinet and tapping my foot to *Boppin' the Blues* by *Carl Perkins,* the doorbell chimes. I look up, sensing the energy in the room has changed, and watch as three men walk in wearing expensive suits. Two taller men take a seat in a booth facing the door while the other one wanders over toward me. He has a false air of confidence surrounding him as if he is trying to impress the other two men at the booth.

I try and summon my brightest smile before I speak. "Hi there, how are you today? Welcome to *Coffee Kat*. How can I help you?" I try to shake off the uneasy feelings playing hockey down my spine.

He leers at me before his eyes travel down my body and back up to focus on my breasts for a while. I turn away and he lifts his eyes to meet mine. I don't know why, but there is something about this guy that gives me the creeps. An involuntary shudder of disgust zings through my body. I keep my fake smile plastered on my face.

"I want two short black and a flat white." His tone is commanding. Rude.

I try to be polite, and though I wanna tell him where to go and it's not that hard to learn some friggin' manner's, I keep the smile on my face as I ask, "Of course, would you like anything else with that today?"

"If I wanted something else I would have asked for it." As I said – rude.

I'm taken back by the sudden irritation in his voice. I try to think of what the hell I may have said wrong to get this reaction. I start to shake, but concentrate on relaxing. Shaking it off, I square my shoulders and straighten my back. As much as I want to hide away in the corner, I know I have to be strong. *It's okay, you're okay. Just breathe, ring up his order and he'll go away.* "Ok, no worries. Would you like me to bring them to your table once they're ready?"

"Well, I'm not just gonna stand here all day and wait." He snarls and shakes his head, like I've said the stupidest thing ever.

He speaks so harshly; I flinch and cower before I square my shoulders and move on. This dip shit is *not* going to intimidate me in my workplace. "That will be $11.65 please," I speak sickly sweet and paste on another fake smile.

He narrows his eyes and for the first time since he entered, I realize how dark and scary they are. I take an involuntary step back. He notices my discomfort and it's like I've made him happy that he was able to scare me. His stupid lips twist up in a smirk. *Just slap his smug face. No, I can't. I'm at work I need to act professionally. No slap him he deserves it… No! Yes! No! Fuck, I'm losing my mind. I need to stop talking to myself or answering myself, oh how does that saying go? Concentrate! I have to work! Right, work!*

As I gather myself and glance up to where the guy was standing, I see he is no longer there. I switch my focus to the counter and the money is sitting right there. I gather it up and stash it in the cash register. I shake my head and berate myself for zoning out. *Well at least you didn't have to speak another word to him, that's a bonus.* I giggle to myself while I clip the order receipt on the coffee machine for Kat.

Once the order is ready, Kat ducks back to the kitchen. I prepare myself by taking a deep breath in and blowing it out, giving myself a little pep talk. *I can do this. Go over there, put the drinks on the table and walk away. Breathe-in, breathe-out, breathe-in, breathe-out. Fuck, STOP IT I'M NOT GIVING BIRTH! I'm delivering coffee for fuck sake. Let's just get this over with. If he gives me too much trouble, Kat's in the kitchen, she'll sort him out.* I smirk to myself at that thought.

I round the counter carrying the tray of coffees, look up and *Bam!* A pair of the most gorgeous green eyes I have ever seen are staring back at me. They sparkle like emeralds, so vibrant. I grip the tray harder as I lose myself in their depths. They draw me in as if seeing straight through me. A hum runs through my body turning into a butterfly feeling deep down in my belly. I feel the air around me thicken, heat rises in my cheeks from deep down in my toes. I'm mesmerized by their color and collide with a hard body. Coffees fly everywhere and I land on my ass.

"Ow... shit," I mutter to myself, geez just my luck. As I struggle to pick myself up off the floor, I glance around to check the damage I have done. I quickly realize I have collided with the dipshit with no manners and he's screaming at me.

"You stupid bitch, do you know how much this suit cost? More than you make in a fucking year. Fucking Hell, you are gonna pay for this do you understand me?"

I nod frantically and finally find my voice. "Oh My God." My voice is squeaky; I clear my throat so it doesn't sound like I'm about to cry. "I'm so sorry, please let me help you clean up the mess. Please, it was an accident. I didn't mean.... I-I'm s-sorry, please... let me grab some napkins or a cloth or something, I'm so sorry."

I'm stuttering now and fumbling my words, barely able to contain my sobs. My eyes glaze over and I'm trying really hard to hold back the tears. But, first one, then another slide down my cheeks. I tense up waiting for the blow that's sure to come, but it never does. I notice the other two men starting to stand at the same time Kat rushes from the kitchen straight up into this guy's face.

"Hey, asshole!" She steps up even closer and glares at the man, venom spews from her eyes. "Back the fuck off her. She didn't mean to knock into you, it's not like she lined you up and thought, fuck it I might just throw this tray at you. Trust me you would have known if she was lining you up because I would have been standing on top of the counter over there cheering her on and filming your stupid ass. Then later tonight, my friend and I would sit and eat popcorn, replaying this scene over and over again."

"Are you for real, Bitch?" The guy is not intimidated by Kat.

"You have no idea how real I can get, dipshit," Kat snaps back.

He reaches over to grab hold of my arm and I instantly cower, flinching away.

Kat gets back in his face and through gritted teeth, she hisses, "Go on! Touch her. I'll hit you so fucking hard *Google* will have trouble finding you." She turns her head and softens her voice as she speaks to me, "Brookie, go back to the kitchen and clean yourself up while I show this fucker the door and hopefully smack him with it on the way out."

I bite my lip and nod trying not to laugh at the incredulous look on the guy's face. When Kat's angry, some of the funniest shit comes out of her mouth and I friggin' love how she always has my back. As I slowly turn to head back to the kitchen, the guy seems to come back to the present and starts yelling at me again.

"BITCH THIS ISN'T OVER WITH, YOU…"

I don't stop and hear Kat snap her fingers. I know from past experience; she has done it in front of his face. I can't stop the giggle that escapes as I push through the kitchen door. I whack my hand across my mouth and I can still hear her yelling at that sorry excuse for a man.

"Hey, don't fucking talk to her. You talk to me. You need to chill the fuck out mate and calm your farm it was just…"

I can't hear her anymore as I rush over to the sink and start to clean up.

I let out the breath I didn't realize I was holding and examine the mess I'm in. Fuck, I can't believe what came over me. When I rounded the counter, all I remember was looking up and being captured by those emerald green eyes with thick lashes. I couldn't breathe or break away. It seems like invisible rope was pulling me to him, as if he could read my every thought and see into my soul. Then, I bumped into that big idiot and I was jolted back to reality when all hell broke loose. I'm thankful Kat was here because I don't know what I would have done otherwise.

I stare at myself in the mirror noticing my eyes are a bit bloodshot and puffy from crying. I calm myself down by taking deep breaths, still picturing those eyes, the power that exuded from him. I have never felt anything like it before, it was like we knew each other on some weird level and I couldn't pull myself away. It was a surreal feeling. I'm trying to figure out the words to explain it, but I have no friggin' clue how.

⁓ ❧ ❦ ⁓

Dominic

We pull up to the curb in front of a little café nestled in between some older houses and I start tapping my fingers on the armrest wondering again why we have come here instead of one of the usual spots I go to for coffee. When Sergio, one of my men opens my door, I step out. I scan the surroundings, something so natural that most of the time I don't even realize I'm doing it anymore. It's ingrained in me to do so. I notice a few people on the street stop and stare at my limo, but that's normal and I brush it off. I glance at Antonio, my best friend and *capo Bastone* (underboss). He's tall like me standing 6' 3", broad shouldered and fit, but that's where the similarities end. He has short brown hair, I have black. His eyes are brown, mine are green. He rounds the back of the SUV to stand next to me and I nod at Sergio in thanks. "Stay near the car, we shouldn't be long." Sergio nods back as we start to walk away "Tell me again, Antonio, why are we here?" My tone conveys clearly; I'm not impressed with this idea.

"I told you, Boss. Aaron asked if we could meet him here because he wanted to meet on neutral ground. Apparently, this place is quiet at this time of day so we won't be heard by anybody."

I give a short sharp nod to let him know I understand, but I'm still not impressed. He knows I like to have control of every situation in my life and I don't like to be blindsided. "This information, Aaron has, had better be good"

Antonio nods and mumbles "I hope so, Boss."

As we are about to enter the café, I hear footsteps to my left. I swing around quickly to see who is coming toward me. A tall man in a suit with short, greased back brown hair, lean in stature, steps over and shoves his hand out ready to shake mine.

"Hi, Mr. Grasso, nice to finally met you. I'm Aaron Pillsbury." He puffs out his chest and extends his hand further for me to take.

It's as if I'm supposed to be honored I'm in his presence. I want to laugh and punch him in the face at the same time. Who does this *cazzo* (dick) think he is? I nod my head in greeting and watch as his attitude deflates with my rejection. I smirk and take a quick glance at Antonio noticing the smirk playing on his lips as well. I chuckle low in my throat thinking this day may turn out better than I had planned. I push the café door open, ready for this to be over already. I hear Antonio tell him just how it is.

"Aaron, the way you approached my boss, you're lucky you're not dead."

I chuckle a bit louder.

After we stride in, I sit down at a booth facing the door so I can see what is going on outside. Antonio takes the seat next to me after telling the *cazzo* what we want. I start thinking about what I have to do today. I have another meeting at 1pm and then I might go out to one of the clubs I own tonight. Before I can think of anything further, Antonio nudges me bringing me back to the present.

"Boss, let's get what we need out of this *cazzo* and get out of here."

I nod and open my mouth with a reply, but the person in question sits in front of me.

"Fucking hell, that was a mission to order the coffees. The stupid bitch behind the counter wouldn't stop chatting me up. Don't get me wrong she's a looker, and I would bend her over in a heartbeat, but the sweet innocent act she was playing doesn't do it for me. It pisses me off."

Antonio speaks up before I have a chance to, I'm ok with it because I don't have the patience to deal with this prick right now. I want to find out the information and leave.

"So, what have you got for us?" Antonio doesn't beat around the bush.

As Antonio and Aaron get into the details, I zone out. I really don't give a fuck what connections this idiot has. I tap my fingers against the table and think what a waste of time this is. It has to be one of the most ridiculous meetings I have ever had. This guy is supposed to have some connections who would be useful to us, but so far all I've seen is, he's an arrogant piece of shit in a suit who thinks he's better than everybody else. He's one of those types who likes to throw his money around and let everybody else do the hard work. I have always hated those types of people. I sit studying this little coffee shop liking the vibe it has going on, tapping my foot under the table to a beat of some fifties song coming through the speakers above. I think I may have to make this place a permanent coffee stop. I guess I'll have to wait and try the coffee first before I make any definite decisions.

I'm trying hard to ignore this piece of shit in front of me, and I'm about two seconds away from telling Antonio this is a waste of time and we're leaving when I look up. My heart slams against my ribs when I lock eyes with the most gorgeous woman I have ever seen in my life. Her blonde hair is in a messy knot on top of her head with a few curls hanging loosely around her face. She's petite, probably would only reach to my shoulders and her eyes.....the bluest I have ever seen. I could get lost in them for days. I'm captivated and drawn into their depths so deeply, I can't seem to pull myself away. *I need to know who this angel is and make her Mine!*

Where the fuck did that thought come from? I shake my head to get rid of those thoughts and concentrate on taking her in, committing every detail to memory.

She's so small, I would probably scare the shit out of her if I stood up. I'm big and intimidating, in my line of business my size comes in handy, but right now it may work against me. My stomach twists at the thought.

Antonio nudges me to attract my attention, but before I can look at him and respond, the stupid fucking piece of shit who was sitting with us, has walked straight in front of my angel. They collide causing her to drop the tray of drinks which spill down the front of him. She's knocked onto her ass, covering her with the spilled drinks as well. My head snaps up and anger bubbles within when I hear him yelling at her. She's struggling to stand and gather herself. I frown when she flinches and cowers away. Tears slide down her face. I feel protective of her and my anger spikes, I'm ready to explode. I'm at boiling point and want to rip this guy's head off. How dare he speak to her like that.

I stand, intent on doing exactly that when a petite redhead comes flying out of the kitchen. I stop and watch as she gets into the prick's face and starts giving him a serve. I turn to let Antonio know I'm about to handle this guy, but he's tuned out and is staring straight at Red. Next thing I hear is Red telling my angel to go and clean herself up. I catch her eye and see she is biting her lip trying not laugh, it's the cutest thing I have ever seen.

Antonio steps over to where Red and the dickhead are still going at each other. I step to Antonio's side as he growls, "Is there a problem here *figa* (cunt)?"

"Yeah, this little bitch thinks she can speak to me like trash," Aaron spits out

"Call her a bitch again and see what happens?" Antonio crosses his arms over his chest in an intimidating stance.

"Don't you remember who I am?" Aaron waves his hands around as if we should feel privileged to be near him.

"Si, I do! But, do you remember who *we* are?" Antonio rocks back on his heels and nods toward me.

I smirk. "Now you're fucked."

All the color drains from the prick's face and his expression is one of sheer panic. He opens his mouth to say something, but Red cuts him off by snapping her fingers in his face. "Hey." We all turn to her as she continues. "Do you know who *I* am? My name is Kat, nice to meet ya. Now, FUCK OFF out of my café."

"More like Tiger," Antonio says under his breath with a slight smirk on his face.

"Okay, mate, are you gonna leave or am I going to have to make you?" Red stands with her hands on her hips.

"You listen to me you trailer trash bitch, *nobody* speaks to me like that do you under.......Ooooff." Aaron doesn't get a chance to finish what he's saying before Red brings her knee up and thumps him in the balls.

"Don't you ever call me trailer trash again you piece of shit. NOW, GET THE FUCK OUT!!" Red yells at the piece of shit as he writhes on the floor trying to catch his breath.

I look over at Antonio, he has a megawatt smile pasted on his face and I can't help but chuckle. *Hmmm…* Red has a temper and Antonio is fucked, I can see it written all over his face. He's smitten, he wants her and will stop at nothing to get what he wants, just like me. We *always* get what we want.

As I look down and watch the piece of shit trying to pick himself up off the floor, I think my day just got a little more interesting. I look out the door and nod at Sergio so he can come remove this *figa*. Sergio walks in, picks him up, throws him over his shoulder like he weighs nothing, and starts heading for the door. I mumble low so only he can hear me, "Keep him close."

"Right, Boss" Sergio nods as he leaves.

I'm not worried the asshole will try anything with Sergio. He's built like a tank and looks scary as fuck with his dark eyes and pretty much his whole body covered in tattoos. You would have to be crazy to try anything with him. I turn my head back to Red to apologize, but Antonio is already on it.

⁂

Brooklyn

I breathe deep, calming myself down and shake out my hands before splashing water on my face. Thank god I don't wear makeup to work besides moisturizer, otherwise, I would look a lot worse than I do now. I hear Kat yelling, then the front door opening and closing. I need to get myself together, only a couple more hours and I can go home and snuggle up with Evie and watch a movie. I may even make popcorn. I giggle to myself as I remember what Kat said to that idiot and then I realize as I'm walking out of the kitchen I don't have another apron to put on. Damn!

"Oh shoot, Kat, I don't have another apron is that gonna be a problem?"

I look up, my breath leaving me as three sets of eyes swing my way *Shit!* The two men from earlier are still here, standing there commanding the room. Is it just me or does it seem like the room shrank? I'm not sure what to do so I stop in my tracks, waiting for the screaming to begin again. When the yelling doesn't happen, I take a deep breath, square my shoulders and start walking again. I stand beside Kat in case she may need me. Feeling the tension around the room, I force myself to look at Kat. I need to be strong. I calm my breathing as my eyes gravitate toward his. I note the width of his shoulders, his strong jaw, he's so powerful. When I lift my eyes to his, I see the fire in them causing my body to come alive. *What the hell is wrong with me?*

"That's ok, Dollface it's not a problem" Kat puts both hands on my shoulders giving a little squeeze, bringing me back to earth. Looking me over from head to toe, probably to see if I'm okay.

"I'm okay," I whisper. "I think the fall just caught me off guard."

She nods, satisfied with my answer and faces the two men standing in front of us. They're gorgeous, and so friggin' tall, they tower over us. They exude power and confidence. Mr. green eyes captures my attention again. My fingers twitch wanting to run them through his short black hair. *Fuck, what is happening to me?* I have that weird feeling again like a live wire running through my veins. I turn my attention to the other man and calm my thundering heart. I would be amazed if they couldn't hear it, I take a deep breath to calm myself down, but as I do I breathe in their intoxicating scent. My mouth waters, I wipe my hand over my mouth making sure I'm not drooling. I jump when Kat speaks up again.

"Ok guys, shall I replace your drinks on the house or shall I be kneeing you guys in the balls and having your other man out there come and drag you both out too?" Kat motions to the door with a tilt of her head, where indeed there is another man standing on the other side of the glass door leaning against a shiny black SUV. *Holy shit I wouldn't want to meet him in a dark alley.*

I snap my eyes back to the men in front of us noticing they both wince at the thought of anything going near their balls let alone a knee. I bite my lip trying not to giggle at the expressions on their faces. The guy on the right speaks first after looking at Mr. Green eyes and him giving a small nod.

"Do you mind us sitting down and getting two short black coffees please?"

"At least he knows his manners." I snort, then quickly snap my head up when Mr. Green eyes speaks.

"Are you ok, Angel?"

I nod my head then look away. Shit, he has an accent just like his friend. His voice is deep and smooth. I swear I feel it right down to my toes as a tiny little shiver runs down my spine, *Wow!* Oh, and the way he called me Angel, my belly flips, and the butterflies are back full force as heat starts to pool low in my belly. At the same time, I feel heat creep up my neck, I'm so embarrassed right now I just want to hide. *For God's sake, I'm a twenty-three-year-old woman I shouldn't be acting like this.* Mr. Green eyes opens his mouth to say something else and I think I may burst. Kat cuts him off thankfully because I don't think my body could have handled it otherwise.

"No probs, take a seat and they'll be ready shortly." Kat starts to turn away, but then thinks better of it and says, "You guys start any shit like your friend, and I don't care how big or powerful you are, I *will* make sure you leave here limping." With that, she turns around, flips her hair over her shoulder and walks back to the coffee machine.

I stand biting my lip trying not to laugh when I see them wince again and cup themselves like they are experiencing extreme pain just thinking about it. I try not to laugh but a little snort escapes before I can stop it. I start to turn so I can grab the mop and clean up the floor, and see Mr. Green eyes quirk a perfect dark eyebrow. A smirk plays on his lips as he goes to sit back down. Oh, those lips. Hmm, that bottom one. I would love to nip and bite. I lick my lip again imagining it was his. I'm snapped out of my thoughts when I hear a throat clear. Pulling my eyes up to his. I swear I see hunger and amusement in those gorgeous emeralds of his. I turn and head toward the kitchen again. I need to get myself under control.

Three

Dominic

I can't stop staring at her, she is absolutely breathtaking. From the expression on her face, I suspect she was thinking naughty thoughts – hopefully about me. I clear my throat so I could break whatever was going on in her head before my restraint completely went to shit. I'm so fucking hard it hurts, and I know if this table wasn't here, I wouldn't be able to hide a damn thing. My thoughts drift back to when she returned from the kitchen and I finally got a good look at her with no apron. I had to control myself or I would have thrown her over my shoulder and stormed out of here. Oh yeah, I would have had my way with her, given the choice. Tight blue jeans and black shirt with the slightest bit of cleavage to tease, the way they hugged all her curves had my man down south rising to attention. I realized I was gawking and switched my attention to Antonio, he was fixated on Red. Thank fuck he wasn't staring at my Angel, I didn't want to have to beat the shit out of my best friend. I'd save the beating for that fucker, Aaron Pillsbury. What kind of name is that anyway? Pillsbury? He'll keep, I want to let him sweat it out in the back of the SUV before I teach him some manners. For now, I'll have a coffee and enjoy watching my Angel.

Antonio nudges me and clears his throat. I was zoned in on my Angel, breathing in the beautiful scent she is wearing. I had no idea he had been trying to get my attention. "What's up *Fratello* (brother)?" I sit back and attempt to adjust my package, again *Fuck!*

"You were off on another planet there for a while. I wanted to see if we were on the same page with these girls."

"Si, I'm thinking we are. Angel's mine." I growl a little more forcibly than I intended to.

"*Bene* (good) because the feisty little Tiger is mine," he growls back

I chuckle low in my throat knowing this is about to get interesting. Antonio can be hot-headed and Red is probably going to give him a run for his money.

Our coffees are placed in front of us. I glance up and Angel is gazing at me, a gorgeous look on her face like she is drowning in me. Fuck, what I wouldn't do to know what she is thinking right now.

"Ahhh, *Grazie*, (thank you) Angel"

"You're welcome, anytime. Just call me. I-I meant come t t-to the counter." She blows out a deep breath and mumbles to herself, "I can't believe I'm stuffing this up."

I bite my lip to stop the laugh that wants to escape and reach out, placing my hand on top of hers to stop her fiddling with her fingers. I feel her jolt at the contact and have to take a deep breath myself as I feel like an electric current just ripped through my body. I'm transfixed by the connection, breathing in her intoxicating scent but I hear the faint gasp that slips from those luscious lips of hers. My eyes lock on hers, they have dilated and her breathing has changed. It hits me square in the chest, she is feeling what I am. *What the fuck is happening to me?* I clear my throat and when I'm finally able to speak, my voice is huskier than normal.

"What's your name Angel?" It takes her a moment to answer, but when she does, her voice is also that of an angel. I squirm and adjust myself under the table again.

"Brooklyn." Her breathless voice just about does me in.

I suck in a deep breath as my thoughts go wild. How would she feel underneath me, writhing in pleasure? What sounds would she make as I brought her to the edge? Would she scream my name as I ...?

Shit, Dom. Stop! Get it together before you explode in your pants like a sixteen- year- old boy and scare her off!

I clear my throat again and shake my head to clear the images I had created in my mind.

"What's your friend's name, Angel?" I indicate Red with a nod of my head. I watch as her shoulders slump and a frown crosses her face. It dawns on me, she thinks I'm interested in her friend. *Shit.* I trace slow circles on the palm of her hand with my thumb trying to reassure her before I go on. "This is my friend Antonio." I tilt my head in his direction. "He would like to know."

"Oh… um… yeah, that's Katherine but she prefers to be called Kat." A slight blush colors her soft cheeks and I have to hold back a moan wondering how far down that blush goes.

My Angel turns toward Antonio and graces him with the biggest smile I have seen, it's one of those smiles which would brighten up the darkest day. My stomach knots with a sting of possessiveness. Jealousy. *I* should be the one receiving that smile. I give her hand a little squeeze trying to draw her attention back to me. I know it's irrational, but I don't care. I'm a selfish bastard and that smile is *mine*.

Shit, I'm fucked and by the look Antonio is giving me he knows it too.

"And your name?" she says jolting me out of my thoughts

"Oh, I'm sorry. Dominic and it's a pleasure meeting you, Angel" I turn her hand over in mine lift it to my lips and plant a gentle kiss. Her hand is so soft I don't want to release her. As each second passes, it gets harder to regain my control.

"Dominic," she repeats in her breathless voice again. Then something changes, her body tenses up and the expression on her face becomes blank. She snatches her hand from mine and backs up a step as she mumbles, "I'm sorry, I better get back to work." With those words, she turns and hurries away.

What the fuck just happened? I know she felt what I felt, so why is she pulling back? I watch her walk away noticing the sexy sway of her hips. Fuck she's gorgeous! I know I'm not finished with this little one just yet, actually, I'm only just getting started. I remove one of my business cards from my pocket, drink the now lukewarm coffee in one gulp then slowly make my way over to my skittish Angel at the counter. Her back is to me so I murmur her name. I watch as she tenses up before her shoulders loosen. She turns around with a smile on her face. This is not like the one she had before, this one is forced. I'm not exactly sure what happened in the last five minutes to cause me to lose her, but I'm going to find out. "I just wanted to give you this. My contact details are on there and the name of my club." I slide the card across the counter and her eyes widen. "Maybe we can grab a drink tonight, your friend can come to. I know Antonio would love to get to know her a little better. How about we say nine? I'll put your names on the list at the door under Brooklyn Angel and Katherine Tiger."

My lips twitch as she struggles to hold back a giggle at the pet names. I chuckle low in my throat when she doesn't succeed "Oh and make sure you wear that perfume you have on." I wink before turning and head to Antonio who is waiting by the door watching Red, but not before I catch her blush again. *Hmmm...* again I wonder how far down that blush goes.

Brooklyn

"Oh wow, Brookie, I can't believe you got that guys number. Don't get me wrong, he was a friggin' hot tomalie, but boy oh boy, his mate was smoking bacon." I laugh at the look on her face, shit, she cracks me up. Before I can form a response, Kat goes on. "Did you see his eyes, they were dark like melted chocolate you want to coat yourself in? I have a feeling they are gonna haunt me in my dreams if you know what I mean?" She wiggles her eyebrows sighing wistfully and it cracks me up harder.

Kat's focus returns to the road and I reach down and run my finger over the spot where I can still feel Dominic's lips on my skin. I swear it still tingles and I shiver remembering the feel of his soft lips on me. Mmmm, but nothing compares to the feeling when he first touched my hand. It was like electric shocks were pulsing through my body. At first I thought I was imagining it, but when I looked into his eyes, I could have sworn that he was feeling it too. I run my hand up my arm as I feel goose bumps break out.

"Brooklyn Harper Mackenzie!"

"Hmm, what? Huh? Why are you full naming me?" I scrunch up my nose and look over at Kat realizing she is staring at me. "Um, shouldn't you be watching the road?"

She bursts out laughing and I'm wondering what is so friggin' funny as I look around. I finally realize we are parked out the front of my place. I must have been really zoned out to not notice we had reached our destination and Kat had parked the car.

"First off, we're here and secondly, I have been sitting here calling your name for like five minutes and you haven't answered me. Are you ok? Are you still thinking about that asshole from earlier today?"

Shit, she looks really concerned. I hate that I have worried her when in fact I was mooning over a full bottom lip I would love to taste. Electric shocks and dreamy green eyes, I feel myself heating again. *Shit get a hold of yourself Brooklyn don't you have enough to worry about?* And, that one thought knocks me back to the here and now. Now, what was she saying? Oh, that's right, the dipshit from today. Surprisingly I wasn't at all bothered by him. I'd actually completely forgotten about him until Kat brought him up.

"No, I'm good. He was such a jerk, he barely registered on my radar after you got rid of him." I turn and smile at her. I better tell her we are invited to a club tonight. After Dominic and Antonio left we were so busy, I completely forgot. I only had a chance to tell her that Dominic had given me his business card.

"Hey Kat."

"Hmmmm."

"I meant to tell you we've been invited to a club tonight for drinks with Antonio and Dominic. He said he would leave our names on the list at the door." I giggle to myself when I remember the names he was going to use.

"Oh yeah, cool do you know what kind of club it is?"

"Nah, he didn't mention it. The card he gave me said it was called *DESTINY*. I can't go anyway; I think I'll have a nice hot bath then snuggle with Evie and watch a movie. I mentioned it in case you might be interested in going." I shrug.

"No, I'm not going without you, it would be awesome to party with my girl again." Kat winks. "I can't even remember the last time we went out together."

"I was out with you today," I smirk.

"Bitch! You know what I mean."

I laugh at the look on her face

"Hey, but in all seriousness, I can't go. I have sweet pea and she comes first. Sorry, Hun."

"Nah, that's cool." Kat shrugs. "I'll crash at your place again and we can have a pajama party, watch movies all night. How does that sound?"

"Sounds like a plan. Evie will love it and we can have popcorn too."

We are both laughing as we step out of the car and head toward Gwen and Harry's place. We're still laughing when the door opens and Harry starts chuckling at us, while we wipe our eyes as tears from laughing so hard trickle out.

"Good evening, girls. It's good to see you laughing, you must have had a productive day at the café." He chuckles as he points us to the kitchen where more giggles and laughter are coming from.

Shit, it's so good to laugh again. I try to think of the last time I laughed this hard. I'm pulled out of my thoughts when I hear Evie belly laugh at something Gwen has said. It's such a great sound that I giggle. Evie turns her head and as soon as she sees it's me, she jumps off the stool, bounces over to me and leaps into my arms. I hug her tight and kiss her cheek while brushing some of her blonde curls out of her face.

"Hi sweet pea, I missed you today. I hope you were on your best behavior for Gwen and Harry."

"Oh, yes Mommy I was, I have missed you sooo much. Come look, we've been baking cupcakes and cookies. Look, come see." Evie drags me over to the bench to have a look at what they have been up to, I can't help but smile at her excitement.

"Oh Wow, what a fantastic job! They look amazing, I may have to taste test these." I reach over to grab one but freeze midway when Evie yells at me.

"Nooooo! Mommy not yet." She shakes her head at me and continues, "they're not ready yet. Nanny Gwen says we have to wait for them to cool down so we can decorate."

"Oh, ok. I'm sorry, they already look so good."

My daughter looks so serious; I glance at Kat and Gwen and bite my lip to stop myself from laughing. I'm pretty sure they're doing the same thing.

Harry saunters in shaking his head. "Let me guess, you got in trouble too." I nod and he smirks as he continues, "I've been trying to get one of those cookies all afternoon, but every time I get near them, I'm getting barked at to not touch. I was told, if I can't contain myself, I should leave the kitchen." He pouts like a little boy which brings a smile to my face. "Just one damn cookie or cupcake, that's all I'm asking for. I'm not picky, I just wanted one or the other. Do you know how hard it is being in a house where you smell all this yummy food and you get a smack on the hand for trying to have a taste?"

He lowers his head and his big puppy dog eyes are pleading with me to understand his dilemma. I giggle and look over at Gwen to see if his antics are working on her. I catch her just in time to see her rolling her eyes and trying to hide a smirk behind her hand. "Stop your complaining old man, you'll get one when they're ready. But, if you keep this up Evie and I will eat the whole lot in front of you. Now shoo, get out of the kitchen. You can't be trusted." Gwen waves her hands at her husband.

Harry turns to leave but not before he throws over his shoulder, "You're lucky you're my wife and Evie is my Granddaughter and I love you both. Damn cookie Nazi's." He grumbles as he stomps off down the hall.

Evie bursts into laughter first which starts us all up again. Evie and I are so lucky to have these people in our lives. Mr. and Mrs. Peterson have started calling Evie their granddaughter and told her she could call them Nanny and Poppy, it puts the biggest smile on her face. It also puts a smile on my face because since my parents passed away, we don't have any family besides Kat. She's not blood but she may as well be. I remember my Dad and Mom use to say when we were younger, *"Kat darling, remember you will always have a home with us. You are no guest in our house, you are family."*

I miss my parents so much; I still remember the last time I saw them so vividly. I had invited them over for dinner one weekend so we could catch up. If I had known that would be the last time I would see them, hugged them, I would have held on tighter and told them I loved them a million times more.

As I finish cleaning up the kitchen I wipe my hands on the tea towel that's thrown over my shoulder. I look around the kitchen making sure I haven't missed anything. Salad and Vegies are done, the roast is cooking, only another ten minutes left and I have the cheesecake in the fridge for dessert.

"Darren," I call into the lounge room. "Did you pick up the wine today?"

"YES! God dammit," He yells as he walks into the kitchen. I flinch at the tone of his voice but he acts as if he doesn't notice. He stands close in front of me, grabs hold of my chin and roughly tilts my head up so I'm looking into his dark eyes "I told you I did, earlier," he spits at me. I'm so taken off guard, I suck in a deep breath.

"I'm sorry." I don't know what's going on lately because I'm used to the harsh words and a push here and there, but lately, it feels like I'm disappointing and failing him more, and he gets a bit rougher with me each and every time.

"You're sorry? You're lucky your parents are on their way over or I would teach you a lesson." He drops my chin and storms off. I don't know what to do or say, so, I stand there watching him walk out and wonder again about what's going on. I know he doesn't get along with my parents, it's the reason I don't see them as much as I'd like. He feels as if he has to prove something to them and tells me he shouldn't have to feel that way in his own home. I can completely understand, but they are still my parents and I love them dearly. Regardless of how Darren feels, I have them over at least once a month for dinner, but this new turn of events with his mood swings has really thrown me off. I feel like I'm treading on eggshells more than normal most days. This isn't the first time he has mentioned teaching me a lesson, he's said it to me a few times before and I really don't want to find out what he means. I'm standing in the kitchen, trying to work out how I made him so angry, when the doorbell chimes. I shake off my thoughts and head to open the door.

All through dinner, Mom and Dad ask me about what's been happening and comment on how much Evie is growing into such a bright little girl. They agree I'm doing a wonderful job with how I'm raising her. I smile broadly and think how much I love spending time with them. I tell them about a small work party we are having in a couple of months and ask Dad about his golf game last weekend. I *ask Mom about her book club which she attends every Tuesday night. While they answer my questions, they also ask me about the work party. I notice how Darren is acting tonight, strange. It was like my parents arrived and whammo, he's playing the part of the doting fiancée, talk about a complete change in the space of five minutes. I feel like I live with Dr. Jekyll and Mr. Hyde lately. He seems to have been worse than normal in the past few months, or has it been longer? I'm really not sure, but the days he's nice and understanding are becoming few and far between. He's never been a really nice person now I think about it. My stomach roils at the realization. I have been more worried as the pushes and nasty words became more frequent so I gave my best friend, Kat a call and told her what's been happening. I wish I hadn't now because it worried her terribly. So much, in fact, the next day I received a package in the mail with a burner phone and a card which read:*

Brooklyn,

I know you said not to worry and that everything will be fine.

Just in case it's not, my number is already programmed

Stay safe

Love Kat

Xx

I wasn't sure what to do at first, I stared at the phone thinking I would never need something like this. But, a part of me said to keep it and to hide it before Darren found out.

I'm drawn from my thoughts when I hear a throat clearing. I look up and notice no one is talking, they are all staring at me. I'm gripping my napkin so hard, my knuckles are turning white. I quickly release it, clear my throat and stand.

"I'm sorry I was just thinking about getting the dessert ready, I won't be long." I excuse myself and quickly leave the room. I let out the breath I didn't realize I was holding as I enter the kitchen and make my way to the fridge. As I reach for the door of the fridge, I'm grabbed by the wrist and spun around so fast I trip over my own feet. I catch myself on the kitchen bench.

Darren leans down and hisses low in my ear, "just fucking wait, once your parents leave, you will be taught a lesson." He releases me and walks away.

Fuck, what's gonna happen when my parents leave? With his threat, I can't help but feel queasy and brace myself on the counter trying to get my breathing under control. Pouring myself a glass of water, I hope to settle this feeling I have in my belly. I take a deep breath and then another before heading toward the dining room carrying the cheesecake. I place it on the table before I take my seat.

Mom pats my hand and gives it a little squeeze before turning to me with a worried look on her face. "Are you ok sweetie? You look pale and your hand is cold."

"I'm fine, it's been a busy day." I give her what I hope is a reassuring smile as I start handing out dessert.

"Try not to over work yourself, it isn't healthy." Mom pats my hand.

I smile and nod and avoid Darren's eyes which feel like they are burning a hole through me.

By the time dessert is over, Darren has gone back to being the doting fiancée. I didn't realize how late it had gotten until Darren says he is going to put Evie to bed while I say goodnight to my parents.

"Oh Mom, thanks for coming over." I give her a big hug and a kiss on the cheek.

"And, thanks Dad for the fantastic bottle of wine you brought over, it was delicious." He wraps his arms around me in a big bear hug that makes me giggle.

"You're welcome, baby girl." He plants a kiss on my forehead before turning and taking Mom's hand. He leads her down the path toward their car.

"Drive safe," I call out and wave as I watch them leave the driveway and head down the street.

As I'm closing the door, Darren moves in behind me. He places both arms up caging me against the door and hisses in my ear, *"upstairs now."* Before I can say a word, he walks away. I don't know what to do, but I do know not following his order is going to get me in more trouble. I hurry upstairs to our bedroom. When I push open the door, Darren is pacing the floor. I can't help feeling he isn't the man I thought he was. No, this is a man I don't recognize anymore.

"Who the fuck do you think you are?" When he yells at me, I flinch. I don't know what to say so I keep my mouth shut. I don't want to anger him any more than he already is.

He stops pacing and stalks toward me while staring at me like I'm the scum of the earth. *"You are fucking worthless. You need me because no other man would ever put up with your shit. You need to start earning your place, you and that little bitch down the hall belong to me! You will do as I say, when I say. Or, there will be consequences, do you understand me?"* He grabs my hair pulling my head back roughly, a cry of pain slips from my mouth and my eyes seem to glaze over. He bends down close to my ear and hisses, *"You are so pathetic. Remember I can take all this away from you in a heartbeat. I will not have you disrespect me again, this is my house and you will show me some respect. Do you understand me, bitch?"*

I try and nod my head but he's still holding me by the hair. He pushes me to my knees and unzips his fly. I try and hold back my sobs as best I can, I know what's coming. He slams his cock into my mouth and grabs my head so hard, I can feel some of my hair coming out by the roots. I try not to gag while I wait for him to finish. I say a prayer that this will be over soon and I can crawl under the blankets and pretend I have a better life. He grunts and explodes into my mouth. I try to swallow without gagging. I feel his hand on the side of my face, his thumb running over my cheek. I try not to flinch at the contact. "Why do you insist on pissing me off? When are you going realize, you're pathetic and worthless? You need to remember, you are nothing. Nothing without me. DO you understand me, Brooklyn? NOTHING!"

Tears stream down my face, he's still gripping my hair and I can't move. As he lets go, he hesitates for a minute. I feel a burning sting across my face and I'm thrown to the floor like trash. He turns and makes his way to the door, pauses and looks back at me with the evilest smile I have ever seen. Chills dance down my spine, the cold, hard edge of his words slice through me like a knife. "Push me, Brooklyn, and see how far I take this." The bedroom door slams behind him.

I curl up on the floor hugging my knees to my chest and burst into gut-wrenching sobs. It was then I realized, things weren't going to get any better, they were only going to get worse. I had to work out a way to get Evie and me away from this MONSTER!

Four

Brooklyn

"Mommy….Mommy….is that ok?"

"Hmmm, sorry sweet-pea I missed what you were saying?" I shake my head to get rid of my dark thoughts and concentrate on what Evie is saying.

"Oh Mommy, you're silly." She shakes her head at me "I was saying, nanny Gwen says if it's ok with you, I can stay over tonight and help finish off the baking. Can I Mommy, Pll lee ease. I'll be good I promise."

I glance at Gwen and she nods her head to confirm it's fine.

Evie pleads with me to say yes. "Please… please….please, Mommy, please…" Evie places her hands together like she is praying and levels her puppy dog eyes at me.

"Ok, ok." I hold my hand up "I give up, you can stay." Before I can get another word out she is bouncing around like the energizer bunny, I burst out laughing at her enthusiasm.

"Aunty Kat, did you hear? I get to stay and make all these cookies pretty."

"I heard, Babydoll." Kat smiles down at her and winks. It's obvious my best friend adores her.

I clap my hands to get my daughter's attention. "I have one rule - you have to promise to make special ones for Aunty Kat and me."

"Yes, Mommy we will. Nanna Gwen, I get to stay but we have to make special ones for Mommy and Aunty Kat, is that okay?"

"Yes of course precious girl, I think we can manage that" Gwen smiles down at Evie and pats her head as moves toward the fridge.

The biggest smile spreads across my girl's face, her gorgeous baby blues twinkle like stars. My heart lurches with joy knowing how happy she is.

"You girls wanna drink?" Gwen pulls lemonade from the fridge and places it on the bench before grabbing cups from the cupboard.

Kat, Evie and I all nod and take a seat on the bench.

After we have our drink and catch up for a bit, filling Gwen in our day, I grab Evie an overnight bag from home. We say our goodnights with big hugs and kisses. Then Kat and I make our way to my place to decide what to do for the rest of the night.

"Sooo..." Kat starts in a whiny voice I have heard before when she wants me to do something. I know what's coming so I turn my back to her flee down the little hall toward the kitchen.

After a couple of minutes of silence, I crack first and ask "Sooo, what?" I already know what Kat wants to say, but I need her to get it out already. Sometimes it's like pulling teeth with her. I smirk at her over my shoulder, she narrows her eyes at me which makes my smile bigger.

'Okay, stop it! I hate how well you know me."

"Sorry."

"Sodoyouwannagototheclubtongiht?" Kat speaks at lightning pace and it's like the whole sentence is one friggin' word.

"What the fuck was that? Can I get the English version now?" I laugh.

"Oh, shut your face, bitch" she smirks *"Did you want to go to the club tonight?"* She speaks slower and emphasizes each word.

I'm not sure what to say so, I turn and start looking through the fridge to buy me some more time to think of an answer. But Kat's onto me she knows me as well as I know her.

"Brooklyn Harper Mackenzie, do not ignore me I asked you a question?"

"Shit, why do you keep full naming me today? You can be so annoying."

"Listen here, bitch, we need a night out. It's been like forever since we have had a drink together and just danced the night away. Evie is safe with Gwen and Harry so you have no excuses, come on. Please?" There's that whiny voice again.

I straighten and close the fridge door before turning to Kat. Now I know where Evie has learned to do that puppy dog look, 'cause Kat is the master of that look and I find it very hard to say no to her. Guess we're going to a club tonight.

"It's not the fact I don't want to go, Kat, I'm just worried. With everything that's gone on over the past couple of months, I'm really not interested in seeing anybody, even if it is for only one night."

Kat drops the smile, wraps her arm around my shoulders and gives me a squeeze. "I know Dollface, but you can't stop living your life. Maybe this is what you need, a night to let loose and have a bit of fun. Plus, it's Wednesday night so we won't have a late one because we both work tomorrow. I know these guys seem dangerous with their brooding good looks and mesmerizing eyes…" She signs wistfully. "But, where was I? Oh yeah, but these guys seem different you know, the good kind of bad."

She has a faraway look on her face and I snap my fingers to bring her back to the conversation. "Hey, don't just feed me lines because you wanna get laid."

A serious look crosses Kat's face. "Dollface, I would never do that. What I'm trying to say, is these guys don't seem like the type to hurt a woman, you should have seen them when you were in the kitchen." She shakes her head as if she still can't quite believe it herself and that gets my mind going.

What if Darren finds us and he sees me with another man? Stop Brooklyn! Take one day at a time, that's all you can hope for right now. Evie's safe and Kat's right, I need a night out.

"Ok we will go, but if its crap we're coming home. Promise me, Kat" I thrust my pinkie finger out waiting for hers to latch on and we kiss the back of our hands so it's a sealed bond. It's stupid, but we have always done it.

"I promise." Kat fist bumps the air. We crack up laughing and run upstairs to find something to wear.

————————————————————————

Dominic

I button my suit jacket as I step from the car and nod toward Sergio in thanks. Music blares from inside *Destiny*, glancing up I see the purple neon sign shining in this otherwise dark street. Then I notice the line to get in, looks like it's going to be a good night all round. I walk up to Demetri, one of my most trusted men on the door. Nodding my head in greeting, I grab the VIP list and add my Angel and her friend. Fuck, I hope she turns up. My lips turn up as I recall the expression on her face when I told her what names would be down on the list. I hand the list back to Demetri and make sure everything is good. I really don't need any more drama today, especially when my Angel could be here soon. I check my watch - 8.45pm, plenty of time to grab a drink and take a seat in my booth while I wait for her to show up. I really hope she turns up, I don't know what I'll do if she doesn't. It's not like I can drop by her place and demand to know why she's not here. I don't even know where she lives, I don't have a way to contact her except where she works. If she doesn't turn up, I'll be at the café door right on opening to find out why. *Geez Dom get a fucking grip and be patient*. Fuck, I hate waiting. I want to see her again, feel her soft skin, smell her sweet scent. My mouth waters just thinking about her and that scent! It's exactly what I thought heaven would smell like, honey and vanilla. I wonder if she tastes the same. *Shit, stop!* I'm getting hard as a fucking rock just thinking about the beautiful girl and it's not good when you're standing out the front of your club with so many people around staring at you. I need a drink that's what I need.

"Boss are you alright?" Demetri asks.

"Si *Fratello* (brother). I'm fine, it's been a long day. I think I need a drink"

"Right, Boss, well everything is good out here unless you have anything you need me to know or do?"

"Si, two lovely ladies will be here about 9pm, their names are on the list." I motion to the clipboard in his hands. "They are very special to me and Antonio so, no fucking with them and most definitely NO fucking flirting especially with my Angel or, you may piss me off and we don't want to do that now do we?" I raise an eyebrow at him and scowl, he gets the message.

"No, Boss. Definitely not. I would never mess with what's yours and Antonio's."

"I'm glad we're on the same page. Just make sure no-one messes with her." I repeat myself so he knows I'm not fucking around.

"Right, Boss." He nods and waits for me to turn away and head inside. I smile when I hear him exhale hard.

I head down the long hallway toward the double doors which open into the main area of the club. The hallway isn't dark, 'ambient lighting' thanks to a few neon signs on the walls leading to the doors. To the right before entering the club is a coat room where Theo usually works. He's tall, lean build, brown hair and wears glasses. He's smart, an excellent hacker and loyal. I greet him like I do everyone else - a chin lift as I push through the double doors.

I scan the room to make sure everything is in order. Bright multi-coloured lights flash around the dark maroon colored walls and wooden dance floor. The DJ sits in the corner on a small raised wooden platform. Large booth seating lines both sides of the room with smaller tables and chairs scattered around the dance floor. I glance to the stairs leading up to the VIP section to make sure my men are doing their jobs.

I stride to the long bar with its purple lights running under the edge of the counter. A *Destiny* sign is displayed in brilliant neon above the glass shelving which holds the finest spirits available. Janet and Amy, our barmaids are serving a couple of customers. The minute Janet locks eyes on me, she sashays over batting her eyelashes

"Hey handsome," she purrs as she slides a scotch over to me "I didn't realize you were coming in tonight, you should have called me." She pouts and pretends to pick something off the too tight top she's wearing which emphasizes her fake boobs. I try hard not to roll my eyes at her.

She has always been a little pushy, but she also knew what we had was only a simple hook up. A one-time thing. Six fucking months ago! Fuck, it was never going to be anything more but something tells me Janet isn't accepting it. Maybe it's my fault, maybe I wasn't clear enough with her. I could never see myself settling down with her, or anyone else for that matter. That is, until today. When I looked into the most breathtaking ocean blue eyes I have ever seen and my fingers itched with the urge to run through her golden blonde curly hair, I was gone. Smitten, I want nothing more than to strip her naked and examine every one of her luscious curves.

"Dom, baby." Janet purrs again and tries to rub my arm, I quickly pull back. I don't want her to touch me and she should know better than to do that. Hearing her voice, it's like nails on a chalkboard. I have to put a stop to this now before my Angel turns up.

"Hey Janet, how's things tonight? Everything good?" I strive for casual as I look around the club.

When I turn back, she stares at me for a moment. She's probably hoping I'll drag her to the back office for a quick fuck. *That's never going to happen again.*

"Is everything okay, baby? You look tense, would you like me to relieve some of that tension for you?" She licks her lips.

I feel nothing in my pants. Normally, when a woman licks her lips like that, my dick starts to stir, but I'm not even tingling. Hmm, interesting, considering I only looked into Angel's eyes and my dick was instantly hard as a rock to the point of pain. "No, I'm feeling good actually, just wanted to make sure everything was running smoothly."

Janet moves closer and places her hand on my arm. "Baby, come on, let me relieve some of that tension."

Anger bubbles inside me as I lift her hand from my arm and place it back on the bar. Does she not take a hint? "Look, thanks for the offer, but I'm not interested. I told you at the time, it was a one-time thing only."

That did it! I watch as a sneer crosses her face and she opens her mouth to say something I know will be nasty. I lift my hand to cut her off before she starts.

"I wouldn't if I was you. I don't hurt women, but if you say one thing to piss me off, I may change my mind. Do you understand me?" I would never lay a hand on a woman but she doesn't know that. "I told you what it was from the beginning so don't act like I promised you the world." I spin on my heel and make my way over to my booth.

I don't usually explain myself to anyone, so it pisses me off that I've had to this time. I sit down beside Antonio before I completely lose my cool.

I don't sleep with many women because, in my line of work, I don't have time to worry about them or have them involved in my life. Sometimes it's good to have a little company to take the edge off and that may make me an asshole, but I don't promise them anything besides a good time. It's hard to trust in my line of work, and don't get me wrong, I would love someone to call my own, but before today I didn't think that would ever happen.

Now I've met Brooklyn, I have a feeling things are going to change and for once I'm not worried about the changes to come.

"Boss, everything looking good for tonight?" Antonio asks.

"Si." I give him a chin lift. "Everything get cleaned up after I left today?"

"Si, the asshole won't be bothering anybody again. After you left, I made sure I had my own fun."

I chuckled low, knowing exactly what his kind of fun entailed. Antonio has a thing for torture. The man didn't have the best upbringing and he has his own deep, dark secrets I'm sure he's never told anybody. I know a little, but I'm sure there's a lot more. I don't push him, it's his past and God knows I have my own memories which haunt me. But, knowing that piece of shit crossed several lines of disrespect toward us and toward the women, I can only imagine what else happened after I left.

"*Bene*" (good). I take a sip of my drink and close my eyes as I feel the smooth burn slide down my throat. I remember the tears running down my Angels cheeks and watching her chin wobble as she fought off her emotions. It caused my heart to squeeze in my chest and I never want to see that abject look of panic and fear in her eyes again. It tore me up inside and I want to kill that piece of shit all over again. My fists clench with anger, but the asshole has been dealt with now. I try to relax and take another sip of my scotch. I look around when I feel eyes staring at me from across the room. *Holy shit* I take a deep breath to get my lungs working again.

My Angel is standing near the doors staring straight at me and I can't take my eyes off her. It's as if the rest of the world has disappeared and it's just her and me. My eyes drink her in, she is more breathtaking than when I first saw her at the café. She's wearing a gorgeous white dress which hits just above the knees and is cut enough at the top to see a hint of cleavage. The rest of the dress hugs her body like a second skin. I glance around and realize I'm not the only one staring. It pisses me off because those mother fuckers need to realize, she is MINE! The jealousy and possessiveness I feel for this woman is unlike anything I have ever felt before. I have never been a jealous person, but she is different. It's like she's my beacon calling me home. I need to claim her, make her mine in every way possible. *Mine, Mine, Mine....*

⁂

Brooklyn

The cab pulls up to the front of the club and I glance at Kat. She is wearing a black dress with a thin red belt, red heels and has red painted lips to match. With her fair skin and red hair, done like a pin up doll she looks absolutely smoking hot. I peer down at my simple white dress, my naturally curly blonde hair is out, my makeup is natural and I'm wearing nude heels. Maybe I should have worn the red dress Kat tried to insist I wear, but I really didn't want to stand out, I wanted to blend in.

Kat gives my hand a squeeze before we exit the cab. "Hey, cheer up Dollface. You look hot!" How does she always know what I'm thinking?

Stepping onto the footpath, I look up and notice the purple neon sign which reads - *Destiny* and butterflies start to form in my belly. Kat and I approach the doors.

"Excuse me, Miss." A burly bouncer speaks with an accent which reminds me of Dominic's. He has a bald head and a lot of tattoos, if he wasn't smiling at me, he may have scared the crap out of me.

I return his smile before speaking. "Hi, sorry to barge up here, but my friend and I have been put on some list. Do we still need to line up?" I look at the line and hope we don't because the line is long and there's a chill in the air.

"No, *Signora* (ma'am) I'll check the list and if you are who I think you are, you can go straight in."

"Cool." I feel my face heat as I say the names Dom said he would put on the list. "Brooklyn Angel." I point to me and then to Kat "and Katherine Tiger."

The bouncer checks his clipboard with a smile curling his lips. I swear, honest to God, I hear Kat growl.

"Fucken Tiger, I'll show him, Tiger. I'm a kitten — soft, cuddly and cute." Kat mumbles under her breath and laughter bubbles inside me. The bouncer speaks before I completely lose it.

"Enjoy your evening *Signorine* (ladies)."

He waves us past, Kat and I both smile and thank him before we enter the long hall leading toward a set of double doors. I observe the array of neon lights and the various shades of colors illuminating the hall. We smile at a man off to our right who's standing with his arms crossed over his chest. He's next to a girl collecting coats from various people.

"Have you been here before?" I whisper to Kat

"Nah, I think it's pretty new. I have heard about it though. Apparently, some mob boss bought it."

"Are you serious?" I hiss and grab her arm, pulling her to a stop.

"I'm not sure, I don't go out much so I really wouldn't have a clue. It's probably just a rumor. Don't stress about it. Come on." Kat gives my hand a squeeze.

She pushes the double doors open and the first thing that hits me is the blaring music the DJ is playing, it's one of my favorite songs - *Hot in Herre* by *Nelly*. Geez, it's pretty crowded in here tonight and I can't believe how nice it is even with the odor of sweat soaked bodies dancing together. I had a feeling it might have been a bit dingy, but this is nice. Warm and cozy. I absorb it all from the beautiful wooden floor boards on the dance floor to the booths with little tea light candles placed in the center of each table to add a bit of mood lighting. Colored flashing lights dance off the dark maroon walls, the bar is illuminated with purple lights. Glass shelving holding bottles of spirits is overlooked by a large neon sign announcing the club's name – *Destiny*.

WOW! I look to Kat wide-eyed to see what she thinks, but she is staring off to the other side of the room. I squint to take a closer look and notice two large men taking up a whole booth. I realize it's Dominic and Antonio. Fuck, it feels like the place gets smaller with them here. Dominic must feel my eyes on him because he turns and looks into my eyes. My knees weaken and there it is again - a feeling running through my body like I'm coming home. It's such a weird feeling I have never felt before, not even with Darren. *Ugh, No I'm not gonna think about him tonight, this my night and I'm going to enjoy it.*

Kat grabs my hand and motions to the bar, I nod my head to agree because I don't think I can find my voice right now. Not that she could hear me over the music anyway.

"How can I help you?" The girl behind the bar plasters a fake smile on her face.

"Can we please have two Vodka's and orange?" Kat asks.

"Coming right up." She starts making our drinks.

I reach for my purse and feel a hard body press up behind me, large hands rest on my hips. I freeze but relax when Dominic sniffs my neck and whispers in my ear. "Angel, you look breathtaking and you smell divine, good enough to eat. You don't need to pay; I have it covered." I relax into his arms; a shiver runs through my body at the sound of his intoxicating smooth accent and the huskiness of his voice.

"I can't let you do that, it's not right. We can pay for ourselves." I turn my head to look up at him and I'm captured by his gorgeous green eyes and beautiful smile. I'm so captivated I almost don't hear what he says next. "I know you can *il Mio Amore*, but you don't have to. It's taken care of." He winks at me.

I think I melted from the sound of his voice as his accent washed over me. I don't care if he just called me a bitch, it sounded so sexy. *Shit, Brooklyn stop. You're probably giving him your crazy eyes right now.* I lick my bottom lip, watching as his eyes track the movement. I know when I speak I'm going to sound breathless, but right now I don't think I care.

"Ok, Dominic." Yep, breathless voice just like I thought.

But, I don't care because I swear I hear him suck in a breath. It makes me smile inside, knowing I can affect this man who dominates every space he is in, as much as he affects me. I'm jolted out of my thoughts when drinks are slammed down on the bar. I flinch and try and step out of Dom's hold, but he pulls me closer. When I turn my head, I see the girl standing there giving me a scathing look. I feel Dominic tense up and he flexes his fingers on my waist. I'm about to say something when Kat speaks first.

"What's your problem, bitch?"

"Nothing," she sneers. "They slipped from my grasp and I put them down harder than I intended." There's a big ass fake smile on her face.

"Geez, love is everything about you fake?" Kat asks.

"What the fuck did you say?" The girl slams her hands on her waist and shouts her reply.

"I said." Kat makes air quotes with her fingers. "You *really* need to buy yourself a personality because everything about you is sooo fake." Kat holds up her hand and starts counting off on her fingers. "Your boobs, your smile, your tan and most definitely your personality. Your hair is probably fake too."

"You fucking bitch, who the hell do you think you are? You think you can talk to me like that. Antonio? Dominic? Are you gonna let this bitch talk to me like that?"

I glance at Dominic and Antonio and they both shrug their shoulders. I turn back to the chick behind the bar and watch her deflate a little before an ugly sneer crosses her face. I look back at Dominic and he opens his mouth to say something, but Kat cuts him off.

"Bitch." Kat slams her fists on her hips and shakes her whole body, she's really pissed. "Why don't you show some self-respect and walk away." Kat spins around, and with a chuckling Antonio on her heels, she stomps toward the booth the guys were in when we arrived.

I pick up my drink to follow then hear her mumble something I don't quite catch, but I think Dominic did because I feel him tense and growl deep in his throat. It was so low I may have imagined it, and with Dominic's arm around me, it's hard to concentrate. I shrug it off.

When we make it to the booth I hear Antonio explaining to Kat. "I would have gotten involved, but I'm pretty sure you had it under control and Tiger, I don't hurt women. *Ever.*"

"Good to know you don't hurt women and I did have it handled. I don't need a man to fight my battles for me." She glares at Antonio. "And, stop calling me Tiger!"

This should be an interesting night with these two. I look at Dominic and I can't help but smirk. He winks at me like he knows exactly what I'm thinking.

Five

Dominic

As we take our seats at the booth, I suck a deep breath in through my nose to calm myself down, otherwise I'm going to most definitely scare my Angel off. It took everything in me at the bar to not say anything or interfere. Antonio gave me a look as if to say he was about to rip the bitches head off, but I gave a small shake of my head and nodded to Kat. She seemed to have everything under control, and I didn't want to make things worse by creating a scene with it being the girls first time here. Fortunately, Kat was more than capable of taking care of the situation. Just thinking about the little spitfire Antonio has to handle, makes me chuckle. Fuck, I hope he knows what he's doing, she's more than his match.

I take another deep breath in and catch a whiff of Brooklyn's intoxicating honey/vanilla scent. It's driving me crazy, I swear to Christ it's going to be my undoing.

"Thank you for the drinks, but really we can afford to pay for them," Brooklyn speaks in a soft voice and I have to lean down to hear her over the thumping beat of the music.

I whisper in her ear, "I never said you couldn't, Angel, but please let me spoil you for tonight." I feel her tense so I pull back and wink. She blushes, and because I'm so close, I feel the small shiver that runs through her body.

"Thank you." She smiles and fuck, the power of it hits me straight in the chest.

I'm in Love with a Stripper by *T-Pain* starts to play "Ah, Dollface, I love this song; come dance with me." The next thing I know, my Angel is being hauled to her feet by Kat and dragged off to the dance floor. They're giggling their heads off. *God, she's beautiful, she doesn't seem to realize how gorgeous she is.*

I lean back in the booth and watch Angel sway her hips to the beat. She mesmerizes me, I'm engrossed in watching her dirty dancing with Kat, my cock thickens and swells. I tear my eyes from the erotic sight before I get up and drag her out of here, caveman style. I readjust myself under the table. *Fuck, get it together Dom. Shit, you're not a horny teenage boy looking at a pair of tits for the first time.* My cock responds to my thoughts and I get even harder, I readjust myself again. What is it about this girl that's making my head spin? I can't seem to act my age around her.

"Boss, I'm not sure about you but I think I'm in love," Antonio says from beside me.

I turn to look at him and think he must be fucking kidding, but his expression is the most serious I have seen in a while. His eyes are locked on his woman on the dance floor. I turn back to watch the girls dancing and focus on my Angel dancing around, enjoying herself. Could this be love? Fuck! Fuck! My heart is banging out a military tattoo in my chest, I feel like someone has sucker punched me. I'm in love with this girl and I barely know her. "Fuck," I mumble.

Antonio laughs and slaps me on the back as he gets to his feet. "Tell me about it, Boss. Who knew that instant love shit actually happens." He shakes his head and chuckles. "I don't know how to explain it, all I know is I haven't stopped thinking about her since we left her café today. When she walked in here tonight, I felt this weird connection I have never felt before. It was like she was coming home to me. Fuck I sound like a fucking pussy, but there's something about that girl."

I want to turn around and tell him to grow the fuck up and act like my *capo Bastone,* but fuck if he isn't telling the truth because if I'm being honest, I felt it too. "*Fratello,* I know what you mean." I take a swig of my drink. "I don't know about you, but I'm thinking we better go claim our girls before some vultures try and dance with them."

Sure enough, I look out to the floor to find there are about a dozen guys hanging around the edge staring at Brooklyn and Kat. Time to put a stop to this shit, we need to take them to the VIP area. I look at Antonio and know he's thinking the same thing as me when he nods his head toward the stairs.

I get ready to move when Antonio sidles over close. "What do you want to do about Janet?"

I look toward the bar and see Janet throwing death stares at the girls. I shake my head, that bitch never learns. "Leave her to me, I'll deal with her."

Antonio nods "Ok, but are you sure you don't want my Tiger to deal with her? She's more than capable." He chuckles.

"Si, I believe so too, you've got your hands full with that one *Fratello.*"

"Si, and it's going to be fun to tame her," Antonio speaks so low I barely hear him over the music as we make our way over to the girls.

I grab Angel around the waist bringing her back into my chest and start moving my body to the beat of the music. She tenses up and I lower my head to the crook of her neck, breathing in her scent, as I whisper in her ear. "Angel it's me, you're safe. I would never let anything happen to you, and I sure as shit won't let anyone touch you." My words seem to relax her and she starts to move with me. Feeling her soft body relaxing into my hard chest brings a smile to my face. I lift my head to glare at the vultures still hanging around in the hopes they may get a dance. They back the fuck off and I'm met with a couple of arms raised in surrender before they turn around and walk away. I go back to dancing with my Angel and try to remember the last time I danced. I don't think I ever have except when my momma tried to teach me. I close my eyes and breathe Angel in, when I feel her completely relax, I hold her closer so there is no room between us. Lifting my head, I catch Janet's eye at the bar. She's standing there staring, mouth open, eyes wide. *Now, do you get it?* I will be speaking to her about the show earlier, anger flares when I remember her threatening Kat as we walked away from the bar. I don't think anybody else heard it, but I sure as shit did. After tonight she can kiss her fucking job goodbye.

"We're going to take you girls up to the VIP lounge, so you can dance there. There are a private bar and lounge area which are more comfortable than the booths." I whisper in Angel's ear and feel the shiver run through her body. I know if she answers me, she'll have that breathy quality to her voice I like so much and it will be my undoing. I'll say "fuck it" and drag her ass out of here. I grab her hand and start moving toward the stairs before she can say a word because I will lose what little control I have left. I look over my shoulder to make sure Antonio and Kat are following, he gives me a chin lift and leads Kat off the floor.

⁂

Brooklyn

As we thread through the crowd toward the stairs leading to the VIP section, I peer over my shoulder ensuring Kat is following. Antonio is dragging her from the dance floor, I think he may have been a bit jealous of other guys trying to dance with her. I smirk at her and Kat gives me the evil eye which causes me to burst into laughter.

"What's so funny, Angel?" Dom leans close and whispers in my ear.

I can't control the tremor which runs through my body or the heat pooling between my legs. When I hear his voice so close to my ear, it's like he owns my body, it triggers something deep inside me.

"I was thinking, Kat and Antonio would make a good couple. From what I've seen so far, he doesn't put up with her shit and she definitely won't put up with his. It's interesting to watch it's like *Batman* and *Catwoman* meeting for the first time and I'm wondering who will win."

Dom chuckles and it makes me giggle again. We make our way up the stairs to the VIP section and I take the opportunity to look around, taking it all in. It's gorgeous up here with deep maroon walls, black leather couches, small tables with tea light candles on each and a smaller bar area with purple lights around the edges. A neon sign behind the bar says *VIP*, it's very elegant.

"WOW! This place is gorgeous, Dom." I sink into a soft couch and run my fingers over the luxurious leather. *Talk about luscious.*

"I'm glad you like it, and I'm very pleased I can hear your beautiful voice up here." Dom sits beside me.

I feel my face heat and glance down to where my fingers are intertwined in my lap. I can't help my nervousness when he speaks like that to me, it floors me. I have never been complimented so much in my life, let alone one day. I'm not sure I know how to handle it considering Darren never had anything nice to say. *No! Don't go there, we're having a great night, let's not ruin it by thinking of him.* I shrug off my thoughts when Dom grazes his fingers down my arm causing goose bumps to pebble my skin.

"Where did you go, beautiful?" He leans in and murmurs in my ear.

"Hmmm… What?" I turn my attention back to Dom. "I'm sorry, babe, I zoned out for a minute there." I gaze into his eyes, fuck they're gorgeous.

"I like you calling me, babe," Dom says quietly.

Fuck, I did call him babe. What the hell? I barely know this guy and I'm calling him babe, he probably thinks I'm some lovesick fool. Shit. Love? LOVE? What the fuck is wrong with me? The first guy to be nice to me and I'm gonna scare him away. Fuck!

"I'm sorry, so sorry it just slipped out. I'm sor…" Dom places his fingers over my mouth effectively shutting me up.

"Shh, it's ok. I like it. It sounds sexy coming from you." He caresses my cheek, runs his index finger from my temple to my bottom lip and tucks a finger under my chin to lift my face up to his. I flinch, freeze up, waiting and bracing myself for what's to come.

I see it in his eyes the moment he realizes something is wrong. He drops his hand and places it on my hand in my lap. I look down and realize I'm digging my nails into my leg. Shit, could I be any more screwed up? I know it's coming, he'll realize I'm too much trouble. I knew I shouldn't have come out tonight, I just mess things up. I'm so pathetic, I'm such a failure. I feel like I'm going to cry, my bottom lip trembles. I'm surprised when Dom speaks.

"Shh… Sweetheart, I swear I would never hurt you. Seeing that look in your eyes, the sheer panic and fear breaks my heart." He speaks softly so as not to let everyone know what we are talking about and it makes me like him even more. He's protecting me.

"My beautiful, Angel. Who hurt you?"

I don't know how to answer. I know I'm not ready to talk about it right now, and especially not here in a club. I shake my head as a rogue tear runs down my cheek.

Dom brushes his thumb over my cheek and captures my tear, he follows it with a light kiss. "Ok, we don't have to talk about this right now, but hopefully soon you'll trust me enough to tell me your secrets." He kisses me on the forehead. "Shit, you smell good." He rests his chin lightly on my head and it brings a smile to my face. I'm still smiling when he sits back.

"That's better, you are absolutely gorgeous, but when you smile, it's like I'm looking at the sun for the first time in my life."

"God, I love your accent, where are you from?" I attempt to change the subject, because if he continues speaking like that, I may melt into a puddle on the floor. I know it's lame but I also couldn't think of anything to say that wouldn't make me sound so desperate for his attention. Dom looks at me and smiles, I think he knows what his words are doing to me and he knows what I'm trying to do, but he doesn't seem to mind.

"I'm from Italy. Born and raised until about a year ago, when I moved here. And, yourself?" His thumb rubs tiny circles in the palm of my hand.

"I was born right here in Newcastle, but my Mom, Dad and I moved to Sydney when I was twelve. That's when I met Kat. She's my Best friend."

"So, what brought you back to Newcastle?"

"Um…Oh…Um… It's a long story, I won't bore you with details but I really missed Kat and I wanted to give my daughter a better life and…" I stop dead, realizing I have just dropped a bomb. But, I guess if he can't handle knowing I have a daughter, that's his problem, not mine. This is who I am. I come with a gorgeous little mini me and I will not have some guy I barely know get pissed about the fact I have a beautiful child and…

"I bet she's as gorgeous as her momma, no?"

I'm completely caught off guard. I didn't expect that response at all. I must be staring at him like a deer caught in headlights if his low chuckle is anything to go by.

"Um… She's gorgeous, cheeky, full of life and very smart. She gives Kat a run for her money." I laugh as I remember her bouncing around Gwen's kitchen earlier, and how excited she was about decorating cookies. I wrap my arms around myself, I'm missing my little sweet pea.

"How old is this little Princess?"

"She just turned five and her name is Evie, she's my whole world."

"I have no doubt in my mind that's true, your whole face lights up when you talk about her." He caresses my cheek with his fingers and instead of flinching away this time, I lean into his touch. It's warm and comforting.

"That's better, relax, you're safe with me."

I stare into his captivating eyes of his and I'm lost in the look he is giving me. It's like I'm his world and I *am* safe. I'm completely mesmerized and it takes me a minute to realize Kat is saying something to me.

"Hey, Dollface, do you wanna get another drink?"

"Yeah, sure" I stare back at Dom and something passes between us. I'm not sure what it is exactly, but it makes me feel all warm inside. I reach out and grab Kat's outstretched hand, she pulls me onto my feet and we head to the bar.

"Fuck, Brooklyn, Antonio is one of the most annoying people I have ever met. Geez he's lucky he's sexy and those eyes, mmm..." She closes her eyes and her lips turn up into a smile.

I giggle and nudge her with my shoulder, she rolls her eyes and continues with her rant "Anyway, it's lucky he looks like he does, otherwise I would slap him so hard skittles would fly out of that dirty ass mouth of his."

I burst into laughter, I can't help it she just cracks me up. I give her a sideways hug as we sidle up to the bar. "Fuck, I love you girl, you say the craziest shit sometimes."

"I'm guessing you're having a good night. You and Dom seem to be getting along." She winks at me.

"I'm having a great night, thanks for talking me into coming out tonight. Dom's nice, I don't know why, but there's something about him that draws me in." I shrug.

"Tell me about it," Kat mumbles, her voice is so low I'm lucky to catch it. I don't call her on it, but she knows I heard her.

I smile and wink at her, in true Kat style she rolls her beautiful baby blue eyes before giving me a tight hug.

Six

Dominic

I sip my drink and watch the girls walk towards the bar. I feel the seat next to me compress as Antonio sits down. His lips are pursed as he tries to hide his amusement. It's actually a good look on him, I haven't seen him this happy in years.

"Boss, I'm thinking that little spitfire right there…" Antonio points to Kat "…is like a dream come true."

"Why, because she won't take your shit?" I try not to laugh.

"Yeah, and the fact that when I look at her I see a future." Antonio sighs and runs a hand through his hair "I sound like a complete pussy. Fuck!"

"You know you can always be honest with me. I may be the *Capofamiglia* (Boss), but you are like a *Fratello* to me and it's always been that way. It's like I know I can tell you anything.

I'm about to tell him, I think I'm feeling the same about my Angel when I notice the girls heading our way. I give Antonio a small nod so he knows we will finish this later. When I turn toward the girls again, I notice a guy in front of Brooklyn and I don't like the look of him. When she attempts to move away, the *cazzo* (dick) grabs her arm.

"What the fuck?" I catapulted to my feet and moved forward in time to see Angel flinch slightly. If I hadn't been watching so closely, I may have missed it. She squares her shoulders and says something to him, but it's so loud in here I can't hear it. The prick pushes Kat out of the way causing her to trip and fall to the floor – Antonio is not gonna be happy. The prick raises his hand as if he's about to hit Angel. My anger goes from serious to explosive at warp speed. As far as I'm concerned, no-one touches a woman, and most definitely not my woman. I'm on him in a millisecond, my fingers dig into the back of his neck and I lean real close so I can whisper in his ear, "let go or I *will* teach you some manners."

"Hey, don't fucking touch me, I just wanted a dance with the bitch." He twists and pushes me away.

I nod my head locking eyes with Antonio who's standing on the other side of him, helping Kat off the floor.

"Escort this *cazzo* out and he is *never* to set foot in here again"

"Who the fuck do you think you are?" He glances to his side spots Antonio and turns back to me.

I lean close so only he can hear me and growl in his ear. "I'm your worst fucking nightmare"

I see the flash in his eyes when it registers who I am. His face pales as he starts rambling on with shit. "I'm sorry man, you know how woman get. Sometimes they need to be shown who's boss." He tries to justify his actions.

"Well, I'm about to show you who's boss." I push him toward Antonio who grabs hold of him and drags him to the back of the club. Kat follows hot on his heels, yelling in the *cazzo*'s face.

I turn to face my Angel, still trying to rein in my anger. "Th-Thank you. I appreciate it," she mumbles.

Before I can say anything, she spins on her heel and hurries away.

What. The. Fuck?

"Angel wait!" I call out and she stops dead in her tracks. She turns and locks eyes with me, I watch as her shoulders slump and she lets out a breath like she was holding it in the whole time, maybe she was. I make my way toward her, careful not to scare her off. It's then I notice, her eyes are glassy and a single tear rolls down her cheek. I move closer, wrap my arms around her and bend to whisper in her ear.

"*Hey il Mio Amore*, it's ok I've got you." I hold her closer, her body sags against me and she's shaking. Shit, she's crying. Hard. *I'll kill that motherfucker when I get my hands on him.*

I sweep her into my arms, cradling her small body against my chest and make my way to the lounge. I rub my fingers over her back in soothing circles, trying to calm her down. I whisper everything is ok and I promise her again, I won't let anybody hurt her. I know for sure now, that this woman is a victim of abuse. The signs are right in front of my face, the freezing up when someone touches her and the flinching when someone yells near, or around her. Someone has badly hurt my Angel, and I won't stop until I find out who, and dispose of them. But, for now, I will hold her and be her rock.

"I-I'm s-s-sorry I didn't m-mean to make you a-angry." Brooklyn sobs into my neck.

I place my fingers and lift her chin so I am looking into her eyes. "Angel, my beautiful Angel, you could never make me angry." I hope to God she believes me.

Her eyes search my face and I feel her body relax against me. Thank fuck she believes me. The last thing I need is for her to be scared of me before I get a chance to get to know her and to see if she can accept me for my flaws, and my job.

"I d-didn't make you angry?" Her voice is husky and shaky.

"*il Mio Amore* no, but that asshole made me very angry when he put his hands on you. NO-one touches you unless you want them too. Do you understand that, Angel? I *will* protect you."

"You promise?"

"Always, my darling." Shit that just slipped out. *Don't get scared, please don't get scared.* I'm pulled from my thoughts when she holds me tighter and buries her head against my chest.

"Please hold me. I'm so tired of being scared," she whispers. I'm not sure she meant for me to hear her words, but I did, and I'm going to sit here and hold her all fucking night if I have to.

I'm not sure how long we sit with her clinging to me, but I don't really care. Nothing else matters, but the Angel in my arms. I glance up when I hear Antonio and Kat come back upstairs.

"You should have let me finish him like cheesecake, Antonio. You didn't need to interfere. I told you, I can look after myself." Kat hisses through clenched teeth as she stomps closer.

I try not to laugh at the pair of them, but they have been going at each other all night and it's quite amusing.

"Kitten, if you want cheesecake, I'll buy you some and you can finish that all by yourself. Sound good?" Antonio smiles at Kat but she glares back.

"Kitten?"

"You didn't like Tiger."

"Humph, better I guess."

"I still like Tiger."

I feel a slight movement in my arms and I look down. Brooklyn is biting her lip, trying not to laugh. I wink at her as I chuckle, I'm getting lost in those beautiful eyes of hers, feeling her body now fully relaxed.

"Did you get dropped on your head when you were born?" Kat asks.

"Yeah into a pool of sexy." Antonio wiggles his eyebrows.

I watch Kat and wait for what she'll say next. She's biting her lip to prevent herself from laughing, but in the end, the laughter wins out. It's like a chain reaction setting Brooklyn off, then Antonio and I laugh along with them.

When Kat manages a breath and starts to speak, I wait for another comeback, but she shakes her head and growls, "fucking men!"

"How about we get you girls home? I'm pretty sure Brooklyn has had more than enough excitement for one night." She clings to me tighter and I realize she doesn't want to let me go. It's as if she's afraid I'll disappear. I cuddle her close. "Angel, I have a few meetings tomorrow and Friday, but if it's okay with you, can I come see you sometime Friday evening or Saturday? It's getting late and you look like you could do with some sleep." To confirm my point, Brooklyn places her hand over her mouth and yawns, making me chuckle.

"I am a little tired. I'm working tomorrow and Friday. Saturday I'm taking Evie to the beach, so I will leave it up to you."

I see insecurity and doubt in her eyes, maybe she thinks I'm just feeding her lines about wanting to see her again and keeping her safe. I'm guessing it doesn't matter what I say, she probably won't believe me until I show her. I lean down and kiss her forehead. The blush I love so much creeps down her neck. Fuck, I can't wait to see how far down it spreads. *One step at a time Dom, we don't want to scare her off.* "Si, sounds good to me. I'll call. Come on, let's get you home." I lean forward and kiss her on the forehead again like it's the most natural thing for me to do. I stand and head toward the stairs still holding her in my arms. Fuck she feels good, like she belongs there.

"Babe I can walk, you don't have to carry me."

I look down and give her a wink. I love hearing her call me, babe, it sounds so right. "I like holding you close against me." I lean down and kiss her forehead again because I can, and because I ache to keep touching, and kissing her soft skin.

Brooklyn

Building sand castles with Evie is one of my favorite things to do. Watching as she runs her fingers through the sand, runs off to find leaves, little twigs, and shells to help decorate her creations. I love watching how her little mind works.

"Mommy...mommy, can we make a big one this time? I love it when we make big ones"

"Hmm? Of course, Sweetpea, anything you want"

The sun is shining as I sit here listening to the waves crash against the rocks. I haven't seen or heard from Dom since Wednesday night. I guess he's been busy or he figured I wasn't worth his time. I'm disappointed, but I can't blame him. Maybe it's for the best. Watching the boats in the distance my mind drifts back to the moments my life changed forever. I remember the fights, harsh words and rub my arm absently as if the bruises are still there. I know I can't put Evie and myself through that again.

"Bitch! You think I'm with you because of love?" Darren spits in my face and throws me to the ground so hard it knocks the air from my lungs. I know I'll have fresh bruises and grazes tomorrow. I curl up on the floor waiting for the next blow to come. I puzzle over what I had actually done wrong to bring on his anger. I'm brought back to the present with a sharp kick to my side. "I had to fucking stay with your worthless ass because YOU decided to get pregnant. Fucking bitch."

I attempt to banish the thoughts plaguing me and concentrate on listening to Evie giggling. She's trying to sing along with the words on the radio I brought along with us. Hearing her giggle and happy has to be the best sound in the world. I can't believe I could have lost this. *No, I'm not going to think about the past now. It's bad enough he stalks my dreams at night, I'm not going to have him ruin my days too. Fuck that!* I bend down and pick up another shell and place it in the pile Evie already has and help her build our beautiful sand castle.

The hairs on the back of my neck prickle, I feel like I'm being watched. I try not to panic and look around to see if I'm just imagining it. I wasn't. Dominic is leaning against a black, shiny car. He's wearing blue jeans and a tight black shirt, watching us. Fuck, the man is sex on legs. He pushes off the car and heads toward us. As I watch him approach, a fluttering feeling in my belly like butterflies are going crazy....actually, screw the butterflies it's more like a herd of elephants dancing the tango. I chuckle to myself.

Evie grabs hold of my leg a bit tighter than normal when she looks up to see the tall, dark stranger nearby. I rub my hand over her back in a soothing motion and assure her everything is fine.

When Dominic reaches us a spark ignites inside me, it feels like I can let go, I'm safe. It's as if this is where I'm meant to be, who I'm meant to be with. Why can't I stop these feelings when he looks into my eyes, they seem to suck me in and won't let me go. If I'm being completely honest, it all scares the shit out of me.

A gorgeous smile lights up his handsome face and I can't help but return it. He crouches in front of me until he's eye level with Evie, but she shies away. Dom offers her his hand. Evie looks at me to see if he's okay. I nod and smile when she reaches out to shake Dom's hand. He gives her a bright smile and she smiles back. There must be something comforting about his smile because I slowly feel Evie relax and watch as she takes a couple of steps closer to him.

"Hi there, Princess. My name is Dominic, what's yours?"

"Hi, I'm Evie, but my mommy calls me Sweetpea."

Dominic laughs

"Well, Evie it's a pleasure to meet you. Would you like me to call you, Sweetpea or Princess?"

"Um…" Evie pauses with her little finger to her lip, like she's pondering a serious problem. I try and stifle my giggle. "I like Princess because my mommy says we make sand castles and I'm the princess. Right mommy, I'm the Princess?" She tugs on my shorts

I laugh, crouch down and run my fingers through her gorgeous blonde hair. "Of course, Sweetpea, you are my Princess."

Without warning, Evie turns her big blue eyes on Dominic and asks, "are you here to hurt my mommy?"

I don't know what to say and stand. I begin gathering our belongings and hear Dominic talking to Evie.

"No, Princess, I would *never* hurt your momma or you. As a matter of fact, I came to see if you two lovely ladies would like to have lunch with me."

"Oh, mommy can we please? I'm hungry. Please... pleeeease..." Her hands are clenched together, her eyes wide as she begs me to say yes.

"Oh, Sweetpea. I... uh... I don't think it's such a good idea" I'm flustered, I don't know what I should do. *If I spend any more time with this man, I'm sure I will get my heart broken and I don't think I could survive it. I really shouldn't be thinking about this stuff right now, I have enough to worry about. What if Darren finds us? What if he sees me with Dominic.? Shit! What am I going to do?* I'm jolted from my thoughts when Evie tugs on my shorts.

"Oh please, mommy plllleeeease?"

I glance down, her little eyes sparkle with the possibility of a fancy lunch. When I turn to Dominic, his eyes are pleading with me too. *Ahhh, shit, how can I say no to both of them?*

"Okay Sweetpea, but we can't stay out late. We'll have to go and get you changed first and get all this sand off you."

"Okay, mommy. Yes!" Evie fist pumps the air as she bounces up and down, she stops as another thought comes to her. "Can we get ice cream too?"

Dominic answers, trying not to laugh. "If it's okay with your momma, after lunch we can get some ice cream."

"Um, yeah okay. I'll take her to get ready, I can meet you there if you like? I don't want to make you wait around. We live just up the road so let me know where and..."

Before I can continue, Dom cuts me off "It's not a problem. I can wait, I have all day to spend with you. I'll drive you ladies home so you can get changed."

I look at Dominic then turn to his car "It's ok we can walk, it won't take us long. I wouldn't want to get sand in your car."

Dom slides his hand up my arm, and I feel the prickle of goose bumps. "Brooklyn, it's fine. It's just a bit of sand."

"Um.." I twist my fingers in each other as I squirm, Darren would have been livid if we'd put even one grain of sand in his car.

Dominic laughs, it's such a wonderful sound, I get lost in it for a moment then realize he has grabbed mine and Evie's hands and is leading us toward his car. The feel of his rough hand in mine and listening to his smooth accent causes a shiver to line dance down my spine. My logical brain has gone into hiding and all the reasons I had to not go to lunch don't seem to matter anymore.

"Come on you two, we need lunch and some ice cream for my Princess." Dominic throws a wink my way. *I'm done, completely and utterly done, Turn the timer off and take me out of the oven.* I giggle at my thoughts. Fuck, I think the weirdest shit sometimes.

Seven

Dominic

I stand in Brooklyn's kitchen waiting for my girls to get ready for lunch. I notice how little of it represents my Angel. There are a few pictures on the fridge, one of Evie and Kat snuggled on the lounge together and another of the three of them on the beach. It's obvious they are the very best of friends. I move closer and smile at a photo of Evie dressed up as a princess and another with her face painted like a butterfly.

"Do you like my mommy?" A soft voice from behind startles me.

I turn to find Evie studying me. I sink to my heels so I can look in her eyes, so much like her mommas. Hopefully, she will see as well as hear the truth in my words when I answer her.

"Si, I like your momma, very much." I tuck a renegade blonde curl behind her ear before I go on. "And, I like you as well, Princess."

A small smile pulls at her lips before it drops and she frowns before speaking again. "You promise you won't hurt her, like my horrible ex-daddy did?" She focuses on my eyes again and I see the tears welling in hers, her bottom lip trembles. It takes all my control to rein in my anger at the man who hurt my Angel and broke this poor little one's heart.

"I promise I will *never* hurt your momma." I inhale a deep breath before I pry further, I don't know how well I'll handle the answer I expect. "Why do you call him your ex-daddy?"

Evie squares her little shoulders, so much like her mother. She sniffs back her tears and when she answers me, her young voice is strong. I can't believe how brave this little one is.

"Aunty Kat told me, men should never, ever hurt their little girls or their mommies. She said he's not a good man and sure isn't my daddy."

I drag my fingers through my hair. "Well, your Aunty Kat is a smart woman and you are a very brave little girl."

"My mommy is the brave one, he hurt her so much." She sniffs again. "She's been sad for a long time. At night when she thinks I'm asleep. I hear her crying. Sometimes she wakes up and screams. I wish I could make her happy again." She sniffs again wiping her nose and the tears with the back of her hand. Her smile returns with full force before she continues, "today she was happy and smiling, my mommy was different. Please make my mommy happy like that all the time."

My heart squeezes in my chest and I'm trembling with pure rage. The *stronzo* is dead when I get my hands on him. *Antonio and I are going to give torture a whole new meaning when we get our hands on the asshole.*

I gently place my hands on Evie's shoulders and draw her closer. I place a finger under her chin and tilt her face up. "*Principessa*, I promise, your momma and you are safe and no-one will ever hurt you again. You are mine now and I will do everything in my power to make sure you're both happy."

That earns me a bright smile and she relaxes her shoulders as if a big weight has been lifted off them. I need to change the subject before I lose my temper, my little Princess does not need to see that, she has already dealt with enough at her young age.

"So, Princess what kind of Ice Cream do you like?"

Brooklyn comes down the stairs and my eyes almost pop from my head. She's absolutely breathtaking in a white sundress with a flower print which hits just above the knees. I can tell the sun kissed her today and her blonde hair bounces on her shoulders.

Fuck, one look and I'm hard as stone. What is about this woman that throws me for a fucking loop? I pick my jaw up off the floor and subtly adjust myself. Not subtle enough, a smile spreads across her face as her eyes are drawn to my discomfort.

"Are we ready to go?" she asks.

"Angel you are breathtakingly beautiful." My voice sounds huskier. Evie giggles and I look down to find she is staring straight at me. I give her a wink. Hopefully, she didn't notice me trying to adjust myself. I have to get us out of here before I say, *fuck it* and take her on the nearest hard surface. Definitely not something Evie needs to see.

I gather Evie's small hand in mine and move close to Brooklyn. I wrap my arm around her waist, lower my head and place a soft kiss on her temple while I breathe in her scent. "Come on ladies, time for lunch." I lead my ladies from the house.

As I drive toward the *Surf House*, I glance over to see Brooklyn is twisting her fingers in her lap. I reach over, grab her hand and rub my thumb over her pulse point. She trembles. *Fuck, I love how she responds to my touch.* I glance in the rear-view mirror to make sure Evie is ok before turning my focus back to the road.

"What's wrong, Angel?' I hope my soft voice is soothing.

She flinches at the sound of my voice and shakes her head. I chuckle a little because I know she was deep in thought, and by the looks of the blush creeping down her neck, it was probably something dirty. *Interesting...*

"Um... well th-there's a bit of sand in the car, but I promise I'll..."

I cut her train of thought off with a soft growl and realize my mistake the instant she freezes beside me. *Shit, I'm a cazzo.* I rub her hand again, giving it a soft squeeze before I speak. I feel some of the tension leave her body.

"Listen to me, darling. I don't care about sand in the car and I don't want you to worry about that kind of shit anymore. It doesn't matter, the only thing that matters, is we have a nice relaxing lunch followed by ice cream." I give her a wink to lighten the mood and it brings a gorgeous smile to her face.

"Whatever happened in the past is not what is happening here and now with us. I told you on Wednesday night, I would never hurt you and I meant it. I gave you my word and I never break my word." She nods her head and relaxes back in the seat.

After turning into the carpark, I slot the car into a space. When I step out, I have to adjust myself again. *Fuck, being in a car surrounded by her scent, has me going crazy.* I shake my head as I move to the other side of the car and open Brooklyn's door. I then open Evie's, I'm almost knocked to the ground when Evie leaps on me and tries to climb me like a tree.

"Sweetpea, be careful you nearly knocked Dom over! Maybe you should walk?" Brooklyn rushes over to us. "I'm so sorry Dom, really sorry I don't know..."

I hold up my hand as I laugh. "Angel, stop. It's fine. I'm honored she wants me to carry her." I lift the child into my arms. "You weigh next to nothing huh, Princess?" Evie smiles as she nods and then shocks me by planting a kiss on my cheek. I could easily fall in love with this precious little girl.

"Ok ladies, let's go." I gather Brooklyn's small hand in mine.

<hr>

Brooklyn

What can I say? Lunch was perfect - great food, a fantastic view of the beach and even better company. I still have that nagging voice inside my head telling me this may be a bad idea, but I'm trying hard to ignore it. Bringing Dom into our lives right now could be one of the worst mistakes of my life. I don't want to get him caught up in the mess I have created for myself. I don't want to get him hurt and that's what could happen. Darren could find us tomorrow and I have no doubt in my mind he would try and hurt Dominic.

I chastise myself, thinking about my past sends chills down my spine and achieves nothing. Evie and I have had one of the best days of our lives and I don't want to bring myself down thinking about such rubbish, there's time for that later. I want to enjoy the rest of today with a man who brings a smile to Evie's face and peace to my heart. I don't think I've heard Evie laugh this much in a very long time. I believe Dominic when he says he would never hurt us, but can I allow a relationship to develop when at the end of the day I'm still fighting demons from the past?

I watch Evie eating her ice cream, I can't remember how long it's been since I have seen her this happy. A smile spreads across my face and I break into laughter when she trips and lobs her ice cream down the front of Dom's shirt. *Shit, I shouldn't be standing here laughing, maybe this will push him over the edge.* I hurry closer to them. When I reach Dom, I realize he's not mad. He is actually smirking and biting his sexy as sin lip in an attempt to hold back his laughter. He eventually loses the battle, and yet again, I find myself transfixed by the sound of his deep husky laugh.

"Little *Amore*, if you didn't like my shirt you could have just told me." Dom bubbles with laughter.

"How about we head home and I'll see if I can clean up your shirt. Evie, I think it's bath time for you." I glance at my watch and see it's almost 5pm. I hadn't realized it had gotten so late. Wow, the day has flown by.

Dom looks at his own watch. "Sounds like a plan." He waves his hand in the air. "Not the shirt part, but I didn't realize how late it was."

Shit, maybe he had plans. "I'm sorry we have kept you out all day." He probably has work to do or somewhere to be. Wait, what does he do for work? I haven't asked, but he must be someone important. He has an aura of power around him. It starts me recalling what I do know about him....

I saw how people looked at him last night and again today at lunch. He drives an expensive Lexus and he had a bodyguard the other day. Hmmm, Antonio was calling him, Boss. Boss of what? I should ask, but, instead, I find myself saying, "You must have better things you need to be doing, rather than hanging out with us. I'll understand if you need to leave." *Shit did I say that? Talk about being needy, let's have a pity party for one shall we and be done with it? Fuck, I'm pathetic.*

"I have nothing that can't wait." He growls low in his throat again, but this time I don't freeze up. Instead, heat pools low in my belly, and when his arm wraps around my waist, I lean into him. I hear him breathe me in and mumble, "good girl" into my hair as he presses a kiss against my head. I relax into his hard chest and inhale his intoxicating scent as I wrap my arms around his waist. When I pull back a little and peer down at Evie, I see the huge grin on her face. She bursts into giggles and points her little fingers at me. I look down, I have ice cream all over me too.

Dom chuckles low in his throat. "Ok ladies, I think it's time to get my girls home and cleaned up." Dom gives my ass a squeeze and I swear a tiny moan slips out. *Damn!*

I look at Dom and watch as a sexy smirk curves his lips and he raises a perfect dark eyebrow. Then slowly, oh so slowly, I watch his tongue dart out and lick that bottom lip. *Oh, hot damn, I want to taste that lip of his.* As if reading my mind, he places a soft kiss on my cheek and whispers in my ear.

"Baby, I'm hanging on by a thread here. Please stop looking at me like you want to devour me." He pauses for a minute and I think he's finished. I can't explain why I begin to feel rejected and try to pull away, but he pulls me back into his hard chest and continues. "I want to rip your clothes off and fuck you…" He pauses and looks into my eyes and I find myself melting against him. "But, we are in public and we have to get my Princess home for a bath."

Shit, I completely forgot where we were, I was so caught up in the moment. *Shit!*

Dom must have seen my alarm, and as if he could read my mind, he shakes his head, telling me everything is fine. He gives my ass another squeeze before bending down and scooping Evie into his arm. With me under his other arm, we make our way to the car and like the gentleman he is, he opens my door and then Evie's. He places her into her car seat, ensuring she's safe. I was a shocked when I first saw a child's car seat in his car and I asked about it. His answer? *"I sent one of my men out to buy it for my Princess, she must be kept safe."* Maybe, I should have felt scared or worried, but I must admit it was kind of sweet that he knew Evie needed a car seat, and it made me melt a bit more for this caring man.

I add bubble bath into the running water for Evie's bath. I'm swirling my hand around making sure the temp is just right when Evie comes bouncing in, giggling.

"Mommy, is my bath ready?"

"Nearly. How about we get you ready to hop in?" She turns around and I start taking her piggy tales out.

"Mommy?"

"Hmmm...?"

"I like Dom, he makes you smile and laugh."

I spin her around and look into her eyes, tears are near the surface. "Sweetpea, what's wrong?"

She bites her lip and sniffs back her tears, it about breaks my heart. "I don't want you to be sad anymore. Can Dom be with us always?"

I swear my heart cracks a little. I run my fingers across her cheek and catch a stray tear. "Shhhh, Sweetpea please don't cry."

She moves into my arms and gives me a big hug. "Dom won't hurt us, mommy. He promised and I believe him," she whispers in my ear.

I pull back a little and feel a tear slide over my cheek. Evie wipes it away. "I believe him too, Sweetpea." I watch as a megawatt smile breaks out across her face. "Ok, no more tears, let's get you into the tub."

I finish stripping her off and she climbs up the small steps to help her get in. "Nice and slow, I don't want you to slip and fall." I hold my hand out to help her, but she laughs.

"Mommy I know, I'm a big girl now. I can do it by myself." I watch as she lowers herself into the water. "You can go now."

"Okay, call out when you have finished playing and I'll come and wash your hair, I'll just be outside the door."

"Okay, mommy."

I feel a little thrown off by the conversation I had with Evie. I don't want her to get hurt anymore because of me and my stupid mistakes. She has already been through enough. I question *again*, what the hell I'm doing with Dom. I know he would never hurt us physically, I wasn't lying when I told Evie he wouldn't. It's weird to think, considering we have only known each other a couple of days, but I feel it deep down in my bones. He's a good man. But, what about emotionally? I can already see Evie getting attached to him and eventually he will leave, everybody does. Except Kat, she has always been there for me. No matter what happened, she was always there.

Maybe, deep down I was hoping I wouldn't need to reveal the shit from my past and we could be like any other couple. Unfortunately, I don't have that option because eventually the past will catch up to me and I'll either be dragged back to hell or I won't make it to my twenty-fourth birthday. I remember the words Darren said to me a couple of nights before I left.....

I was on my knees in front of him and he had just finished in my mouth. He had ripped my head back so hard, I felt my hair coming out at the roots. I tried so hard to stop the scream that came out of my mouth. He bent down to get in my face and gritted out, "You're a good little slut, that's all you're good for and don't you forget it. You belong to me. You and that little bitch down the hall, and if I can't have both of you, then nobody will." He spat in my face and I don't remember anything after that because he knocked me out. I woke up on the floor the next morning with a crying Evie lying beside me. I hugged her tight, trying to work out what the hell I could do.

I must have been completely zoned out because I slam into a hard body and freeze instantly. I cower, waiting for a blow that never comes. *Shit, I'm so pathetic.*

"Angel, are you okay?" A deep voice asks.

Dom has his hands on my arms and a concerned look on his face. I know he noticed my terrified reaction, but he doesn't say anything. *God damn the man is sexy!*

I clear my throat before I answer. "Um… yea, I'm fine, just waiting for Evie to be ready for me so I can wash her hair."

"Are you sure? You looked pretty zoned out there for a minute." He rubs his hands slowly over my arms, it's comforting and I find myself wrapping my arms around his waist. I feel safe in his arms and it's like his body was made for mine. I fit perfectly against him.

I snuggle into his warm body, breathe in his fresh scent and run my hands up and down his back. He has no shirt on and I'm feeling his hard, sculpted body for the first time. *Wow! Oh wow, um, what do I do now? Shit.* I start to pull back, but he tightens his hold. Not so tight that he's hurting me, but the right pressure to help me relax into him again. And that's when I feel it, a hard ridge poking me in the stomach.

He's hard! For me? Oh my god, he's hard for *me*. I clear my throat and take a small step back so I can look into his eyes. "Why don't you have a shirt on?" Dom chuckles low in his throat and I feel the vibration run through my body. I squeeze my legs together to relieve the sudden ache that's appeared.

"There was ice cream on my shirt, remember? I'm sorry if it makes you uncomfortable, I can put it back on if you want? I just don't have a spare one in the car."

"NO!" I say a little louder than I should have. "I mean, no it's fine. Sorry, I forgot. I'll fix it for you if you can go grab…"

Dom smiles at me. "Already taken care of *il Mio Amore*." He points down the stairs toward the laundry. "It's hanging up in the laundry."

"You did it yourself? I'm so sorry I should have taken care of it before I fixed Evie…" Before I can finish what I'm saying, Dom cuts me off by placing a finger over my lips.

"Angel, you are not my slave, I can fix my own shirt." He pulls me back into his arms.

"You're Hard!" *Shit! Why do I keep blurting this shit out? He probably thinks I'm the craziest bitch alive.* "Sorry, I swear I'm not crazy."

This time, Dom doesn't hold back. He cracks up laughing and it's so loud it makes me laugh.

"Firstly, I don't think you're crazy, secondly, I love that you say what's on your mind and thirdly, Si I'm hard. I've been hard since you first turned those baby blue eyes on me."

"That can't be possible." Dom slides a finger under my chin and tilts my head up so I'm looking into his gorgeous emerald eyes. "Do you wear contacts?" Dom chuckles again and he has a sexy smirk on his lips again.

"No, I don't, do you? I swear they are the most beautiful eyes I have ever seen; they are absolutely mesmerizing. The first time I looked into your eyes it made my whole world flip on its head and I felt for the first time in my life like I was actually living. Before I met you, it felt like I was walking around with blinders on, going through the motions of living. One look at you and it was like you flipped a switch inside me, all of a sudden the sun was brighter, the air was fresher and the ocean was clearer."

Holy Shit! I am absolutely speechless and I have no clue how to respond to his words. So, instead, I stand on tiptoes and place my lips on his. It's soft at first like we're testing each other. As the kiss grows firmer, more insistent, his tongue swipes across my bottom lip. I gasp in surprise and he takes the opportunity to slip the muscle inside my mouth to caress and tango with mine. As the kiss intensifies, I let him take control. He slides his hand into my hair holding me so close it feels like we don't have a millimeter between us. I suck on his bottom lip moaning a little, he groans and pulls back to rest his forehead against mine. We're both breathing heavy. I run my fingers across my swollen lips and swear they are tingling. I have never felt so much passion and need in my life, my whole body is on fire. I'm brought out of my lust filled haze when Dom mumbles, "fuck, even better than I thought."

I realize I have basically climbed the poor man like a tree, my legs are wrapped around his waist and my hands are tangled in his hair. I try to untangle myself, but Dom has other ideas and holds me tighter to him. We rest for a minute, forehead to forehead, and try to catch our breath.

"Sorry." I feel embarrassed.

"Never be sorry for kissing me like that my Angel, it took everything in me to pull back instead of turning you around and taking you up against the wall."

"Oh… okay." What am I supposed to say to that? I have never had sex against a wall before, fuck, I've only had sex once in my life and it's not like I can remember it.

I clear my head of those enticing thoughts as Dom keeps speaking, but not before he gives me a wink. "Before we go any further we have a little girl to put to bed and some things to talk about."

I'm sure he must know exactly what I'm thinking about. As if she was aware we were talking about her, Evie calls out "Mommy, finished."

I lock eyes with Dom and nod my head before I call back, "I'm coming, Sweetpea." I get a squeeze to the ass and I swear I hear him mumble, "I wish you were." I'm not too sure what he meant, but I really don't have a chance to ask before he is sliding me down his hard body. I feel every hard ridge and muscle and although I try to stifle a moan, I'm not successful. Dom chuckles as he turns toward the stairs, but not before he smacks me lightly on the ass and throws over his shoulder, "I'll put the kettle on while you sort out my Princess."

"Ok babe, sounds good." *Here I go again calling him babe... what in the ever-loving shit am I thinking calling him that and worst yet I kissed him? It's gonna make it much harder when I have to let him go. Not that I wanna let him go, but I don't think after the talk he wants to have, he is going to willingly stick around.* I turn and head back into the bathroom, he's right, I need to sort out Evie first and then we can talk.

Eight

Dominic

As I walk down the stairs heading to the kitchen, I adjust myself *again!* I've lost count how many times I've had to do it today. Fuck, get it together Dom, you're twenty-six-years-old. You're not a sixteen-year-old boy anymore. I reach over and switch the kettle on. While I search through the cupboards for coffee cups, I replay that amazing kiss again. Fuck it was hot, probably the best kiss of my life. It about killed me to pull back, but we have to have a chat first. I don't want to get in deep with this woman if she can't handle my job. Fuck, who am I trying to kid here? I'm already in deep, any deeper and I would be fucking drowning. *Fuck!* How did this happen? Yesterday I swear to Christ I had a pair of balls, I'm a fucking Mafia Boss! But, one look from her, and I was gone. When I met Evie it was like the final puzzle piece, I didn't know I was searching for, clicked into place. Fuck I hope she can accept me because I have already decided they are my life now. I don't know what I'll do if I lose them. I need to make her mine. I have never wanted anything as much as I want those two beautiful girls. *Fuck, I'm a pussy!* I rake my fingers through my hair while I contemplate how I'm going to make my Angel fall in love with me. Antonio was right when he said this was love.

My thoughts are cut off abruptly when I hear glass smash followed by a blood-curdling scream.

WHAT. THE. FUCK?

I bolt from the kitchen and take the steps two at a time to get to them as quickly as possible. I shout out Brooklyn's name as I frantically search the upstairs rooms. I swing a door open with a bang and find my girls huddled together on the floor. I rush over, sweep them both into my arms and move them away from the window.

"What the fuck happened?" My voice is abrupt, but I'm too pumped up to care right now. I see the terror in their eyes and Brooklyn points to the floor. In amongst the glass on the carpet is a brick with a note attached to it. "Fuck," I say to nobody in particular, but I feel Brooklyn tense in my arms. *Shit, you're scaring her you cazzo, settle the fuck down.* I take a deep breath and let it out slowly. "I'm sorry *il Mio Amore*." I kiss Brooklyn's temple and feel some of the tension leave her body. I gather myself and concentrate on the girls, I need to make sure they weren't hurt. I carry my girls into the hallway and set both of them down. I crouch down in front of Evie and stroke the tears from her cheeks. "Are you hurt Principessa?"

She shakes her head, but her voice is soft, shaky when she speaks. "No, it just scared me. What is Princi... Princi...?"

"Principessa. It means Princess in Italian."

She gives me a tiny smile as she sniffs and wipes her hand under her nose. I hug her to me and glance at Brooklyn who is pacing back and forth, tears stream down her face.

"Fuck, he's back. He knows where we are! Shit, what have I done?" Her eyes are wild with fear.

"You didn't do anything, Angel." My voice is soft, soothing but when I reach for her she steps back and waves her arms around frantically. "He must have seen you with me. I need Kat. We need to get out of here, go somewhere so he can't find us again."

I'd heard enough. There is no way she's leaving me, being scared off by some fucking bastard. I'll make damn fucking sure she gets that through her head. I don't care what I have to do to prove I can protect her, but she is not leaving. Period! I sit Evie down then stand and pull my Angel into my arms. This time she doesn't resist me, she buries her head in my chest and her body shakes as she sobs. I run my hand over her back and whisper in her ear. "You can't leave me, darling, not when I have finally found the missing piece to my heart."

The words get her attention and she looks straight up into my eyes. Her eyes are red and puffy from crying, but still mesmerizing. "You don't understand Dom; I don't have a choice. I can't stay if he knows where I am."

I caress her face with my fingertips. "Then help me understand." She shakes her head. "You're not the only one with scars and secrets *il Mio Amore.* How about we call Kat and Antonio, ask them to come over and we'll sit down and talk? We can try and figure this out together. You're not on your own anymore, and I promise you, with all that I am, I will protect you and my Princess."

She nods slowly, but I can still see her struggling to believe me. It annoys me that she won't trust me, but with her past, I can understand why she is fighting it.

"Mommy everything is going to be okay. Dom will take care of us." Evie sniffs and gives Brooklyn a hug.

"Princess, how about you take your momma into the bathroom and get cleaned up so I can clean the mess up in the bedroom? Once we're done, I'll call Aunty Kat and Antonio."

Evie smiles and steps toward me. I bend down to see what she wants. She plants a kiss on my cheek and whispers, "I trust you." Fuck I love this child. I hug her tight and kiss the top of her head. When I release her, she takes Brooklyn's hand and starts to pull her toward the bathroom.

I make quick work of cleaning the glass up off the floor, I don't want to be away from my girls for long while they're both so upset. I pick the brick up and start to head for the bathroom. I contemplate whether or not I should just throw it in the bin, note and all. But, I want to know what this sick fuck wrote to my Angel. I'm pretty sure she's already read the scrawled note. I knock on the door, it opens and my girls step out

"Let's go downstairs to the kitchen and we can call Kat and Antonio, let them know what has happened." Brooklyn nods and grabs hold of my hand like it's the last time she'll ever hold it. I give it a squeeze and encourage Evie to go ahead of us. She starts to run off downstairs. "Easy little *amore*, I don't want you to fall."

In the kitchen, I settle Evie at the breakfast bar and head to the fridge. "How about a glass of warm milk, Princess?" I look over my shoulder.

Evie smiles widely. "Can I have a cookie as well?" She gives me her puppy dog eyes and I know when she pierces me with that look, I will probably never be able to tell her, no. Yep, I'm fucked. I've fallen victim to the charms of a five-year-old girl. Me, a hardened Mafia boss, sucker punched by a rugrat. I chuckle and glance at her mother to make sure it's okay. When she gives me a nod I grab a container, marked 'cookies' from the bench, remove the lid and hold it toward Evie. "Here you go. Can you sit here and have your snack while momma and I talk?"

"Yep, I'm a big girl."

"Angel, why don't you put the kettle on and give Kat a call. I'll call Antonio."

"Um… Okay, I can do that." As she attempts to pass me, I grab her by the waist and pull her into my chest. Holding her in my arms calms us both down. I take a deep, soothing breath of her scent. *They're fine, they're safe.* I whisper in her ear, "One step at a time, darling. We'll work this out together, si?"

"If you say so, Dom." She pulls from my arms far too quickly for my liking, but I need to call Antonio and I'm guessing she needs to talk to Kat. So, I step back and take my phone from my pocket. I hit Antonio's name and put the device to my ear, listening to it ring while I watch Brooklyn flip the kettle on and pull a phone from the kitchen drawer.

Hmmm… I'll have to ask her about that later.

"Boss," Antonio's voice is loud in my ear. Shit, I must have zoned out for a minute because I didn't realize he had picked up.

"*Si capo Bastone*, I'm at Angel's. I need you here *now*, grab Kat on the way."

'Kat is with me now; we'll be there in ten minutes." He disconnects the call, he knows from my tone, I want them here urgently.

"Angel," I speak quietly. She's a million miles away, standing, staring at the phone in her hand.

"Hmmm… I'm sorry what?"

"Kat and Antonio will be here in about ten minutes, they were together. How about I make the coffee and you put a movie on for Evie? Then we can talk."

Brooklyn's twisting her fingers so hard, her knuckles are as white as snow. She also biting her lip and drawing blood. Tears drip from her chin, it breaks my heart to see her so upset. I approach her carefully, take the phone from her hands, place it onto the counter and draw her into my arms. "Angel please don't cry, I promise things will be okay once we talk." Fuck, I hope they will be.

"I'm sorry it's just..." She gazes up at me with her tear filled blue eyes. "I'm so scared."

"I know, darling. A lot of shit has happened tonight."

She pushes away. "I'll set Evie up with a movie and be back in a few minutes."

Brooklyn moves close to Evie and runs her fingers through her curls. "Hey Sweetpea, what movie do you want to watch?"

"Um... Cinderella please, mommy." Evie sounds tired when she speaks.

"How about you watch the movie and see if you can have a little sleep?"

"Okay, mommy" Evie opens her mouth wide in a big yawn.

Five minutes later the front door crashes open, I go on instant alert and slip my hand into my pocket. When I hear Kat and Antonio coming through the small entryway, I relax my grip on the gun.

"Shit, Kitten, what did that door ever do to you?" Antonio chuckles.

"It was in my fucking way, so sue me," Kat yells. "Brooklyn, where are you? What the fuck is going on?" Kat locates us in the kitchen and rushes up to Brooklyn. She grabs hold of her arms and inspects her from head to toe.

"Ssshh." Brooklyn point to the small living room where Evie has fallen asleep.

"Shit, sorry Dollface, I didn't realize." Satisfied Brooklyn and Evie aren't physically harmed; Kat turns on me. "What the fuck have you done to her?" Kat pokes her finger into my chest.

Antonio grabs her around the waist and drags her back into his arms. "Easy, Kitten"

Kat snaps her head back to glare at her captor then spins in his arms so she faces him. He then receives the 'poking' treatment. "You listen to me. I don't care who you are, you ever touch me again without my permission and I will have your balls in a vice quicker than you can say, motherfucker. *Capisce*? Now back the fuck up!"

I stare at Antonio and I can see him struggling to hold back, he doesn't release her. I put my hands up to stop whatever is about to come out because right now we have other things we need to discuss. "Please, calm down. I have done nothing and I mean *nothing* to Brooklyn *or* Evie." I take a deep breath to calm myself down. Knowing she is thinking I would hurt my girls, pisses me off. "And, I never will!"

Kat stares at me hard, she's trying to judge if I'm sincere. When she relaxes in Antonio's arms, I figure she believes me. Thank fuck, I don't need her up my ass while we try and work this shit out.

"You can let go of me now, you, you,.....aargh. Just let go of me." Kat glares at Antonio

"But, why? I love it when you're feisty." Antonio chuckles but lets her go.

I indicate the table. "Let's sit down and have a coffee. We need to talk and we need to keep the volume down. My Princess has just gone to sleep and I don't want anyone to wake her up."

"Who the hell do you think you are, barking out orders?" Kat slams her hands on her hips.

Brooklyn steps closer to her friend and pats her shoulder. "Kat, please, sit and chill. It's been a long night."

Kat acquiesces and takes a seat at the breakfast bar with Brooklyn. Antonio leans against the door frame with his arms crossed over his chest.

"Okay, girls, first things first. How do you like your coffee?"

"Blonde with a pair." The girls speak in unison and start giggling like school girls.

I raise my eyebrow and shrug at Antonio because I don't have a fucking clue what that means. He shrugs while trying to hide a smile. Fucker!

"Babe, it means white with two sugars, please." Brooklyn stops laughing long enough to put me out of my misery. Her eyes travel over my still naked chest and I watch as her eyes go wide. Her tongue slips out and licks her bottom lip and that does it. I'm fucking hard, again! When she speaks in that breathless tone I love so much, I have to close my eyes and concentrate on not coming in my fucking pants. Fuck!

"You have a tattoo!" She eye fucks the ink on the right side of my body which begins on my chest and travels all the way down my rib cage. She squirms in her chair and I know she's squeezing her legs together. She's turned on by my tattoo!

"Quit eye fucking him Brookie." Kat nudges her. "Tell me why we're here and what was so fucking urgent?"

Kat's voice seems to snap her out of whatever thoughts Brooklyn was having. I should thank Kat because I was about to snap and take my Angel right here on the kitchen floor, and I didn't care who else was here.

"Oh… Yea… Um… he's back." She whispers and peeks up at me through her eyelashes.

"What do you mean, *he's back*? Who's back?" Kat looks at Brooklyn wide-eyed and if I'm not mistaken, I see fear there too.

"Darren," Brooklyn speaks quietly. She looks to me for reassurance. I nod my head and keep eye contact so she'll continue.

Kat grabs her hand. "How do you know? What happened?"

Angel seems to space out and her words come in a rush. "We were upstairs and I was giving Evie a bath. I was waiting for her to be ready to um… wash her hair and I was thinking about things, like the mistakes I've made and how Evie has been through so much already and I don't want to put her through anymore. Um… I ran into Dom outside the bathroom… and he had no shirt on because Evie spilled ice cream on him… and then we were kissing and um…"

"Brooklyn." I reach over and put my hand on hers. "Angel, I think Kat meant, how do you know Darren has found you?"

"Oh… um… I'm sorry." She's getting flustered and I watch as a blush creeps into her cheeks.

"It's okay, my darling." I wink at her. "Tell Kat what happened *after* you got Evie out of the bath when you were getting her dressed."

Brooklyn turns her focus back to Kat. "I'd just finished drying Evie off and was helping her with her pajamas. I turned to get her hairbrush so I could plait her hair for bed when all of a sudden there was a smash. I heard Evie scream or it could have been me, I don't know. It was a brick with a piece of paper attached to it laying in a pile of glass on the floor, then Evie's door crashed open and we were safe in Dom's arms." She finishes with tears streaming down her face.

"Oh, Brookie, it's ok. Thank fuck, you're both safe." Kat pauses for a moment. "The brick didn't hit you or Babydoll, did it?"

Brooklyn shakes her head and wipes her eyes. "It missed us, but not by much." She hiccups on a sob. "What am I going to do, Kat?" Her hands shake as she lifts the mug to her mouth and takes a sip of her coffee.

Kat inhales deeply before turning to me "I'm sorry, Dom for yelling at you and accusing you of hurting Brooklyn and Evie."

I wave a hand in the air. "It's okay Kat, I understand she's like your sister and you want to protect her."

I lean forward and run my fingers lightly over Angel's cheek. "Do you think you could tell me everything now so I can have a good understanding of what's going on?"

Brooklyn leans into my touch, nods her head, takes a deep breath, then lays it all out for me…….

"It's a long story. I had just turned eighteen when I first met Darren Jacobs, well, officially I should say." She shrugs and glances at Kat who encourages her to continue. "He was actually my neighbor, but I never really paid him much mind. I hadn't been interested in boys before, well boys weren't really interested in me. Anyway, it didn't matter. I was always busy with my nose in a book or hanging out with Kat. She used to tell me all the time, he was watching me and it creeped her out. I ignored what she said because I knew he couldn't be interested in me. As I said, I had just turned eighteen and was standing out front of my parent's house waiting for Kat to turn up. She'd come down from Newcastle to visit me and to take me to the movies for my birthday. While I was waiting, Darren came out and started talking to me. He'd talked to me a few times, just idle chit chat most of the time so I didn't think anything of it. He said he worried about me because I was young and he thought I was a bit naïve. He insisted I could get mixed up in trouble without being aware of it so he said he would be there if I ever needed a friend or someone to talk to. I thought it was a bit strange at first because when we'd talked before, it was a *hello, how are you?* or *it's a great day*, that sort of thing. It bugged me a bit at first, but I brushed it off thinking it was quite sweet of him to be concerned.'

Brooklyn paused and sipped at her coffee before going on. "Later that night, Kat and I were on our way back home and decided to stop and grab a bottle of wine to celebrate. When we got back to my parent's place, Kat received a phone call and had to rush back home. I decided to go to my room, have a shower, lay in bed to watch a movie and have a glass of wine. You know, just to relax. After I showered and got comfortable, there was a knock at my window and I thought maybe it was Kat not wanting to wake my parents up. I got out of bed and opened the window. It was Darren. I was shocked and he made me nervous, but then he smiled at me and told me he knew it had been my birthday. He said he felt bad that he'd forgotten to wish me a belated Happy Birthday when he'd spoken to me earlier in the day. I was still nervous, I'd never really spoken to a boy before, but then he asked if I wanted to go take a walk with him. I was skeptical about his motives. Like I said, we'd never even spoken that much and now he wanted me to sneak out of the house and take a walk with him. I explained to him that there would be a better time to get to know each other, now wasn't it. But then I started thinking - I had never snuck out of the house before, and I thought why not? Live a little! And, if I'm being honest I was excited that a guy would want to spend some time with me."

I'm not sure where this is going, but I have a bad feeling lodged in the pit of my stomach. I look over at Antonio, he raises an eyebrow and I know he's thinking this can't be leading anywhere good. I glance at Kat and notice how glassy her eyes are, filled with tears. Yeah, I'm not going to like this. I already hate the motherfucker and want him to die, but I think long, *very* long torture is definitely going to be called for.

I focus on my Angel as she speaks again. "I did sneak out and as we walked, he grabbed hold of my hand. I remember jumping a bit, no boy had ever touched me before let alone held my hand. I was unsure at first, but Darren said I wasn't to worry, this was just us getting to know each other. Because I was stupid, I shrugged my shoulders and believed him. We chatted about the stuff we liked and it turned out we had I lot in common. Somehow, we ended up at one of his mate's homes. I told him I should probably be getting back home so I wouldn't get caught, but Darren said he needed to call in real quick. He told me he'd left something there earlier and had to grab it. I agreed, we would go in and grab it then leave because I needed to get home. Inside the house were at least a dozen people. Drinking, playing music and stuff. Darren convinced me to stay for one drink and explained it would be rude if we left without saying hello to a couple of people. So, stupidly, I agreed."

Brooklyn sighs and finishes her coffee.

"Darren grabbed us a beer each and we ended up sitting outside around a fire. It was nice at first, but then I'm not sure what happened. I started to feel dizzy and nauseous. I told Darren I needed to go home because I wasn't feeling well. He helped me up and we said goodbye to his friends, but as we entered the house I felt like I was gonna throw up so I raced to the bathroom. Darren, being the gentleman I thought he was, held my hair and rubbed my back while I brought up everything I'd eaten that day. I told him how sorry I was and that I'd had a glass of wine before he'd turned up at my window. I must be a lightweight because that and the beer were all I'd had."

Brooklyn takes a deep breath. "After washing my face, Darren helped me out of the bathroom. I don't remember much after that, it's pretty much a blur. I remember Darren taking me into a room, kissing me and trying to slide his hand down my pants. I had a feeling of falling onto something soft and that was it. Nothing. Until I woke a couple of hours later to find I was naked with Darren beside me. I was trying to remember what had happened when Darren woke up, but there was no easy smile or sweet touch. I could see he was upset with me and I wasn't sure what I'd done wrong. When I asked, he told me I'd passed out while he was trying to make love to me. He said I'd begged and begged for him to touch me and make me his, but then when things started to happen, I blacked out. I told him I was sorry. I didn't know what had come over me, but he wouldn't hear anything I had to say. He got up and dressed and ordered me to do the same. I was upset and disappointed I had let him down, but he told me there was nothing I could do to fix the situation. He regretted taking me there and said it was time to leave. I was desperately upset at myself at this point and was trying to hold back the tears that threatened to fall. I hated to disappoint anybody, and couldn't forgive myself for throwing myself at the first guy I was with and stuffing it up."

Brooklyn starts to play with her coffee cup as tears roll down her face. I rest my hand over hers and it seems to jolt her out of whatever memory she was reliving. "Would you like another coffee?" I rub my thumb over her hand and watch as the tension in her body eases and she relaxes a little.

"I would love one, thank you."

"Me too please, if you don't mind." Kat pushes her cup to me and I notice her tear-drenched face.

I take the cups to the sink and flip the kettle back on. While I wait for the water to boil, I rinse out the mugs. From the corner of my eye, I see Kat lean over and give Angel a hug before wiping the tears from her face.

I'm bubbling with anger; I'm pissed about what I'm hearing. I want to find the fucker and kill him. Slowly. *Very* slowly. I glance at Antonio and the expression on his face tells me he is every bit as pissed as I am. The kettle boils, I make the coffees and place the four full mugs on the bench before leaning on it and waiting for Brooklyn to continue.

"Thanks, Babe." Brooklyn smiles and takes a sip. "After that night, I didn't see Darren for a few weeks. It upset me because I knew I'd hurt him and there was nothing I could do to make things right. I started feeling 'off', constantly throwing up and exhausted, but I passed it off as having caught a bug. When I didn't start to get better, I made an appointment to see the doctor. I figured I probably needed antibiotics. He examined me and didn't think it was flu so he ordered a bunch of tests. I was pregnant. I was devastated because I didn't remember having sex. I honestly believed I was still a virgin. I left the doctor's office with a bunch of instructions and was in a daze as I headed home. I stopped at Darren's place, but he wasn't there so I left a note in his mailbox asking if he could contact me. I said we really needed to talk. A couple of hours later he called me and I asked if we could meet up because I really needed to talk to him. He was angry, said I'd hurt him and he didn't want anything to do with me. I started crying and I let slip I was pregnant. The silence was deafening, I thought he'd hung up but I could hear his heavy breathing. I remember repeating over and over again how sorry I was and that I didn't mean to hurt him. I also told him I hadn't meant for me to get pregnant. When he finally spoke and said he would meet me to talk, I was relieved. It gave me some hope we could work things out and all would be fine because I knew, no matter what, I was not giving up the baby."

Brooklyn sipped her coffee. "The following week we met up for lunch and I told him again how sorry I was. I explained I was shocked to find out I was pregnant because I thought I was still a virgin. Darren was quiet while I spoke, but then it was like a switch flipped and he became angry. He couldn't believe I didn't remember us having sex. I was quiet for a while, not sure what to say, I didn't want to hurt him more than I already had. He said I would have to prove I really cared about him by moving in with him so we could raise the baby together. He was buying a house in Parramatta which was just over an hour away from where I lived in Bundeena. I was a worried at first, not sure what to do. He insisted it was the only way I could prove to him I really cared about him and our relationship. So, much to the displeasure of my parents and Kat, we moved in together. I knew I didn't love him, but I thought over time it might change. I'd always had both my parents and they had a special kind of love, they were true soul mates. It was what I wanted, someone to love me like I was their whole world. I hoped Darren could be like that and I really wanted a family for my child. I moved in and Evie was born but nothing changed. Darren always had an issue with me. He would say nasty things or push me around a little bit. He complained I was either too fat or too skinny. If dinner wasn't on the table at the right time he wanted to know why. I would explain the baby was sick or something, but it didn't stop him from being angry. If the baby was sick it was my fault, if the baby was crying it was my fault, he would constantly tell me how pathetic and needy I was. At first, it was words or a push here or there. He was hardly ever home so it wasn't completely horrible, then something happened about a year ago. I'm not sure what, but when he came home it was like he was a completely different person. The nasty words and the pushing continued, but he started slapping and kicking me. From the day we moved in together, he refused to have sex with me, but then he demanded I suck him off. He'd hold my head while he forced his dick down my throat and almost rip my hair out while he forced himself in and out. I guess you get the picture."

Her eyes plead with me to understand what she's been through. I clench my jaw and give a little nod letting her know, I understand. If it's dick play he wants, I'll give him some he'll never forget when I catch up with the fucker.

"I'd been planning to leave for a while, but I had to wait for the right time. I had saved little bits here and there from the grocery money he gave me because I didn't have a cent to my name. I had a daughter to look after so I couldn't just pick up and leave without at least something to help us start over. But, one night he came home before I had a chance to make dinner and he shoved me so hard into the wall it took my breath away. I fell and hit my head. I lay on the floor waiting for the next blow to come, but he turned away from me and went after Evie. She'd come out to see if I was okay, she would have heard me scream."

My Angel closes her eyes and I watch as tears slide down her cheeks, she's trying to wipe them away with her hand but it's not working they just keep coming.

"H-he threw h-her across the f-f-floor for trying to get in the middle of us." Her voice chokes on her sobs, it breaks my heart.

I look over to see Evie's sleeping form before turning back to Brooklyn, waiting for her to finish. When she doesn't go on, I let go of the death grip I have on the bench, move closer and gather her hand. Her eyes lock on mine and something passes over her face, but it's gone before I get a chance to work out what it was.

She sighs. "I couldn't believe I had let his abuse get that far, but I was so scared. I am *still* so scared. He always told me he owned us and he would take Evie from me or he would kill us both if I ever tried to leave. The night he hurt Evie had to be the last, so the next morning when Darren left for an early meeting, I summoned every bit of strength I had left, grabbed Evie and got the hell out of there with Kat's help." I pass her a tissue and watch as she looks over at Evie before Kat leans forward to hug her.

I take a deep breath in and let it out slowly. *Fuck me!* No wonder my Angel was skittish when I first touched her. I drag my fingers through my hair trying to work out where to start, what to do first. I pace back and forth trying to come to terms with everything she's told me. I try to calm myself down before I leave this house right now, find this *stronzo* and break his fucking neck. I glance at Antonio and notice he's clenching and unclenching his fists. He wants to kill the fucker as much as I do. I temper my rage and take a couple of deep breaths before asking, "Angel, how did you end up getting away?"

"About 6 months ago, I rang Kat. We hadn't spoken in a while, Darren and Kat didn't get along. Darren hated that we spoke at all, he said she was a bad influence and we didn't need her near our family. Kat insisted there was something off about him." Brooklyn peers into her mug as if seeking answers. "I should have listened to her. He forbade me from speaking with her so I would sneak calls to her. Kat's instincts told her something was wrong, but I told her not to worry, everything would be fine. The day after I spoke with Kat, while Darren was at work, I received a package in the mail. It contained a cell phone and a note from Kat to keep it hidden. I didn't think I would need it and she was just being silly, but in the end, that phone saved our lives. When Darren was in the shower that morning, he thought I was still sleeping, I messaged Kat and told her my plan to leave. Three hours later, after Darren left for his meeting, I messaged Kat we were ready and she came and took us away and brought us here."

Brooklyn sniffs and wipes her eyes again. "I'm sorry Dom. I know it's a lot to take in, but I wanted you to know the whole story. Looking back now, I know how stupid I was to think he might change. I wish I'd left a long time ago, then maybe Evie never would have been hurt." She gazes up at me with her gorgeous blue eyes. "I un-understand i-if you don't want anything to do with me now..... It's ok.... I... Uh... "

Is she fucking kidding me? I'm not leaving, I'm not going anywhere. After I put the motherfucker in the ground, we're going to have a life together. I stride around the bench and sweep her into my arms. I kiss her forehead softly. "I'm not going anywhere. You and Princess Evie are stuck with me."

Brooklyn pleads with me to understand. "But you don't understand, Darren could hurt you. I don't think I could live…" I place my finger over her lips.

"Listen to me, darling. Okay?" She nods. "Good girl." I place a kiss on her head and take a deep breath, calming myself with her scent. I select my words carefully so as not to frighten her. "I'm not going anywhere. This fucker should be very afraid of both Antonio and me, not the other way around. Okay? I am one of the most powerful men this city has ever seen, I'm here to stay and you, my Angel, will be by my side the whole time." I kiss her forehead. "I am not leaving you, I am not letting you go. You, and my beautiful Princess over there…." I point to where Evie is sleeping then look back down at Brooklyn. "…are mine."

Brooklyn's eyes widen, she is debating whether or not I'm telling the truth. I hope my words haven't scared her, but before I can worry, she throws herself at me. And, like I always will, I catch her. I bury my nose in her hair and take in another deep breath letting her sweet honey/vanilla scent calm my nerves.

"I'm so sorry Dom," she breaths into my chest.

"Angel." I lean back and wipe away her tears. "This isn't your fault, he manipulated you. You were young and vulnerable. You thought you could trust him because you see good in people. But, *il Mio Amore* I think you know why you can't remember getting pregnant. Please, tell me."

Brooklyn takes a step back, sniffs again, glances at Kat, then turns back to me

"Kat and I spoke about it after I finally left. I think he drugged and raped me. I almost married my rapist!" Brooklyn chokes on a sob.

Fuck! Fuck! Fuck! I feel the tears in my eyes as I reach out and wipe away her tears. "My Angel." I gather her into my arms.

I lock eyes with Antonio and notice, he's gripping the edge of the door frame and his knuckles have turned white. My man hates guys who hit women, but even more, he detests rapists with a vengeance. I give him a chin lift to make sure he's good and he gives me one back as he lowers his hand. "How about another coffee before I explain some shit about me."

The girls murmur a "yes please" and Antonio moves to the fridge to grab the milk. As I walk over to switch on the kettle, I glance at the girls and see they're murmuring to each other. I take the opportunity to talk to Antonio.

"*Capo*… You good?" I drag my fingers through my hair again.

Antonio tightens his lips. "What type of sick fuck moves his victim into his house and then plans to marry them?"

"I'm thinking one that doesn't want to go to court for child payments."

"Shit! I didn't even think about that, what a fucking scumbag."

"A *dead* fucking scumbag. He injured my Angel and hurt my Princess." I gaze over at Evie. I can't begin to understand how anyone could hurt either of them.

Antonio follows my gaze and then looks back at me. "Si Boss, we will get him and he will be very sorry." He turns and walks back over to the girls.

I'll find him and when I do, he'll beg me to end his miserable life.

Nine

Brooklyn

How could I have been so stupid? Not only did I bring this mess down on Evie and me, but now I've put more people at risk. I drop my head in my hands and try to figure out where to go from here. I'm so pathetic.

Kat hugs me tight, after a moment I sit back and give her a weak smile. I look over to where Dominic and Antonio are quietly talking. I'm wondering why he thinks Darren should be scared of *him*. What did he mean by that? I rub my forehead as if that might give me the answers. Nope. Nothing. Dom also said he was the most powerful man in this city. What the fuck is going on? I'm so confused right now; it's been a very long day and I'm starting to get a headache. I lower my head and massage my temples in an attempt to ease some of the tension that's built up in the last couple of hours.

I lift my head and look up when two painkillers are placed on the bench in front of me, but that's not what gives me pause, nope, not at all. I'm captured by the softest green eyes I have ever seen and I swear I get lost in them for a moment or two. This is confirmed when Kat nudges me. A smile curves the lips of that sexy as sin mouth of his. M*mmm*... I still remember the taste... Kat nudges me again and I snap out of my thoughts. Fuck, what is wrong with me? After the conversation we just had, you'd think men would be the last thing on my mind. But nope, my body has other ideas. I feel the heat of a blush creeping into my cheeks. Fuck, what is wrong with me? Get it together, Brooklyn! I try and shake myself back to the present and clear my throat before speaking.

"Ok... Um... Ah... what... what were we saying?"

I glare at Kat when she starts to giggle and when I look towards Antonio, he's got his hand over his mouth to smother his laughter. Dom's no better, he's standing at my side, chuckling. He reaches over, gathers my hand and gives it a squeeze. A feeling of a live wire running through my system is back.

"Sorry, I was in a daze for a moment there." I clear my throat again.

"Ah, Dollface, it's okay. We understand. *I* understand." Kat nudges me and winks, which cracks us both up laughing.

Dom reins in his laughter and wants to get back to the issues at hand. "We ready to keep talking?"

"Yeah Babe, may as well get all this over and done with." I swallow the two tablets with a glass of water Dom had placed in front of me. When I turn to hand him the empty glass, and because I'm feeling brave, I give him a wink. I watch as his lips part and his tongue slips out, he runs it along his plump bottom lip. The sight causes me to bite mine and causes tingles to run through my body.

"Brookie, come on let's get this over and done with." Kat has a wide smile on her face. She knows me too well.

Fuck! Fuck! Fuck! You think I'd be scared about what I'm feeling when I look at Dom, but oddly enough, I'm not. Don't get me wrong, at first I was terrified of him, but it feels like things have changed and there's something about him that makes me feel safe. A feeling I haven't had in a very long time, not since my parents were alive. Shit, I'm not gonna think about this right now. I nod my head at Dom so he knows to go ahead.

"Please, Angel, hear me out." Dominic sucks in a deep breath, fuck, what is he going to say? "The first inkling my family was different came when I was about eight years old, I had found a gun hidden under my parent's bed. I knew my papa had served in the Army and I just assumed it was from then. I was very proud my papa had served our country, that he would put his life on the line to protect the people he loved. A few days later at school, a teacher overheard me talking about finding the gun and of how I proud I was because he risked his life to protect everyone around him. When I got home that day papa pulled me aside and spoke to me. He said *whatever goes on in our family stays within these walls. We don't ever talk about it with anybody else.* I remember wondering why it was such a huge secret, but I shrugged it off, I was too young to fully understand. Papa was a man you didn't disagree with so I agreed I wouldn't say another word about it. He told me *when you get a little older, we will discuss this more.*

Dom glances at me with a worried expression. Maybe he thinks something he's said has upset me. I nod for him to keep going.

"We were a very traditional Italian family. My father worked, while my mother stayed at home and looked after my brother Carmine and me. We were born and raised surrounded by family and friends in Sicily. Everyone knew my papa, even as a young boy I could sense he was important. Whenever he entered a room, the energy would change. People would rush over to shake his hand and kiss his cheek. I looked up to him, he was my hero. I was so proud he was my papa, he never turned anybody away, always listened to whatever they had to say, he always made time for them. If they needed money to pay their bills, he would help. He even went as far as buying them groceries if they were struggling.

Dom paces the kitchen; I'm trying to soak in everything he's telling me. Watching as the muscles in his back flex and ripple, the way he runs his hand through his hair. *Hmmm…*

"Boss." Antonio pulls my attention back to the conversation. "*Bene?*"

Dominic holds up his hand and nods "Si." He turns to me and I notice his beautiful green eyes have lost some of their sparkle, there's a look of sadness in them. I want to curl myself around him and comfort him. But, before I can move toward him he keeps talking.

"One day, when I was about twelve, Papa sat me down at the table in the kitchen. He told me I was older now and starting to become a man. He was worried I'd start hearing things about his life and he wanted to explain it in the best way he knew how. By this point, I'd started piecing things together myself. I'd already heard the whispers and stories going around. I didn't tell him because I knew he'd tell me in his own time. So, I sat and listened. He explained some men in Sicily had formed a secret group and vowed to always protect each other and their families, even if it meant stealing or hurting other people. He was a part of this group. It didn't sound all that bad or scary to me, it was nice to know people cared enough to look after each other. He told me it was time to start helping out the *family* and after school, I would be working with him and Carmine. I was pretty excited because I hadn't expected my father to ask me. As the eldest son, I thought only Carmine would work with him. He explained that since I was so good with numbers, he would start me off by running numbers for him. At the time, I didn't know what he meant by that, but I soon learned. That's how Antonio and I met."

Dom slowed his pacing for a moment and turned toward me. "The years passed and I did my part for the family. Antonio and I became close friends, brothers, and were making our way up the ranks doing odd jobs here and there. Basically, we were doing whatever was asked of us. By the time I was twenty-years-old, I'd become a 'made' man. A couple more years passed, Antonio and I made sure things went the way they were supposed to go and our community was well looked after. When I turned twenty-four, there was talk of a few things happening in other families. They weren't coping as well as us. At the time, Carmine was being groomed to become the Boss, but then there was a massive disagreement between our family, and some of the other families, and a war broke out. In the midst of all the bloodshed, my brother was murdered."

Dom blows out a breath and clears his throat, tears glisten in his eyes. It about breaks my heart. Fuck.

"His death destroyed my papa, he drank more and hardly ever came home at night. When he did come home he used to..." Dom pauses for a minute, and it feels like an eternity before he speaks again. "He would beat my momma like she was his personal punching bag. I only know this because I walked in one morning and she had a black eye and a split lip. It was the first time he'd damaged her face. I saw red and demanded my mother tell me what it was all about. The more my mother told me, the angrier I became. I assumed it was caused by the grief of losing his oldest son but it turns out the *stronzo* (fucker) had been hitting her for a very long time. Long before Carmine was murdered, but he always kept it away from us and left marks where they wouldn't be seen. This was a man I was proud to be related to, the man I called my papa. A man who took an oath to respect women and children and to never cause them harm. I was furious and stormed out of the house. I still remember my momma's cries and pleas to let things be, but I think that pissed me off more. My papa had conditioned my momma to accept that kind of life and the more I thought about it, I realized there had been signs right in front of my eyes. I think I was more upset that I hadn't noticed before then. I couldn't believe I'd let it happen."

Dom drags his fingers through his already disheveled hair.

"Momma would flinch and cower when people got too loud, she was a very shy woman. She married my father not long after she turned eighteen. I'd heard the stories about her papa and what a piece of shit he was. He would beat nonna and momma. I always thought my papa saved her but I was wrong, she was taken from one hell to be brought to another. I pulled my Colt 45 and took off to find him and blow his head off."

I notice he is clenching and unclenching his fists. I'm beyond speechless at this point. I'm not sure if I should be scared and run away screaming or sit here and listen to the rest of his story. I stay rooted to the spot, transfixed by his eyes. It's like they're begging me to understand and listen to what he has to say. I take a deep breath and whisper, "okay." Kat grabs my hand and gives it a quick squeeze.

"When I pulled up at his office, Antonio was walking out. He only had to glance at me to know I was pissed. I told him what I was about to do and why, but he kept shaking his head and telling me to leave it alone. His lack of support pissed me off more, but he grabbed my arm and pulled me down the alley beside the building we worked out of. He explained, I should wait until we came up with a solid plan, because if I stormed in there with guns blazing, it would only end with me in a body bag as well as my papa. He was right, it was a possibility, but I was so angry, I couldn't see reason. Eventually, Antonio said something that made me see reason - I could go in there and deal with things now and the family would be in shambles, or I could wait a couple of days and we could plan this right. So, at the end of the day, we could keep the family together and get rid of papa at the same time. I knew Antonio made a good point, so I tried to relax the best I could over the following days. I agreed I would bide my time for a little longer."

Fuck, where was this going to end?

"It was a well-known fact, a few of us met after hours at a local pizzeria and played cards one night a week. Usually, we'd play a few hands of cards, shoot the breeze then head home or to a job that needed to be done. This particular night, my papa had organized a meeting with another family head to discuss a truce of some sorts. Papa had other ideas, he had plans to take out the other boss - Salvatore Profaci, so he could take over his territory and get revenge for Carmine. We were standing out the front of the building, about to head in when gunshots sounded. We swung around and saw they were coming from a car passing by. Everyone reached for their guns and started firing towards the car while I scrambled to cover my father. When I threw myself on top of him, it was the perfect opportunity to fire. Once the car was gone and the dust cleared, everyone realized the *Boss* was not moving."

The hatred and contempt for his father are obvious in his voice.

"I had the opportunity to do what I thought was right and I took it." He shrugs. "I don't regret it for a second. If he was standing in front of me right now, I wouldn't hesitate to put another bullet in him." He looks straight into my eyes pleading with me to understand. "After the shooting, I became *The Boss*."

And, that knocks the wind right out of me. Fuck! Shit, that's a lot to take in. So, is he still the *Boss*? Even before I even ask the question, I know what the answer is going to be. I feel the energy in the room shift whenever he walks in, the way people look at him and the power and confidence that exudes off him. I ask anyway because I really need to know.

"Are you still the Boss?" My voice is barely above a whisper.

Dom slowly walks to me, as if trying not to scare a wounded animal. He must know I'm teetering on the edge. He leans over the bench and runs his fingers down my cheek. My whole body comes alive with that single touch.

"I am Angel." He speaks softly. "I am still the Boss, the Don, the Godfather, whatever you want to call it."

I blow out the breath I didn't realize I was holding and gaze into his soft green eyes. There's a slight tic in his jaw and worry lines mar his beautiful face. I lift my hand and run my fingers over them. He turns his head and presses a soft kiss into the palm of my hand. Then, he holds my hand against his face for a moment longer then gives it a little squeeze. Damn, he's sexy! He looks so worried about what he has told me, like he's lost his prized puppy. Right now, I'm struggling to take it all in.

He's a Mafia Boss… The big Cheese… No wonder he's not worried about Darren. That's the reason he said Darren should be scared of him. Should I be scared of him too? Should I be running as far and as fast as I can from this man I barely know? He's hurt people, killed his own father, but if I'm being honest, it sounds like his father deserved everything he got. Dominic hasn't shown even an inkling of violence toward me or Evie. He treats us both like we're goddesses who need to be worshiped. I look over at Kat to see she has a soft smile on her face. Fuck, what the hell am I going to do? What the fuck do I say? My thoughts are a mess right now, my brain is turning over at a million miles an hour. I think he's waiting for my response, but I'm not sure what to say to him. Oh, fuck! Holy Shitballs! What Kat said the other night at the club slams into me *with the force of a speeding freight train. **"I think a Mob Boss owns this place."** Fuck! Fuck! Fuck! How did I not put the two together when he gave me his business card with Destiny on it? Fuck!!!*

"Should I be scared?" I wrap my arms around my body and lower my head when I feel a sudden chill come over me.

It's quiet for a moment, I lift my head and look up into his eyes. Before I can say anything further, he lifts me from my chair and pulls me against his warm, hard chest. He folds me into his arms. I tense up at first then relax into his warm embrace. Despite everything, he feels so right. It's as if my heart and my body know we are fine. But, I can't help feeling wary after everything I have been through already. And, how the fuck do I reject him when he's bare-chested and sexy as hell?

"I promise you, my Angel, you will never have a reason to be scared of me. I would lay my life down for you and Evie."

Call me stupid, pathetic or even naïve, but it's like his words permeate every bone in my body and I know he means everything he says. I don't want to ever let go of him. He makes me feel complete for the first time in my life. I think back to the conversation I had with Evie just before her bath, and I know in my heart what I say next is the truth. "I believe you." The tension leaves his body and he leans into me, clinging to me like I have just given him the world.

I lean back so I can see his eyes and notice some of the sparkle has returned, the worry has eased. "Please don't hurt me, Dominic," I beg in a low whisper as I feel him wipe under my eyes with his thumb. I sniff, not realizing I was crying again.

"I won't, I promise." He kisses my forehead "I've told you before, I didn't realize I was missing anything in my life until you looked at me with those eyes. The second you did, I was lost. You are my missing piece, Angel. You and your beautiful Princess. I will do whatever it takes to prove myself to you, to care for you, protect you as you deserve."

The truth is in his eyes as he speaks and I hug him tighter, feeling like the weight of the world has been lifted off my shoulders. Is this what it feels like to be accepted and possibly loved? *Stop it, now! It's too soon to be thinking he loves you. Fuck, can I be any more needy? Darren's words come back to me... "do you realize how needy and pathetic you are?"* I try and stop the words from running on replay in my head when I hear Dom speak.

"Angel, are you ok? What happened just now?"

"Nothing, I'm sorry. I was thinking about everything, it's a lot to take in. I'm sorry." I smile at him.

Dom stares at me for a moment and I see something flash in his eyes, it was gone too quickly for me tell exactly what it was.

"You have nothing to apologize for Angel, I know it's a lot to take in. Just know I'm here and I'm not going anywhere." He places another kiss on my forehead before releasing me, turning and heading to the other side of the bench again.

I sit next to Kat and I watch as Antonio steps toward Dom.

Kat leans over to whisper to me. "Brooklyn, I believe him too." That's a huge statement coming from her, she doesn't really trust anybody least of all men. "He won't hurt you. I have this feeling in my bones, I can't explain it, but I honestly believe he would rather die than cause you or Evie any harm. I have to admit, it's scary as shit that he is in the mob... well, that *he is* the mob. You only have to look in his eyes to see it doesn't matter that you guys have only just met. He already worships the ground you walk on and Dollface," she nudges my shoulder. "You deserve to be treated how he wants to treat you. Try not to over think things, ok? He did what he needed to do to survive and protect the people he loves, babe, and I probably would have done the same if I was in his situation."

I let her words soak in for a minute and recall the last time Darren put his hands on me and hurt Evie. Yeah, if I'd had the chance, I wouldn't have hesitated to put a bullet in his head. Maybe I'm meant to be a Mafia boss's woman. Fuck! I sigh and slam a hand over my mouth to stifle my giggle. I glance at Dom and notice he and Antonio have stopped talking and are watching us. I give him a wink and I watch as the corner of his mouth curls up into that sexy as sin smirk of his. Yep. I'm screwed!

"Angel, how about you and Kat run upstairs and grab a bag for you and Evie."

"Why? I mean what for?" I'm confused, why do I need to pack a bag?

"I would feel more comfortable having my girls under my roof. I need to keep you safe."

Safe? From wh....? Fuck, *the brick*. The reason we're all here. How the hell did I forget about that? Fuck, it's been a long night.

"Of course, sorry," I remember the note attached to the brick. "Can we read the note first please?"

Dom looks at the brick that is sitting by the kettle and gives me an anxious look. Despite his obvious misgivings, he brings it to me. With shaking hands, I reach for it, remove the band holding the note in place and open it out. When I read it, I have trouble understanding the meaning. I place it down on the bench for everyone to see, rubbing my temples again trying to think of what it means......

SLUT

You took something

that is *Mine*!

I'm coming for you.

I give the others a moment to read the note. "I don't understand what I took that's his. I didn't take anything besides a bag of clothes for Evie and me, that's it……" I gasp and slap a hand over my mouth trying to contain my sob. Dom grabs my hand "What is it, Angel?"

I shudder and look into Dominic's eyes then over to where Evie is sleeping. Dom follows my line of sight and immediately realizes what this letter means. "It's Evie, I took our daughter." I burst into tears and within seconds find myself wrapped in Dom's arms and held close.

Twenty minutes later I'm being guided to Dominic's car. He walks beside me with a sleeping Evie in his arms. Kat and Antonio have gone back to her place. As we approach, I catch sight of a dark figure emerging from the shadows at the rear of the car. I scream and push myself up against Dom. He wraps an arm around me and holds me close.

"It's okay, Angel. This is Sergio one of my men who watches over me. He won't hurt you, I promise." Dom kisses my forehead.

Sergio steps nearer and picks up the bag I had dropped to the ground in my panic. I recognize him from the coffee shop. I smile the best I can, given the situation.

"I'm sorry, *Signorina*. I did not mean to scare you." Sergio has a thick accent and holds up his free hand. He glances at Dominic and I see the worry in his eyes.

"No, it's okay. I wasn't expecting anybody to be here." I attempt to ease some of the worry on his face. He looks back at Dom waiting for, I don't know, what?

"Sergio, *va bene, apri la porta.*" *I watch as relief washes over Sergio's face at Dom's word*s.

Sergio nods with respect and opens the door so Dom can place Evie in her car seat, then he moves to another door and opens it for me.

"Thank you, Sergio. I apologize for screaming and worrying you." I climb into the seat.

Sergio waves his hand to indicate there's no problem, smiles, then closes the door for me. When he smiles, he's actually quite handsome. Dominic says something to him in Italian and Sergio heads for his own car.

Dom steps in behind the wheel and starts up the engine. He reaches over, gathers my hand and lifts it to his mouth. After pressing a soft kiss to my palm, he places my hand on his leg. I peer out the window as we pull away. I feel the heat creeping into my cheeks and don't want him to see me blushing. Too late! hear Dom's low chuckle.

⁓⁓⁓⁓⁂⁓⁓⁓⁓

Dom turns the car into a driveway and stops before two huge wrought iron gates. He reaches up near his visor and presses a button. I watch as the gates open to reveal a long driveway lined with hedges on both sides. As we make our way up the long drive until it opens up to a princess driveway with a beautiful water feature in the middle. The sight is absolutely breathtaking.

Scattered lights flicker, illuminating the area. Beyond the water feature stands the most stunning house I have ever clapped eyes on. *House?* How about mansion? The place is fucking huge!

Dom eases the car to the front steps, it's large and wide, leading up to two beautiful, intricately carved, wooden doors. Two columns stand like sentries on guard on either side. Gorgeous picture windows are everywhere. It's stunning, I can only imagine what the inside must be like.

Dom brings the car to a stop and switches off the engine. We sit quietly as I take it all in. I hear the soft tic of the motor cooling before he climbs out and comes around to open my door.

I step out and scan my surroundings. "Wow, babe it's absolutely beautiful." I'm slightly breathless and overawed.

Dom chuckles from beside me, and I realize he has Evie in his arms. "Come on, my Angel, you can explore tomorrow. We need to get our Princess settled into bed."

"Ooops, of course." I hold my arms out. "I'll take her."

"I've got her. Come, let's go inside." He takes my hand, leads me up the stairs and into the house, I mean mansion. Holy Shit!

Ten

Dominic

We cross the entry foyer and I take the girls upstairs where the bedrooms are located. Sneaking a peek at Brooklyn, I chuckle at her *deer in headlights* expression. When we approach the bedroom closest to mine, I throw open the door and cross the room to the bed. I wait while Brooklyn folds back the blankets before laying Evie down, I try my best not to jolt her awake. She snuggles into the blankets I pull over her, oblivious to where she might be. I watch her angelic little face for a moment. Her sleepy eyes flutter open and she gives me a weak smile. I bend down to speak to her and softly stroke her silky hair.

"Hey, Princess. You're at my house where I can keep you and your momma safe. If you wake up and feel scared, we'll be just down the hall. I'll leave the light on for you, okay?" She nods her little head and snuggles deeper into the blankets. "Go back to sleep now." I kiss her soft cheek.

"Ok, Dom," she whispers and then she is out like a light.

"Maybe, I should sleep in here with her, I don't want to impose on you more than I already have. You have done so much for us already and I really do appreciate it. I really do, but like I said I don't want to burden you with any more trouble."

I take Angel by the hand and lead her from the room and down the hall to my bedroom. I close the door, spin her around and wrap her in my arms. Breathing in her scent calm's my anticipation. I run my fingertips lightly over her cheek and smile as she leans into my touch. I place my hand under her chin and lift her face until our eyes lock.

"Listen to me carefully, Angel. You and your beautiful little girl down the hall, are not, and never will be a burden. Not ever! Do you understand me? You are in my home because I want you here. You are in this room because, fuck, I *need* you in this room. You belong here with me. *Both* of you." I hear her sharp intake of breath and before she can say something, I continue. "If you don't want to be in here with me because if you stay, I *will* make love to you, then you are more than welcome to sleep with Evie. I won't push you." I really hope she understands how much I want her here with me. No, I was right before, I *need* her here with me.

"Okay." Her voice is barely a whisper, so quiet, I'm lucky I heard it. But, I did and I still need clarification.

"Okay what, Brooklyn?" I try hard not to get my hopes up or sound eager.

She stares into my eyes and I'm lost in the crystal blue color, they pull me in deeper every time I look at her.

"I will sleep in here with you, if that's what you want."

"Of course, I want you in here, I want to worship every inch of your body, but do *you* want to be in here? I would never force you to stay. If you insist, I will even keep my hands to myself, although I'm sure that would kill me."

Brooklyn giggles. "Yes, I want to stay in here with you, and I know you would never force me to do something I don't want to." She rises to her toes and kisses my cheek. "Thank you."

She smiles shyly and it just about does me in. I give her ass a soft squeeze and bend down to brush my lips over hers. "Through that door," I point to a door on our left "...is a bathroom, have a shower while I go down and make sure Sergio has everything under control." I kiss her softly, turn and head out the door.

Fuck, I need to control myself or I'm going to scare her off. I reach down and rearrange myself, being hard when she's around is becoming a perpetual state of affairs and it's becoming fucking painful. Fuck, I hope she will allow me to make love to her, how the hell am I going to be able to lay next to her, and not want a taste?

Fuck! Fuck! Fuck! Maybe she should sleep with Evie because I'm not so sure I can keep my hands off her. But, I'm a selfish bastard and I want her with me. I mentally chastise myself. *You have more control than this, Dom. She has been through so much already, we are not going to risk scaring her off. We need to take this slow.*

NOW GET IT THE FUCK TOGETHER!

Brooklyn

I watch Dominic leave the bedroom. I can't believe he said I belong here with him. I can't control the butterflies in my belly and the flutter of hope in my heart. I take the opportunity of being alone to study his bedroom. With only the soft light of the bedside lamp, it's difficult to see details. The center of the room is filled with a huge wooden, four-poster bed. It's complimented by matching bedside tables and a large chest of drawers. On the other side of the room are two doors. One I know is the bathroom which Dom pointed out and I assume the other is the closet. I run my fingers over the chest of drawers as I head for the bathroom and notice a framed photo. I can't see it clearly in the dim light so I'll wait and look at it another time because I don't know when Dom will be back and I need a shower.

I open the door to the bathroom and stop short at what is revealed. The room is fucking gorgeous! I feel like I've stepped into a luxury hotel, not that I have ever been in one before, but I have seen pictures in magazines. A huge spa sits on a raised platform in front of the floor to ceiling windows which span the entire wall. The view over the ocean is spectacular, lights from nearby buildings and houses twinkle on the water turned black by the night sky. To the right of the spa is the biggest shower I have ever seen. It's surrounded by clear glass paneling; numerous jets are positioned in the wall. A small wooden ledge allows you to sit and an enormous shower head hangs from the ceiling. You know the ones that make it seem like it's raining? WOW! I cross to the other side of the room where a beautiful long bench is attached to the wall. It has drawers at either end and on top sit two glass sinks. The entire wall above the sinks is taken up by a mirror. Downlights are scattered like diamonds across the ceiling.

It's gorgeous, tastefully done in white marble with gold accents, and the black marble floor ties it all in together. I could easily get used to this bathroom. I make quick work of having a shower, I could have stayed in there for hours letting the jets from the wall massage my body. I've gone from tense to jelly in a matter of moments. I stand naked in front of the mirror drying my hair with the softest towel I have ever felt.

My thoughts drift back to earlier in the evening. The image of Dom standing in my kitchen, watching his muscles flex, eyeing the tattoo running down one side of his body, all hard lines leading down to the sexy V shape of his hips. The happy trail of soft hair traveling down his tight abs to disappear under the waistband of his jeans. Mmmm, I can imagine running my tongue all over his tanned skin, caressing every ridge and valley of muscle. Slowly, oh so slowly, making my way down his body to the prize between his legs. I close my eyes and swipe my tongue across my lips.

Heat pools low in my belly banishing the butterflies from moments ago. I moan and squeeze my thighs together to ease the sudden ache between my legs. I open my eyes and gaze in the mirror. "What the hell is going on with you? You've never felt like this before. You need to get it together because if you go back in the bedroom feeling this way, you'll make a fool of yourself. Yeah, sure he says he wants to make love to you, but why? Why the fuck would he want you? Plain, inexperienced you?" I finish drying my hair and hang the towel back over the rail. *I will not throw myself at him... I will not make a fool of myself... I will not climb that sexy as sin body like a tree... Shit!*

Dominic

After checking in with Sergio and organizing someone to guard the girls when I can't be with them, I head back upstairs. Sneaking a peek to check on Evie, I find her still snuggled up and snoring softly. After leaving the door open a fraction in case she wakes and is frightened by the dark, I make my way to my room.

The thought of Brooklyn waiting for me causes my heart rate to increase. I take slow even breaths, in through my nose and out through my mouth. I don't understand what's going on with me. I'm known for my control, but every time I'm around my Angel, my world tilts on its axis and all control disappears. I can't believe I've only just met her, and I have such deep feelings. I had no idea I could feel this just by looking at a woman. I know I love her. Yeah, I know that sounds stupid and yeah, I know you're sitting there saying – no way! But, I feel a strong protectiveness for her and Evie, like they're my everything. Every time Brooklyn smiles or laughs, I feel it deep in my bones. I know she's 'the one' and I would do anything to make her happy. I hate what she's been through and I know I want to kill the piece of shit with my bare hands, but if she hadn't gone through what she did, then she wouldn't be here with me now. I need to convince her she belongs here, and try and help her to fall in love with me too. I shake my head. These thoughts and feelings make me sound like a fucking pussy, not the hard edge, big time Mafia Boss that I am. Fuck!

As I walk through the door with a bottle of water in my hand for Brooklyn, she steps out of the bathroom. I feel like I've been sucker-punched as the air in my body whooshes out. I grip the bottle with the hold of a Pitbull's jaw and struggle not to follow my instincts, heft her over my shoulder, toss her onto the bed and have my way with her. All. Fucking. Night! The lady is beautiful at any time, but standing there in a full-length light pink satin nightgown, she is downright breathtaking. I swallow the tennis ball sized lump in my throat and hope I have a voice.

"My God you're gorgeous." My voice has a deep huskiness.

Brooklyn is frozen in place, wide-eyed and I watch the blush creep over her cheeks. The light behind her accentuates every curve so I lift my eyes to hers and try to regain control. I clear my throat with a husky cough and try to speak normally.

"I brought you some water." I indicate the bottle as I cross to the bedside table and place it down. "Why don't you crawl into bed and get comfy while I go and get myself ready."

"Um, I better check on Evie first." She heads for the door but I grasp her elbow and turn her toward the bed.

"I checked on her on my way here, she's fine and sound asleep. I tucked the blankets up around her and left her door slightly ajar so she can see the light in the hallway. I feel Brooklyn relax and when I release her, she crawls into the bed. Fuck, she looks good in my bed. I'm not sure how long I stand staring at my vision of loveliness, but when she clears her throat, I hurry to my walk-in closet and change into sweat pants. I stare down at my steel hard cock willing it to behave. I'll terrify her if she sees me like this.

When I've softened a tad, I re-enter the bedroom. Brooklyn is laying on her side facing away from me snuggled up in the blankets. I pad to the bed and ease myself in next to her, trying not to disturb her in case she's asleep. I lay still for a moment, staring up at the ceiling trying to relax and unwind. I jump when Brooklyn speaks.

"Thank you, Dom. I don't know what I would have done if you weren't there tonight."

I roll over to face her, wrap my arm around her waist and draw her back into my chest. I feel her tense, but then she slowly relaxes and squirms into me, trying to get closer. Her ass wriggles against my cock and I'm instantly steel hard again. I groan when she wriggles again, she's fucking killing me.

"You're hard." Her voice if filled with astonishment.

I bury my nose in her hair to hold back my chuckle.

"I'm sorry, I've never felt a man's hard, um... penis, against me before. I don't understand how you could get hard with me."

I'm confused by her words and I'm trying to figure out what she's telling me. Then light flashes in my brain – is she saying that *cazzo* didn't have sex with her? Nah, that can't be true, they lived together for almost five years. There's no way a man could keep his hands off someone as beautiful as my Angel. But, then again, he was a prick.

"What do you mean, darling? Your gorgeous, any man would have trouble controlling their um….themselves around you." I stifle the irritation in my voice and the sudden anger I feel when making that statement. I don't like the idea of other men having those thoughts about my Angel.

"Um…. Darren well…. We kind of never had sex… He said he was incapable of having sex with me because I had destroyed that part of us with what happened the first time. He said I was too ugly anyway. The first, and only time, we had sex was when I fell pregnant with Evie."

Her words tumble out fast, but I manage to catch what she's telling me. Holy fuck, she's only had sex once and doesn't remember it anyway. Fuck! I try and roll her over to face me, but she won't move. She's trembling, is it fear? "Angel," I rise up on my elbow and kiss her temple before slowly rolling her over so I can look into her eyes. This time there's no resistance, she rolls over willingly. There are tears in her eyes.

"Darling, you have no need to feel ashamed. I don't think any less of you because you aren't experienced with sex. That *cazzo* is a fucking idiot. You are absolutely gorgeous, don't let anyone tell you different. Any man would be lucky to have you, sometimes I feel like you would be settling for less than you deserve if you choose to stay with me. I'm not a good man, Angel. I have done some unbelievably bad shit! Some things I'm not proud of, but it's part of my job." I didn't mean to get all deep and meaningful tonight, I'd decided to take things slow, but she needs to know how intense my feelings are for her.

My voice is barely a whisper when I speak. "Angel, I think… I think I'm falling very hard for you. I know it's difficult for you to believe considering we have only just met, but I look at you and Evie and it feels so right. You feel right in my arms, like it's where you belong and…" I trail off, Brooklyn's eyes are as wide as saucers. Have I frightened her? Fuck! Nice job you fucking, *cazzo!*

"You think I would be settling for less with you?"

I nod.

"You say you're not a good man, but would you ever hurt me or Evie?"

I become a little angry with her question, but I shove it aside. "I told you, I would *never* hurt either of you. Brooklyn, I promise I would never harm you in any way. Please believe me."

"I do believe you, and that's why I know I can trust you." She lowers her eyes. "I'm falling for you too. I think you are a good man. I understand you have done some bad things, but I also understand, sometimes there wasn't a choice. I can see, sometimes you were trying to protect someone you loved, I can accept that. I won't accept you telling me you're a bad man when you have shown nothing but kindness to Evie and me." She raises her eyes and there is a determination in them I haven't seen before. Her voice is strong; she is no longer whispering. Her eyes glaze over and she wipes away a fallen tear "I believe you would be settling with me, Dominic. I'm terrified you'll wake up one day and wonder, what the hell have I done, taking on all her baggage and her daughter?" Another tear falls but this time she doesn't wipe it away. She stares at me; the determination has faded to be replaced by fear and worry in her beautiful eyes.

I brush at her tears. "That's not going to happen, that little girl down the hallway is burrowing her way into my heart almost as fast and as deep as you are. I may not have been there to help create her, but I'm here now and that's all that matters to me. I would love nothing more than for her to be mine. Also, since we both believe that the other would be 'settling', we can be the perfect couple which settles together." I lift her chin and brush my lips over hers. "Angel, are you telling me nobody has touched you since Evie was conceived?" She frowns and I feel her stiffen. She opens her mouth to respond, but the words don't come. She nods instead. I rub a hand over the side of her body, my heart thunders in my chest with the happiness I feel in knowing she has only been violated once.

"Why are you smiling?"

I don't answer, instead, I ask her a question of my own. What I do next will come down to her answer.

"Do you trust me, Angel?"

She answers without hesitation. "Yes."

"I'm going to take my time and worship your body the way it should be. If you don't like something I do, or you want me to stop, tell me immediately and I'll stop. Okay?"

Brooklyn nods her head but I need to hear her say the words.

"Is it okay, Angel?"

"Yes, it's okay, Dom.

Eleven

Dominic

I watch her eyes as I run my fingers up and down her side slowly sliding the satin nightgown up over her hips. Leaning forward, I suck her bottom lip into my mouth and bite down with slight pressure. She gasps at the sensation, opens her mouth and allows my tongue to slip in to taste her. A moan rumbles in the back of my throat as we kiss deeply. I run my fingers over the curve of her ass and squeeze before exploring down to her knee. Her skin is velvet soft except for the goosebumps which have broken out. I press myself closer and lift her leg over my hip. I feel the heat and wetness between her legs and moan again. Brooklyn arches her back as she whimpers and tremors run through her body.

When we separate we're both breathless, I feather kisses across her jaw, traveling an invisible line down her throat, listening to her whimpers and feeling her body straining to push closer to mine. I ease her onto her back and kiss her gently before sitting back on my knees and drinking in her body. Her skin is flushed, heated, peppered with sweat. Her eyes flutter open, and a small whimper escapes when I run my hands up over her knees, along the insides of her thighs and bunch her nightgown in my hands. She sucks in a deep breath when I ease the gown up over her head. I see worry when I gaze into her eyes but there is also lust burning brightly. She brings her hands up to cover herself. Nope, not happening. I shake my head as I lean forward, lift her hands up and pin them above her head. I force myself to take things slowly so I don't scare or hurt her.

"Are you okay, Angel?" I keep my eyes locked on hers.

She looks at me wide-eyed for a moment before nodding her head.

I let out the breath I didn't realize I was holding. My eyes roam the most beautiful body I have ever seen. She has a gorgeous hourglass figure, breasts that will fit perfectly in the palms of my hands, punctuated with pebbled brown nipples. My eyes wander further south to the sexy, lacy white panties she is wearing. I suck in a breath when I notice her pussy is bare and I witness the wet patch. I release her hands and lower my fingers to her nipples, feathering the edges of the pebbled nubs. Brooklyn moans and arches her back pushing her breasts harder into my hands.

Leaning forward, I hear her heavy, but steady breathing as I trail kisses from her lips, down her throat and to the sensitive spot behind her ear. I feel her pulse racing under my tongue and suck the skin between my lips. When I allow my hand to caress the soft skin along the side of her rib cage, she arches again, straining toward my touch. When I run my thumb along the underside of her breast, she emits the sexiest noises I have ever heard.

I take a series of deep breaths to calm myself so I don't lose control and blow my load. I draw her hard nipple into my mouth, nip and nibble before swirling my tongue around the hard nub. I suck it deep into my mouth and caress the nub with my tongue before releasing it with a small pop.

Brooklyn rakes her nails across my back and lifts her hips from the bed. When I move onto the other nipple and moan as I suck, she lets out a loud moan of ecstasy. Slowly, I slide down her body, peppering her skin with opened mouth kisses and licks. At her belly button, my tongue swirls inside and around before running from one side of her belly to the other. Her body quivers beneath me, soft moans spill from her lips. I slide her panties off and lower my head between her thighs, nudging them apart with my shoulders. Her clit is swollen with arousal and I run the tip of my tongue over and around the small bundle of nerves. I pin her hips down as she lifts to get closer. Her fingers tighten in my hair, pulling a moan from me. Her breath quickens, she whimpers when I run my tongue along the center of her heat.

"Fuck, Dom. You're not gonna…" Her words trail off on a loud moan when I lick her again and again before blowing gently over her heat.

Fuck she tastes good! I don't think I'll ever get enough of this woman. I slide my tongue deep inside and moan at the sweetest taste I have ever had. I want more. Lifting my eyes, I find her gazing at me heavy-lidded, lust filled eyes. I focus on her face as I suck her clit into my mouth. My finger joins in and I can feel how tight her canal is – fuck! I push a second one in, then curve my fingers until I locate her g-spot. And that does it. I hold her hips down in a firm grip, her eyes roll back in her head, her back arches, muscles tighten and release in an attempt to suck my fingers in deeper. Fuck, she's sexy.

"DOM! Fuuuuck." She turns her face into the pillow to muffle her cries as spasms wrack her body. Watching her pleasure has to be the sexiest moment of my life. I lick and suck her clit, drawing out her pleasure until the spasms eventually disperse. I withdraw my fingers, sucking them into my mouth moaning at her taste, not wanting to waste a drop. I crawl up her body, worshipping every inch with soft kisses and licks. When I reach her mouth, we kiss long and hard, pushing my tongue into her mouth so she can taste her sweetness. Her arms wrap around me, wanting me close. Her nails stroke through my hair, massaging my scalp before clutching the back of my neck. Hearing her moans of pleasure is pushing me to the edge. I'm hanging on by a thread. By the time we come up for air, we're breathing hard. I try to ignore the ache which has been building in my balls since I tasted her. I'm addicted, I want more, so much more. I'm so hard I could explode.

"Beautiful." I place my forehead against hers. "That was the sexiest thing I have ever seen." I watch as she blushes a deep shade of red and tries to cover her face. "Angel, don't hide from me. That was beautiful. You're beautiful."

"No one has ever done that to me before."

I already know this, but I like knowing I'm her first. It makes me feel ten feet tall.

"It won't be the last, Angel." I place a kiss on her nose before laying on my side and pulling her closer into my chest. I kiss her forehead, I can't stop touching her. Brooklyn snuggles into me before pulling back and staring at me.

"What is it, Angel? Are you okay?" I feel panicked which doesn't make sense. I didn't hurt her, did I?

"I can feel you against me, you're still hard." Her voice is barely a whisper and her eyes drop to study my chest.

Thank Christ for that, she's not hurt. I place my fingers beneath her chin and lift her head. "It's okay, that was just for you, si? I don't need anything besides you in my arms and your taste in my mouth." I wink at her to ease the tension and worry in her eyes.

She giggles and slaps my chest, her eyes widen when she realizes what she's just done.

I chuckle and grab her hand. "It's okay Angel, you can hit me anytime, when it's in fun." I place a kiss to her knuckles, then bring her hand down and place it over my heart. I gather her closer and kiss her forehead again. We rest for a moment, I feel her warm breaths on my chest, I try and think of anything else besides her mouth on me or me sliding into her warmth... Shit!

Brooklyn

I snuggle against Dom's chest, his hard muscles pressed up against me. Laying here cuddling, it's like I fit perfectly against him. Our bodies mold perfectly. My head lays on his chest, I listen to his heart beating slowly, feel his chest rise and fall as he breathes in and out. My eyes feel heavy as I'm being lulled to sleep. But, my brain insists on replaying what we have done, well, what he has done. To me. Recalling the feelings of his tongue licking and sucking all over me, the soft kisses he spread over my body, the way he worshiped me like I'm some exquisite and rare dish he can't get anywhere else. I feel the heat rise in my cheeks. The gentle way he held me, not tight enough to hurt, but enough to let me know, he was in control. I thought I would have been scared with it being my first time, yeah, being with Darren doesn't count, but I was far from it. When I escaped, I vowed I would never let anybody else control me, but the way Dom took control turned me on and I want more. Damn it, just thinking about it all is causing me to ache all over again. I squeeze my thighs together, trying to the dull the ache. I know he said tonight was just for me, and I appreciate it, I really do, but I want more. No, I *need* more. I'm not sure what *more* is, but I want it. Desperately. Could I have sex with him? Have his powerful body take mine, pushing in slow, making me burn from the inside out. *Fuck. Just tell him what you want. What if he rejects me? Shit, what would I do then? I'd have to sleep in the other room with Evie. Come on Brooklyn, you can do this. Tell him. For the first time in your life, go for what you want. I send up a silent plea - Please don't let him reject me.*

"Babe, I know..." I pause, taking a moment to gather the courage to ask for what I want. "I know you said tonight was just for me, but..." I trail off. Shit, this is harder than I thought. Dom slides his fingers under my chin, tilts my face up and, when my eyes lock onto his, I become lost in their gorgeous green depths. His eyes sparkle and gazes at me like I hung the moon.

"What is it *Amore Miol grab a fistful*?" The huskiness of his voice sends shivers down my spine.

What was I going to ask? Oh, yeah that's right. "What does that mean?" I know it's not what I meant to ask, but he's said those words to me a couple of times, and I want to know what it means. He pauses for a minute, searching my eyes. I think he's contemplating whether or not to tell me. As I'm about to tell him, it doesn't matter, he continues.

"Do you really want to know?"

I nod my head because I really do.

"It means... My Love"

Wow! I gaze at him and swear I see a blush hit his cheeks. Oh, my God. Dom thinks I'm his Love!

"Please don't freak out. I know we have only just met, but I feel it in my bones. I'm sure we were meant to be together, Fuck! I sound like a pussy." He drags fingers through his hair before sliding his hand down his face. He sucks in a deep breath.

I think he takes my silence as a sign I'm freaking out. I am, but not in a bad way. Not in a way he should be worried about. No, it's good, definitely good. I stare into his eyes and run my fingers across the stubble of his five o'clock shadow.

"You are the sweetest man I have ever met." He raises an eyebrow. I guess being a Mafia boss he wouldn't be used to being called sweet. My lips curl into a smile at his expression. "I promise you I'm not freaking out, and I feel like we're meant to be too *il Mio Amore*." My accent leaves a little to be desired as I repeat the words back to him.

He draws in a sharp breath and his hand travels up to the back of my neck drawing me down toward his lips. We kiss softly at first, my tongue slides across his bottom lip seeking entrance and when he opens, it slips inside. Our tongues twist in an ancient dance of love, drawing a moan from the back of his throat. I ease back and nibble on his bottom lip. Lust and arousal overcome me. "Make love to me, Dom," I smirk when I hear him gasp. I feel powerful knowing I can affect him as badly as he affects me. Shocks of excitement and anticipation cause me to tremble. A slow burn starts in my belly and zips straight to my clit. Droplets of moisture trickle onto my thighs.

Dom locks eyes with mine, he's searching, wanting to know if what I'm asking is true. "Are you sure, my Angel?" His voice is husky, fuck I love it.

"Yes. I'm more sure of wanting you than I have been of anything in a long while." Did I read the signs wrong, maybe he doesn't want to make love to me? "Do you want to, I mean you don't have..."

The words die on my lips when Dom rolls over on top of me. I let out a squeak of surprise which he takes full advantage of by slipping his tongue into my mouth. He claims me with a deep kiss.

The incoherent sound that erupts from me causes Dom to chuckle as he rises from the bed. His movement snaps me out of my fog. Fuck, did I do something wrong? I reach for the sheet to cover myself, but Dom makes a tsking noise. It's then I realize, he is taking his pants off. Fuck. Oh, fuck. I swear my tongue lolls from my mouth. He is so fucking sexy it should be illegal. I rake my eyes over his broad chest and along his sexy as sin tattoo. My mouth has become drier than the fucking Sahara Desert. I suck my tongue back into my mouth and allow my eyes to wander down the rest of his body. I drool over every ripple of muscle, his tight abs and the happy trail of hair heading south. My fingers twitch, wanting to trace every ripple, every valley and hill of pure male muscle. My palms feel the bite of pain as my nails dig ever deeper. The bastard was commando, and fucking hell. He's huge! Not huge like when girls tell their partners *"oh you're so big"* so as not hurt their feelings. No! No! No! Huge as in, I seriously don't think he will fit. "HUGE! FUCK!"

Dom has been standing still allowing me to take in his Adonis-like body. He chuckles when I widen my eyes. I slap my hand over my mouth when I realize my last two words weren't my thoughts, I actually spoke them aloud. Shit! I snap my eyes up to his, and his sexy smirk confirms I had spoken. Shit! Shit! Shit! He's staring at me like he knows what else I was thinking, I feel the heat creeping over my cheeks. I swear until this man walked into my life, I have never blushed so much. You would think I was a fifteen-year-old girl with the way I have been acting. Geez, get a grip, Brooklyn. I'm trying to think of something to say to break the sudden silence. "Will it fit?" Fuck, just shoot me now.

Dom cracks up laughing.

"I'm Sorry." I drop my head into my hands and try not to die of embarrassment. I wish the floor would open up and swallow me whole. Can I be any more pathetic?

Dom places one knee on the bed and leans over me, he pulls my hands away from my face. "Angel, it's okay." When I raise my head, he's right in front of me. Correction, his cock is right in front of me and he's hard. I swear it needs its own postcode. Fuck me! I notice a pearl drop of pre-cum balanced at the tip, and I lick my lips. If I leaned forward just a little, mmmm, I wonder what he tastes like? Dom rubs his thumb over my bottom lip and I flick my tongue out to lick it, he groans deep in the back of his throat. With the small amount of courage I have remaining, I bring my hand up, grasp hold of his hand and suck his thumb into my mouth. As I swirl my tongue around and around, I see the pleasure I can bring him and I suck a little harder.

Dom pulls his thumb from my mouth and I whimper at the loss, but he shakes his head. Shit, I feel like an idiot, did I imagine the look of lust on his face? He must see something in my eyes because he bends down and places a soft kiss to my lips. He sucks my bottom lip into his mouth before releasing it with a soft pop.

"If you kept doing that, I wouldn't last Angel. I'm hanging on by a thread as it is." His voice is huskier than normal.

"Oh." What more can I say?

"Lay back down, Angel." He reaches over and grabs a condom from the drawer in the bedside table.

I sink back against the pillows, his intoxicating scent surrounds me. I feel like I'm floating on a cloud, this bed is so soft. I'm not too sure what I'm supposed to be doing. When I feel the bed shift at the bottom, I look down and watch as Dom crawls toward me, lifting my leg as he moves. He kisses and licks a path over my skin, the scruff of his five o'clock shadow as it grazes against my skin, adds extra sensation to my already sensitized skin. I twist and shift, moan and whimper, then I feel his hot breath between my legs. Reflex causes my thighs to want to close, but they're trapped. The hot flash of his tongue traces lazy circles over my clit, but it's not enough. I whimper and lift my hips. It's just not enough. "Please Dom, please," I beg and he sucks me into his mouth like he's going for gold. My body arches off the bed at the sensation and pleasure he is giving me, but I want more. No, I need more. I whimper when his strong hands pin my hips to the bed. My body trembles with the onslaught of sensations. "Oh, fuck. Fuuuck!" I scream as the orgasm crashes over me like a tidal wave. "Oh, shit!" I'm panting heavy, a light coating of sweat coats my body and I shudder as Dom nips before blowing over my clit to draw out my orgasm. My heart thunders in my chest. When I feel the bed shift, my eyes flash open. Dom is hovering above me with his sexy as sin, crooked smile. "Wow."

Dom chuckles as he effortlessly holds up his weight on his elbows.

"That was amazing," I puff out.

"That's nothing compared to what I'm about to do to your gorgeous body. Are you ready, Angel?"

I moan and wrap my hands around his neck, opening my legs wider for him to position himself, words are failing me right now. His eyes narrow and his eyebrow raises. Oh, he wants me to say it, God I love him. Whoa! Love? I'll deal with that revelation later. I'm more interested in what's happening right now. "Yes, I'm ready," I whisper.

"Good girl." He leans forward and kisses me softly before pushing himself up with one hand and positioning himself with the other. He's so powerful. I should be scared, but I'm not. "This may hurt a little at first, but I'm going to try my best to go as slow as possible, okay?"

"Okay." I feather my fingertips down the side of his face. I feel him push forward and tense up at first, but then I try to relax.

"Relax for me, beautiful, I don't want to hurt you"

Dom eases into me slowly, stretching me wide. A whimper slips out at the intrusion. The sensation causes me to throw my head back on a deep moan at the pleasure he incites. Arching my back off the bed, I push myself closer to him. I want more. Dom's lips are everywhere. I'm breathless, a little lightheaded and moan when I feel Dom's mouth on the spot behind my ear. I love every sensation he is creating. My nails rake at his back and he moans with delight. He hits the sweet spot I didn't realize was there until earlier and I stifle a scream.

"Dominic," I moan as I feel him nibble on my neck.

"Please tell me this isn't a dream, if it is, I don't want to wake up." His moans vibrate through me when he latches onto my ear, sucking and nibbling. His hand slides to my breast causing me to arch into his touch. I feel a slight pinch to my hard nipple, electric shocks race through my body, my veins and arteries providing the conduits. I moan as the pleasure takes over my body and stars dance behind my eyelids. Beautiful green eyes stare at me, blazing with love, hunger, and arousal. The sight intensifies the tremors running through me.

I take a deep breath and relax into the mattress. Dom pushes the rest of the way in. I let out the breath I was holding and feel him do the same. He holds still for a moment and stares into my eyes. I squirm, trying to get used to the feel of him buried deep inside me. I feel so full, turned on and need him to move.

"Did I hurt you?" Is his voice filled with concern or…. pain?

"No, I'm fine, but I need you to move now. Are you okay? You sound like you're in pain." I run my nails up and down his back and feel his muscles tense as a shiver runs through his body.

"Your pussy is so tight, you're squeezing me like a vice." He starts to move. Slow at first, allowing me to get used to his size.

I moan as I fall into rhythm with him. Fuck, it feels so good, like sweet torture. He's being easy with me and holding back.

"Let go, Dom, don't hold back. I won't break. I promise I'll tell you if I hurt." I cup his face, he turns his face into my palm and places a kiss.

"I don't want to hurt you, Angel."

"You won't, trust me. I'm tougher than I look. Please, Dom, I need you." Finally, he starts moving. He runs his hands down my body and latches onto my hips.

"I love it when you beg, put your arms back and hold the headboard."

I reach back and grab hold of the wood panels of the headboard. Dom lifts me up by the waist and I wrap my legs around his back, lock my ankles together and hold on for dear life as he thrusts in and out of me. I push into him hard, taking him even deeper. He latches onto a hard nipple and bites gently, it sends a mixture of pleasure and pain to my aching core. I turn my head and scream out trying to muffle the sound with my arm. Dom grunts and pushes in hard, I feel him stretching me. Fuck, it feels good. If he goes any deeper, I swear he'll pop out through my mouth. I'm struggling to hold on, it's like I can feel him everywhere at once, I want to climb inside his body. He reaches down and fingers my aching clit. I tense my muscles, crying out again with the extra sensation, at the same time Dom groans. He knows exactly where to touch me to cause my body to spark and ignite. Thrust after powerful thrust, he pounds me. I'm floating in ecstasy, I move my hands and drag my nails down his back. It feels like my body is on fire and I'm about to explode. On the next powerful thrust, the planets align, stars dance before my eyes and an explosive orgasm spirals through me.

I'm trying to catch my breath, my heart is racing, then Dom groans my name. It's the sexiest sound I have ever heard. He thrusts, once, twice, as he holds me so tight I can barely catch my breath, he roars and empties inside me.

Breathing heavy, he lowers his forehead to mine. I run my fingers through his hair and watch his eyes flutter closed. A soft moan leaves his lips. I swear I hear him say *mine!*

"Porca puttana!" (Fucking hell) he puffs out "Your muscles, you squeezed my cock so hard I thought it was going to break off. That was the most powerful orgasm of my life."

"Stars," I mumble before closing my eyes. It's all I can manage to say right. My body feels like jelly. I squirm when I feel him getting hard again, my eyes snap open locking with Dom's and I notice the twinkle. A smirk curves his lips and I know I'm in for a long night. When he speaks, I know I'm right.

"Ready for round two *il Mio Amore?*"

Twelve

Brooklyn

I wake to sunshine streaming into the room and blink, slowly wiping the sleep from my eyes. I glance around, trying to figure out where I am. I'm disoriented, but when I stretch I feel a strong arm wrapped around my waist and a hand holding my boob. I begin to panic, but when I turn my head to the side, I see Dominic sleeping peacefully beside me. The past few hours comes rushing back to me. Dom worshipping my body until all hours of the morning, whispering to me - he is mine and I am his. It was the sexiest thing I have ever had said to me and I hold back a moan at the memories, squeezing my thighs together to overcome the delicious ache that doesn't seem to want to go away. I hope he hasn't changed his mind about me. I hope sleeping together doesn't change his feelings for me. I'm not too sure I could handle losing him now. Despite the short time I have known him, it scares the crap out of me, the feelings I have for this man. I have never felt this safe in my life, so precious, so worshiped, as I do when he wraps his arms around me.

I roll onto my side and rise on my elbow to study the man who is capturing my heart. My breath catches, he's so very handsome with his long lashes resting against his cheeks. Even in his sleep, he's sexy and powerful. I run my fingers lightly down the side of his face, I can't believe this man actually wants me. I brush my lips lightly over his and he hums deep in his throat before pulling me closer into his warm, hard body. I snuggle into his chest and feel the warmth of his breath on my face, fuck he smells good. I place a small kiss to his chest and then another because I can! Slowly I try to wriggle out of his arms so as not to disturb him.

Standing on shaky legs, I feel the slight ache in my muscles. Glancing around the room, I'm noticing everything in the new light. Wow! The entire wall behind the bed is ceiling to floor windows like the bathroom with a stunning view of the ocean. I missed this last night in the dim light. I notice thick curtains are drawn back to the sides and a small panel that looks like a light switch. Looking harder I see the panel has the time on it with a couple of buttons, the curtains must be on a timer. I slowly absorb the rest of the room, so elegant. Dark wooden furniture in front of white walls with the same black marble flooring as the bathroom up here and the foyer downstairs. I make my way into the bathroom needing to freshen up before I check on Evie. I hope she slept okay and our noise didn't disturb her. I smile to myself and a warm glow heats my skin, it was a wonderful night.

I throw on my nightgown and descend the stairs after finding Evie was not in her room. I marvel at the foyer and take it all in from the huge crystal chandelier hanging down from the high ceilings to the marble flooring. I feel like I'm in a fairy-tale. I hear music coming from my right so I head in that direction. I stop short in my tracks when I see a huge lounge room with floor to ceiling windows looking out over a gorgeous backyard with a pool the size of the local swim center. Okay, yeah, I might be exaggerating a bit so shoot me. But, it's huge and fancy with a rock formation leading up to a waterfall at one end and a spa off to the side. Beautiful lounges are positioned overlooking the pool, they match an outdoor setting alongside and sit under a huge pergola. Everything is surrounded by beautifully manicured lawns and exquisite gardens. It's breathtaking.

My focus is drawn back to the room before me, large black leather armchairs and a couch dominate the space. Underneath a glass and wooden coffee table sits a magnificent white rug. It screams elegance and there is an open and airy feel to it. On the wall opposite the couches is an enormous flat screen television which takes up close to the whole wall. It's on and playing a music channel.

Antonio is sitting in one of the armchairs and is tapping away on his phone. He looks up when I enter the room. *"Buongiorno,* Brooklyn." He returns his focus to his phone.

"Morning." I take a deep breath and inhale the aroma of cooking, it smells good. Following the direction of the singing, I find Kat and Evie in a beautiful kitchen I could only dream about. A huge breakfast bench in the middle of the room with pots and pans hanging from the ceiling captures my eye. Everything is finished similar to the bathroom upstairs in white marble with gold accents. It's absolutely gorgeous. Stainless steel appliances cause my fingers to twitch, it's a chief's dream. This home looks like it was built for a king, or I guess in this instance, a Mafia Boss. Giggling at my thoughts, I make my way over to the girls.

"Morning girls, what are we making? It smells delicious."

"Morning Mommy. Me and Aunty Kat are making pancakes for Antonio and Dominic. Wanna help?" Evie bright smile lights up her face.

"Sounds great Sweetpea, how about a kiss?"

Evie dives into my arms and gives me a lip-smacking kiss to the cheek before hugging me tightly.

"I love you, mommy."

"I love you too, Sweetpea." Smiling, I cross the room to the sink to wash my hands.

"How are you this morning, Dollface?" Kat sidles up beside me and leans against the cupboards. She's fishing for information.

Last night flits through my mind. Dom worshipping me. The way he held me close like I was the most precious person in the world. And, the kissing. I concentrate on washing my hands, feeling my face become hot. Like any good friend, Kat notices my face and smirks at me. I'm not too sure what to say.

Kat wraps her arms around me in a hug. "Brooklyn, you deserve to be treated like a queen after all you've been through and I think Dom is the right man for the job. You can relax and be yourself around him."

I squeeze her back tighter and when I draw back, I notice her eyes are glassy with tears.

"I love you, Kat, you're my soul sister." Tears prick my eyes, I need to change the subject before we are both a blubbering mess. "How was last night for you?" I smile when she reddens.

Kat wanted to be with us last night, but Antonio wouldn't hear of it. He wanted her to himself and told her she had two options - stay with him at his place or he was staying with her at her place. I'm not too sure how it ended but the back and forth was funny to watch.

"Back at you, Dollface. I don't need to tell you how much I love you and the squirt, you should know by now. That man is so fucking aggravating; I swear he was put on this earth to torment me." She rolls her eyes and we glance at Antonio, he's looking straight at us with a shit eating grin on his face. He winks before going back to his phone. I spin away from Kat as I attempt to hold back my laughter.

"I better call Gwen and let her know what happened last night, she'll be worried about us." I rub my forehead wondering how the hell I could be so inconsiderate in forgetting.

"Don't stress, I already took care of it. I also stopped at your place and grabbed some more of your things. I figured once Dom got you here, you probably wouldn't be leaving for a while, if at all."

Before I can say anything else, *Dear Future Husband* by *Meghan Trainor* blasts from the speakers. Evie squeals, it's her favorite song. She bounces up and down on the bench and claps her hands.

"Random dance party mommy." Evie giggles, jumps down from the bench and begins wriggling around in time to the music.

I smile at Kat and shrug my shoulders. "Come on Aunty Kat let's give Sweetpea what she wants." Laughing, we start to dance and sing around the kitchen, the pancakes forgotten.

Dominic

I roll over and reach for Brooklyn, but come up empty. Did I dream what happened last night? I rub my nose into the pillow. Nope. Definitely not a dream, I can still smell her scent in the bed.

I climb from the bed and head to the bathroom, maybe I can catch her in the shower. I open the door, but the room is empty. Where is she?

Sudden panic washes over me, what if something happened? Would she leave? Could someone have broken in and taken her? Could that asshole have found out where I live and gotten hold of her? I stand up straight and inhale a deep breath. *Stop this, right now. Think rationally.* I hear sounds coming from downstairs, she's probably making breakfast for Evie. *Fuck what is wrong with me?* I rake my nails over my scalp and shake my head. Angel's here. She's safe and so is Evie. *Nothing* and *no-one* can hurt them while they're here.

I quickly shower and dress then make my way downstairs. I see Antonio sitting on the couch, he swings his head toward me, gives me a chin lift and tilts his head in the direction of the kitchen. I look into the kitchen and chuckle when I see Evie, Brooklyn, and Kat dancing and singing at the top of their lungs to a song about someone being their future husband and treating them like ladies even when they're acting crazy. Evie giggles louder as she watches Brooklyn and Kat do some shimmy thing to the words about someone rocking their body right, and something about, even when they're wrong, knowing they are *never* wrong, why disagree? I shake my head and chuckle harder when I hear the next couple of lines. I raise my eyebrow when it gets to a part about opening doors and you might get some kisses. Brooklyn leans her cheek toward Evie so she can kiss it. I look at Antonio and notice he is completely fixated on Kat as she sings about someone buying her a ring, and wanting them to be her one and only.

I stand against the wall, one leg crossed over the other and arms folded across my chest. I listen to the girl's bellows of laughter when the song comes to an end. I want to wake up to this every morning. Evie notices me first and runs toward me. "Dominic, did you see? Did you see? We were having a random dance party." She bounces up and down, giggling and clapping her hands.

I scoop her into my arms and plant a kiss to her forehead. "I saw, Princess. You guys were amazing, but no going on tour till you are at least eighteen. Si?" I try to be serious but Evie cracks up laughing.

"Okay, Dom. We won't leave you." She smacks a kiss on my cheek.

I place her back on the floor and step over to give my Angel a kiss. I place my arms around Brooklyn and feel her body relax into me. "Okay ladies, we've had the entertainment, now what would you like for breakfast?"

Brooklyn looks alarmed. "We were making pancakes if that's okay with you? Sorry, we should have asked first."

I notice she's fidgeting with her fingers again, something she does only when she is worried or scared. "You don't need to ask, Angel. I want you to treat this home as your own." I chuckle when her mouth drops open and her beautiful eyes go wide. I place my finger under her chin, close her mouth and bend down to kiss her softly. I didn't like waking up without you in my arms, Angel," I whisper into her lips as I gaze into her eyes. I feel her tense at my words.

"I'm so sorry, Evie needed breakfast," Brooklyn speaks softly with fear.

I ease her against me and hold her tight. "Darling, It's okay, I'm not angry. I just wanted to hold you and have you to myself for a bit longer." I whisper in her ear and run my nose down her neck, breathing her in. I hear her small gasp and feel her squirm in my arms. I smirk into her neck knowingly, loving how she responds to my touch. Leaning back, I throw her a wink before releasing her and moving over to the coffee machine.

I hear her mumble, "tease."

I smile to myself but I'm worried about how scared she becomes when she misinterprets my words. That asshole really did a number on my Angel, and it will take time, but I am determined she *will* know how it feels to be safe and without fear.

Brooklyn

The air becomes thicker as I watch Dominic walk over to the coffee machine. I try not to drool. Fuck he's sexy! I know, I know, I've said it before, but fuck, he is sexy as sin! He's dressed in a pair of black suit pants which hug him in all the right places. Fuck what an ass! His white singlet vest hugs every muscle perfectly. I feel heat pool low in my belly just watching him. Oh, shit! I lick my lips and remember all the things he did to me last night and all the things I really want to do to him. Right fucking now! Oh, God what is happening to me, I have never felt a need like this before? He's turned me into a sex fiend. "Dominic?" I know my voice is all kinds of breathless right now, but I don't care.

"Si, Angel." He has his back to me and when I glance at Kat she has a smirk on her face. The bitch knows the effect this man is having on me.

"Sweetpea, why don't you show Aunty Kat and Antonio your new room, I just want to talk to Dom for a second, okay?" Evie smiles and nods her head.

I watch as they all leave the room and wait until I hear them on the stairs before I turn back to Dominic. He's looking me up and down with the same hunger I'm feeling for him. I take a deep breath and summon all the courage I can muster. I cross the floor, grab Dom's hand and head for the nearest door. I'm hoping it may be the laundry. Nope, it's the biggest bloody walk in pantry I've ever set eyes on, but that doesn't matter right now. I drag Dom through the door, I know he could stop me at any moment, but he doesn't and that makes me feel good, empowered. Once inside with the door closed, I swing around and push him until his back is against the door. Using a hand at the back of his neck, I pull his head down and capture his lips. I feel one hand thread through my hair and pull my head back, he deepens our kiss. His other hand grabs hold of my ass, lifts me up and pulls me into him. I wrap my legs around his hips and he grinds his hard cock against me. Fuck, he feels good. I moan into his mouth. He swings us around and my back hits the door, the hard ridge of his cock pushes on the spot where I need it the most.

I break the kiss to take in some air and gasp. "What are you doing to me?"

Dom nips at my neck and shivers catapult down my spine. "I could ask you the same thing." I notice his accent has become thicker, more pronounced. His lips crash back against mine, his tongue forces its way into my mouth, taking what I have to offer. I reach down and fumble with the button and zipper of his pants, sighing into his mouth when I finally get them to undo so I can handle the prize. I slip my hand into his pants and caress his hard cock. "Fuck, I need you." I moan and squeeze him through his briefs. I can't think. Fuck, I can barely breathe and my body feels like it's on fire. Pushing me harder against the door Dom slides his hand up my leg, I feel the vibration of his groan zing through my body as he makes contact with the bare flesh between my thighs. Quick as a flash he pulls back, rips my nightgown over my head, and I'm naked and panting with need.

Dom latches on to my left nipple with a growl as his fingers work their way inside me. I'm at the edge, and it only takes a few moments of him fingering my clit before my body tenses up and I explode. I grip him tight and lean forward in an attempt to muffle my scream against his shoulder. "Inside me now, Dom. Please, I need you inside me." I don't give him time to think about anything,

I pull him to me and kiss him hard while I line myself up with the tip of his cock so it's positioned against my clit. I throw my head back and moan at the contact, then push my opening down on him. Dom pushes forward and enters me, stretching me so deliciously. We both let out a deep moan.

"Fuck, you feel good," Dom growls into my neck.

"Don't stop," I moan breathlessly and dig my nails into his shoulders.

Dom growls again and thrusts into me harder and faster. "Fuck, I'm not going to last long."

He hits my sweet spot with a hard thrust and I want to climb up inside him. "Right there." He thrusts and hits it again. "That's it. Fuck!"

Dom's fingers rub my clit, sending my body into a frenzy and I can't hold back any longer. I lean forward and bite into Dom's shoulder at the same time he growls. With his hands on my hips, he pulls me down onto him as he thrusts hard and deep. I erupt with a squeal and with one more thrust, Dom is pushed over the edge with me. His hips piston back and forth as he works through his orgasm.

When we finally quiet, we're hot, sweaty and breathing hard. Fuck, that was good.

Dom leans his forehead against mine and gazes intently into my eyes. There is so much in them, I close my eyes against the intensity. I can't get drawn in too deep because if he leaves me, I know I would never survive.

"Angel look at me."

I open my eyes at his command.

"Did I hurt you?"

"No, babe you were perfect." I smile to ease the worry I see on his face.

He slides me slowly down his body and onto my feet, he slips free and the evidence of our passion slowly trickles down my legs. I tense in his arms. Fuck. Fuck. We forgot to use a condom. I hope he's not angry with me. I feel woozy and light-headed with worry.

"Angel, what is it, you've gone as pale as a sheet?" There's genuine concern in his voice and I feel a lump form in my throat.

I turn away as a tear rolls down my cheek. "I forgot the condom, I'm so sorry Dom. I don't know what came over me. Please forgive me." I can't look in his eyes, I'm afraid of what I might see there.

"Angel." He turns me, and lifts my chin, so I look into his eyes "I'm clean and I have never had sex without one before. You're safe my darling."

"So am I, but what if I get pregnant?" A tear rolls down my cheek and I shake with fear.

He wipes away the tear and gathers me closer. "Is that a bad thing?"

What? What does he mean - *is that a bad thing?* "I don't want to trap you into staying with me and we just met and Darren was so angry with me when I got pregnant with Evie." My words tumble out.

"Forget about your asshole ex, he was no man. Do you *want* to have another baby?"

I search Dom's eyes trying to work out what's going on here. Shouldn't he be angry, screaming at me? He seems fine with all this.

I answer honestly because I do, I would love to give Evie a little brother or sister. "Yes, I would love another baby but Darren....."

He places his fingers over my lips. "I told you, forget that *cazzo*. I want to have a baby with you, I'm not hanging around just for a bit of fun." He sucks in a deep breath. "I want to spend the rest of my life worshipping you, only you. You would look sexy as fuck with my baby growing inside of you, I can't wait for it to happen." He groans and places a hand on my belly. "I want it, but do you? We're meant for each other and I want the whole package - you, Evie, marriage and more children. I thought we were on the same page here, no?"

Oh, no! Have I hurt him. "I'm sorry, sweetheart. I want this, more than anything. I really do. I meant every word I said last night, I swear *il Mio Amore.* I was just worried that maybe you might have changed your mind about wanting me and I don't think I could handle you leaving me."

Dom grabs me gently and pulls me into the sweetest kiss I have ever had. "Thank, Christ. I'm not going anywhere."

"What if I fall pregnant?"

"If you do, I will be the happiest man alive, but if you're not, then that means we have to have more practice." He wiggles his eyebrows, making me giggle.

I reach for my nightgown but Dom grabs my hand and I pause at the sound of his voice. "Angel?"

"Yes?"

"It was sexy as fuck, you dragging me in here and not asking for what you want, but taking what you know is yours."

"You *are* mine," I say the words more for myself than for him.

"And, you are mine. So, no more walking around in nightgowns, especially with no underwear on, in front of other men." He growls and grabs my ass, pulling me closer. Why does the thought of *his* possessiveness turn me on when Darren's filled me with fear? I wonder if I can turn the tables on him a little? I think that might be my mission for the day. I lean up and kiss him. "Okay, babe."

We step back from each other so we can get dressed, but before we make our way back to the kitchen, I give him one more kiss and rise onto my toes to whisper in his ear.

"Sweetheart, always remember, I demand to be the first thing you touch in the morning and the last thing you taste at night"

I turn and pad out to the kitchen, but not before I see the look of possession cross his face. It sends shivers down my spine. Yeah, I've got him thinking. I hear him groan, "Fuck" as I walk into the kitchen. I throw back my head and burst into laughter.

Thirteen

Dominic

As we step back into the kitchen, I grab hold of Angel around the waist and grind myself into her sweet, lush ass. I want her to feel exactly what her words have done to me. I feel small tremors race through her body, and I know I have hit my mark when she reaches out and grabs the edge of the bench hard enough for her knuckles to start turning white. Bending over her, I nip her ear and suck it into my mouth to soothe the sting.

I hear Evie coming down the stairs and run a hand through my hair. Moving closer, I take a deep breath, letting her scent fill me. I don't think I will ever get enough of this woman. "We will finish this later," I growl low and hear a soft whimper slip free when I pull back a little. I want nothing more than to be with my girls right now, and I know it's Sunday morning, but I have business to take care of. I'll have to call a meeting to get this issue sorted out.

"Angel, why don't you and Kat take Evie out to the pool for a swim after you have breakfast?"

Angel glances up from something she is stirring and gives me a puzzled look. "Okay, babe."

I glance at Antonio and notice his arm around Kat's waist.

"Antonio," I nod toward my office. "Call Theo and the men. Tell them I want them here now."

"Si, Boss." Antonio kisses Kat on top of her head then whispers something in her ear, before turning and walking into the foyer with his phone to his ear. Interesting, it looks like things are heating up for them too. I'm a curious bastard, I'll have to ask him about it later. First, we have work to do and an asshole to put in the ground.

"Dominic, is everything okay?" I look down to find Angel biting her lip and pull her into my arms.

"I have something which needs doing this morning."

"Okay." She starts to step out of my hold, her shoulders are drooping and when I look down, she's fidgeting with her fingers. I'm such a cazzo, she thinks I'm pushing her aside. I need to remember, this is all new to her. She's familiar with being used and abused and it will take time for her to realize, I will never hurt her. I drag her back close to my body, she's tense and trembling. I brush my lips over hers before lowering my voice, hoping it will soothe her worry. "Angel look at me." I wait for eyes to meet mine before I continue. "We can talk more about this later, si? But, be assured, this is not a dismissal. This is me protecting Evie and you, okay?" I watch as she absorbs my words, searching my eyes. I feel her relax into my arms and a bright smile spreads across her face. I release the breath I didn't realize I was holding, knowing she understands what I am trying to say and not storming off on me.

"We will talk later I promise, si?" I bend forward and kiss her softly again, when I attempt to pull back, my Angel has other ideas. She wraps her arms around my neck and pushes her tongue into my mouth. I growl and drag her closer into my chest. *Fuck she tastes good.* Angel pulls back laughing when we hear Evie and Kat giggling and making gagging sounds.

"Sorry Babe, but can you do something for me before you go anywhere?" She runs her fingertips up and down my chest, looking up at me through her eyelashes.

I still her hands, holding them against me before I'm tempted to take her right here, right now. Fuck, this woman ties me in knots. "Anything for you, *il Mio Amore.*"

"Please put a shirt on." Her teeth bite down on her lip, as she slowly looks at me up and down before rising onto tiptoes. "If you don't, I may drag you back into the pantry for round two," she whispers in my ear and gives it a little suck as she pulls back.

Fuck! I grab her ass and pull her tighter against me so she can feel how hard I am for her.

"Feel how hard you make me," I growl in her ear. I release her when she starts laughing at my torment. "You'd better get dressed too." I squeeze her ass before giving it a little smack, reminding her of our conversation earlier.

As I descend the stairs fastening the buttons on my shirt, I hear Antonio yelling before something hits the wall. What the fuck is going on? I hurry into my office and see all my men standing around with pissed off expressions pasted on their faces. I look to where Antonio has Joey pinned to the wall by the throat, blood is dripping from his lip.

"What the fuck is happening in here?" My voice is low, menacing. I clench and unclench my fists by my sides.

"Tell the Boss, what you said!" Antonio spits in Joey's face. He attempts to get free of Antonio's hold, with not much success.

"Antonio let go! Joey speak NOW!" I've had enough of this fucking behavior.

Antonio grunts and smashes Joey into the wall one more time before he releases his grip. Joey collapses against the wall, gasping for air and rubbing his throat. His eyes are darting all over the room before they land on mine. That's when I see his pupils are dilated. *Fuck this cazzo is high!*

"I saw the two *puttane* (whores) in the kitchen and asked Antonio if he wanted to double team them with me. He got all fucked up about it."

I grab a fistful of his shirt and drag him toward me none too gently. "*Venite in casa Mia e mancate do rispetto a la Mia Donna, ma chi cazzo sei ti? Che tipo di una testa di cazzo sei tu?*" (Who the fuck do you think you are? You come into my house and disrespect my woman? What kind of a dickhead are you?)

"Well, fuck Boss, I didn't know. I assumed they were a couple of whores here for yours, and Antonio's pleasure." This fucker is digging himself into a deeper hole every time he opens his mouth. He waves his hands around in an attempt to get free of my hold. I let go pushing him back hard against the wall. I pace my office. I'm never this patient, but I can't afford to let Angel hear me. I don't want to scare her off. Fuck, I have to try and rein in my temper.

Antonio gets back up in Joey's face. I've never seen him so angry. "Tell the Boss what you said about his daughter."

My breath rushes out when I hear Antonio call Evie my daughter. Reality hits me with the force of a wrecking ball. My heart somersaults in my chest. Fuck, I have a daughter, the most beautiful daughter on Earth, and this piece of shit said something about her? I stop pacing and approach Joey. I must look like I could murder someone right now because everyone, including Antonio, takes a step back. Everyone except this drugged, fucked, *cazzo* who shrugs like it's not a big deal.

"Daughter? I didn't know, Boss."

"Sergio." My voice is deadly quiet.

Sergio steps up beside me and I can feel the anger radiating off him. "Boss?"

"Take him to the docks." I turn toward Antonio knowing he wants a piece of this shit. I give him a chin lift, there is no need for words. He knows I want this *cazzo* taught a lesson he'll never forget. As soon as the last word leaves my mouth, I bring my fist up and smash him straight in the face. I hear the bone crack. *Fuck that felt good.*

"Si Boss, my pleasure." Sergio kicks the asshole in the stomach causing him to spit up blood all over my shoes. He hauls him up off the floor and throws him over his shoulder.

"Piece of shit," I growl

"*Scusa* (sorry) Boss, that was for your new *famiglia* (Family)." Sergio nods before heading to the door.

I watch as Antonio follows Sergio from my office. When I gaze through the doorway, I see Angel standing near the living room entryway wide-eyed. She turns quickly and hurries away. Fuck! How much did she hear?

"I'll be back," I call to my remaining men as I leave the room. I catch sight of my knuckles and shoes, I never lose control, but it seems I can't help it when it comes to Brooklyn and Evie. I better clean up before I try and explain what just happened in there and beg her to understand. I shake my head as I head upstairs to the bathroom. I have never begged a day in my life or had to explain myself to anybody, but I will do anything not to lose my girls. I hurry to our bedroom. Fuck that sounds good - 'our bedroom.' I head straight to the bathroom. *I can't believe I didn't close my office door, I always close my door during meetings. Cazzo!.*

I stare at myself in the mirror, grab a washcloth flip on the tap and hold it under the water. What am I going to do? I can't change who I am and I need for her to accept me. Bending forward I grab hold of the sink till my knuckles turn white, what the fuck am I going to do if she leaves me? They are *mia vita*. I can't live without them.

"I thought you might need this."

I turn my head toward the door at the sound of Angel's voice. She has a smile on her face and an ice pack in her hand which she holds out toward me. God, she's a vision.

"*Grazie*, Angel." I take the pack from her when she steps closer, and because I'm bent over, Angel takes the opportunity to wrap her arms around my neck and kiss my cheek. I close my eyes and revel in the feel of having her so close. *Christ, I hope this isn't the last time she touches me.* I open my eyes and she smiles up at me. I lift her hands to my lips and kiss her palms gently.

"I'm sorry if I scared you," I say softly.

Angel startles at the sound of my voice and I notice her cheeks becoming rosy. I chuckle when I realize she must have been thinking something naughty.

"Sweetheart, I'll be honest with you. When I first heard the yelling, I was scared, but then I remembered what you said to me earlier. That you would never let anything happen to us and everything you do is for Evie and me. People may think I'm crazy to trust you like I do, considering we just met, but I believe you. I wasn't scared by what I saw. I was awed, seeing Sergio throwing that man around like a bag of potatoes."

Brooklyn squeezes my hands. "Then I saw you standing in the doorway looking powerful and pissed off, that tic in your jaw pulsing. Your nose flaring as you breathed deeply, and your green eyes hard as ice until you saw me and they softened. Do you want to know what happened then, babe, the effect you had on me?" she whispers.

I nod.

"Heat pooled low in my belly watching how strong and protective you were, my whole body ignited. I loved feeling the power you have over me, I wanted you pushing deep inside me. God damn, babe." She breathes in deeply.

Brooklyn leans forward to kiss me again, but I turn into her embrace and pull her closer against me. I lift her ass and grind my hardened cock into her so she can feel what her words do to me. I devour her mouth, when she moans, my cock stands to attention. Fuck, I'm so fucking hard. "Angel," I moan.

She wriggles from my hold and my eyes are plastered to her ass as she walks away, swinging her hips. Fuck, she's gonna kill me, I swear.

She stops at the door and glances back over her shoulder with a smoldering, *fuck me*, expression. "Oh, and babe...."

"Yeah." Fuck knows how I manage to say even that one word.

"Don't ever apologize to me for being who you are. I like who you are. Every. Manly. Sexy. Cell." Her eyes look me up and down slowly as she licks her lips.

Well, fuck me! If I didn't have anything to take care of, I swear she wouldn't be leaving my bed for at least a week. Nope, make that the rest of her life. She sashays from the room with that sexy as sin sway of her hips. "Fuck, Angel. You're gonna give me blue fucking balls."

I hear her giggle as she heads down the hall and she shouts back, "Enjoy the rest of your meeting, babe. I'll be in my swimsuit getting all wet in the pool."

I look down at myself, the zipper of my pants threatens to burst open at any moment. I have never ached so much in my life, it actually brings tears to my eyes. How the hell am I going to get through this meeting now? Fuck! Fuck! Fuck!

It's almost impossible to get the little seductress out of my mind and twenty minutes to relax and bring myself under control. I need to get this over with as quickly as possible. My men turn to look at me when I walk back into the office. I take a seat behind my desk, the men sit and I have their full attention.

"We have a situation that needs immediate resolution. Theo, I need you to find out everything you can on a *cazzo* called Darren Jacobs. I need it now!"

Theo drags out his laptop and starts punching keys.

"Demetri and Michael, you will be guarding Brooklyn and Evie. No-one touches them, do you understand me? You treat them like me, because if they're not happy, I *will* find out and I won't be happy. Understand?" I point to them as I speak in a low, menacing tone. They know I'm not fucking around. "They are *la vita mia*. Don't forget it!". I hear everyone in the room suck in a breath when they realize how fucking serious I am.

"Si, Boss," they answer in unison. They understand exactly what will happen to them if anything happens to my girls.

"Everyone else go about our normal business, make sure the docks are running smoothly."

"Who's got eyes on you, Boss?" Jimmy asks.

"Sergio and Theo. Jimmy, I need you at the docks, any problems let me know. All meetings will be held here or at a coffee shop called *Coffee Kat* from now on. Capisce?."

"Si."Jimmy nods along with everyone else as I get to my feet, I'm ready to end this meeting.

Before I leave, I remember one more thing. "Nico, find out where Joey was getting his drugs and deal with it."

"Si, Boss. I think I know. Leave it with me."

"Bene."

I leave my office and head toward the glass doors which open out to the pool from the lounge room. I stand watching for a moment as Evie giggles and splashes around with Angel and Kat. I need to find this *cazzo* and deal with him quick. I cannot allow anyone to harm my beautiful girls.

My thoughts drift to holding Angel in my arms late last night while she had an unsettling nightmare. I'm not sure if she remembered this morning but I sure as fuck did. Her frantic twisting in my arms trying to escape my hold, the tears, the crying out. I was ready to leap from the bed and kill the *stronzo* with my bare hands, but all I could do was hold her and hope like hell my presence could settle her. He can't get to them here, and hopefully, Theo will find something on him in the next couple of hours. He'll be gone before the week's out. My girls will never have to fear him again.

Angel pulls herself out of the pool and I suck in a deep breath when her body is revealed. My man down south has turned to granite. She is wearing a black one-piece swimsuit. It doesn't have straps at the top, but the middle of the suit has thin black strips crisscrossing over her stomach, hugging all her curves. Fuck! I reach down to adjust myself, the ache is back even worse than before. The woman is a fucking goddess and she's...All. Fucking. MINE!!! I watch as droplets of water slide down her body, I feel jealous, it should be my tongue following every luscious curve. I lick my lips desperately wanting a taste.

Fuck, I need to get it together. I can't go out there looking like half a fucking tree has taken up residence in my pants. Evie and Kat don't need to witness my lack of control. I turn and head toward the stairs, a cold shower maybe?

Brooklyn

I feel self-conscious wearing these swimmers. They're a pair of Kat's because apparently, she couldn't find mine. Yeah, right. We both know where mine were, but they certainly don't make me feel sexy like these do and are nowhere near as revealing. I don't think I have ever felt sexy before. It's Dom, it has to be. I find myself saying and doing a lot of things I never dreamed I would before; I've never had the confidence. He makes me feel like I can let my guard down and be my natural self. If I want to say something without the fear of it coming back on me, I can. He says he is mine, and I am his, but I still have a little voice telling me to hold back. It comes back to me being scared about having been together for such a short space of time, although, it feels like we've never been apart. Over the past years, it's been second nature for me to be alert all the time, being prepared for what might be about to happen. I'm worried this is all a dream and I going to wake up at any minute. I'm pulled from my thoughts when *Play that Song* by *Train* blasts through the outdoor speakers. I love this song. I glance up and see Dominic walking toward us. His presence is commanding, powerful, muscles flex with every step he takes.

He's wearing a pair of board shorts and sunglasses. Fuck me! *Please do.* I lick my lips as I drink in his sexy as sin body. My fingers twitch, wanting to run my hands all over his powerful body. Dom smirks as he approaches, the bastard knows the effect he has on me.

"Mommy"

"Yeah, Sweetpea." I drag my eyes away from the sex on a stick and gaze over at Evie and Kat. Kat is biting her lip and trying not to comment on my reaction to Dom. I poke my tongue out, yeah, real mature I know. It causes both my daughter and her to burst into laughter. I shake my head at the pair of them before turning back to Dom.

"Mommy, this is your favorite song isn't it?" Evie giggles as she splashes the water around.

Dom cocks his head to the side waiting for me to answer.

"It sure is Sweetpea."

"Mommy, we should play Marco Polo. I want to be the fishy out of water." She giggles and claps her hands.

I look back to the pool and see Evie leaning on her elbows which rest on the side of the pool.

"Babydoll, you know you're not supposed to tell us that's what you are going to do, right?" Kat laughs at the disgusted face Evie pulls.

"It doesn't matter. I always win, you never catch me."

Dom laughs at Evie and mumbles something I don't quite catch. The way he looks at Evie, like she is as precious as diamonds to him, makes me melt. It's the way a father *should* look at his daughter, with endless love and pride. Not the way Darren used to look at her like she was a burden, a nuisance he wished didn't exist. Dom actually cares, I see it in his eyes. He genuinely wants to be a part of her life and mine. Why wouldn't I want that? It's everything I have ever dreamed about.

"Mommy, can we please play?"

"Yes, of course. Anything you want"

Kat swims beside Evie. "Okay Babydoll, let's do this. Who's going first?"

"Me!" Evie squeals and closes her eyes. For the next half an hour, Dom discovers what it's like to play games with his new daughter.

While I prepare our lunch in the kitchen, I look outside to where Kat and Evie still play in the pool. It's been a beautiful day, it feels like I'm living in a constant dreamland. No Demons to fight, a man who wants to worship the ground I walk on, a man who claims Evie is going to be his daughter. Hearing him claim her for his own earlier made me feel weak in the knees, this is what a father should be like. A protector, someone who would kill for the ones he loves, maybe it should scare me, but it doesn't. Warm arms wrap around me and Dom's hot breath on my neck as he peppers my neck with soft kisses, causes goosebumps to break out all over my body.

"Mmmm." I murmur my approval and drop my head back against his chest.

"Don't take this swimsuit off, I want to do it with my teeth." I shiver at the command in Dom's deep, smooth voice.

I move my head to one side and look up, licking my lips, wanting a kiss. I turn in his arms, reach up and grasp the back of his neck, pulling his lips down onto mine. I moan into his mouth and run my fingers through his silken hair. Dom growls with sexual frustration, grips me around the waist and lifts me onto the bench. I spread my legs as I sit and he moves between my thighs, drawing me closer into his arms. His hard cock flinches against my belly as he devours my mouth almost frantically. One hand rests on my arse and the other clutches at my head, he tilts it at a better angle so he can deepen the kiss. I moan at the feel of him pressing insistently against me. He groans and grinds into me harder, hitting just the right spot. Wetness rushes to my pussy and I squirm. His tongue pushes deeper into my mouth, he's like a man dying of thirst and I'm there to save him.

My hands trail lightly down his naked back, his muscles flex at my touch. I dig my nails in when he hisses, it sets me on fire. I'm desperate to feel him inside me. A discreet cough breaks me out of my lust filled haze and I pull back from Dom, panting softly. I rest my forehead against his, he is not impressed about us being interrupted.

"What," Dom snaps and glares over my head at the intruder. He tucks me into his body so there is no room between us, it's a possessive move and it feels so good. I run my nails softly down his back and feel the shiver run through him. I don't know what comes over me but I stick my tongue out and lick his pert nipple. He sucks in a deep breath and squeezes me tighter. He's barely hanging on by a thread. Fuck, I feel powerful.

"*Scusa* Boss, I found something. You said you wanted to know immediately."

"*Bene*." Dom's shortness is gone when he speaks again.

"Angel, you feel so good I don't want to let you go, but I have something urgent to take care of."

I nod that I understand and turn my face away so he doesn't notice me pouting. *What the fuck is wrong with you? Pouting because you can't get your own way? Really?*

"Angel, please don't be like that. I promise as soon as I take care of this last thing, I'm all yours. I promise *il Mio Amore.*" He draws my face back to his and plants a soft kiss on my lips before giving my bottom lip a light tug.

"Okay, big man, I have to finish making lunch anyway." I run my hands up and down his hard chest, and because this man makes me feel a little naughty....." but, first I better run to the bathroom and finish what you started." my eyes lock onto his and I squeeze my legs around his waist so he gets my meaning.

"Are you mine *il Mio Amore*?" Fire and passion spark in his eyes.

"Yes." I lick my lips, loving the passion I can ignite in this powerful man. And, the feelings he brings out in me.

He places a strong hand between my legs and cups me. I arch into his touch, silently begging for more as he rubs his palm over my clit. My eyes roll back and a small whimper leaves my mouth.

"This is mine! Il Mio!"

It wasn't a question, but I find myself answering anyway. "Y-yes."

"I'm the only one who will give you pleasure, si?" He raises his eyebrow at me as he pulls his hand away.

I whimper at the loss. I have no words; I'm so tightly wound up so I nod. He frowns, like always he wants words. "Yes, big man." I lean forward and suck his lip into my mouth as I run my hand down his body. I stroke him through his shorts.

He tilts his head back and looks at the ceiling. "*Per l'amor cazzo, non mi puoi dare un cazzo di pausa. Sono solo un essere umano, non ho difese contro questa bella donna.*" (for fuck sake, can't you give me a fucking break? I'm only human, I have no defenses against this beautiful woman.)

I have no idea what he's just muttered, he leans forward and gives me a hard, punishing kiss before he storms away to his office. I burst into giggles.

⁓⁂⁓

Dominic

I'm in a bit of a daze when I leave my office and head back to find Brooklyn. I can't work out what Theo has just shown me. Name, age, job, and next to no details of his past. I haven't read so little on a person unless they were trying to cover something up. What is he trying to hide? Theo is the best there is, he can dig anything up on anybody. It might take some time, but he will get it. For now, I have his address and I have been assured, he will be taken care of by my men. I have to sit patiently and wait while they deal with the asshole. I'm not a patient man, but it's best if I stay with Brooklyn and Evie in case something goes wrong. I'm not happy about staying out of it, but I agree it's for the best.

I run through the information Theo has given me, again. Darren Jacobs is a pharmaceutical Rep. who resides in Parramatta. He's twenty-nine years old, both parents died in a house fire and he was sent to live with his grandmother at the age of twelve. There's a photo attached to the small profile. He looks like a piss ant of a man with gelled back, dirty blonde hair and brown eyes. I'm wondering how my Angel could have fallen for someone like this, then I remember what she said the other night. *"Guys hardly ever paid me attention and I was excited that a guy would want to spend some time with me."* I shrug, it doesn't matter the reason, the fact he hurt Evie and my Angel is a good enough reason to end his miserable, fucking life. I'm going to let my men handle this while I enjoy the rest of the day with my girls. I swing around when I hear the front door open.

"Boss." Antonio gives me a chin lift and moves toward me.

"Everything sorted?"

"Si, I wanted to do a lot more, but I think I made my point."

"I bet." I chuckle as Antonio and I head for the kitchen.

Fourteen

Dominic

As I stride into our room later that night, I have one thing on my mind - stripping my Angel out of the swimsuit she's been wearing today. With my teeth! Fuck! I've been hard all day thinking about it.

Apart from the meeting this morning, I'm not sure I remember ever having such a relaxing day. It's Angel, it has to be. She settles something deep inside me. My money, my cars, this house, all were nothing, just a means to an end. But Brooklyn has changed all that. My house now feels like a home. Hearing the girls laugh in the kitchen and watching them swim in the pool made me feel content, settled. Like I'd found my center. It makes me more determined to have this business with Darren dealt with faster. I hear water running in the bathroom and raise an eyebrow. I thought for sure she would be waiting for me on the bed. I head to the bathroom, place my hand on the door handle and pause. I may scare her if I barge in but I need to touch her, taste her, hold her. Although we have only been together for a couple of days, I have noticed a change in her. She's letting go of her past, gaining confidence. God, I hope I'm right, I need her to be comfortable here. Today has been slow torture, the kissing, and touching, the words spoken from her sexy mouth.

I push open the door and freeze at the vision presented in front of me. Brooklyn is in the shower, her hair up in a messy knot and the sexy swimsuit is still on. Fuck yeah! She had been listening when I told her earlier, *I* wanted to be the one to take it off. I stood mesmerized by the sexy vixen before me until her giggling snapped me back to the present.

"Hey, big man, you took your time coming up. Do you think you can stop staring long enough to help me with my swimmers? It's *hard* to wash with them on."

Fuck! The way she turns her eyes on me and licks her lips when she says, *hard,* shoots flashes of electricity straight to my cock. "Fuck, Angel." I hurriedly close the door behind me, I don't know why, no-one is here besides a couple of my men and they wouldn't dare come up here. Evie is staying with Kat and Antonio tonight to give us time alone.

"What's wrong, Dom?"

Angel has a sexy smirk playing on her lips. I grunt in response, shedding my clothes like they're on fire, tripping over my own feet as I rip my pants from my legs. Brooklyn giggles at my clumsiness. I step into the shower alcove, pull her close and slam my mouth down on hers. She moans into my mouth, I suck it down greedily. I can't get enough of her. Her fingers rake through my hair, twisting the ends and causing me to groan. I pull back and when I gaze into her eyes, I see they are clouded with lust.

"I don't think I can go easy on you tonight."

"Well don't." Her tongue darts out and licks the side of my neck.

Fuck! I'm trying really fucking hard to take things slow so I don't scare her, but she's not helping. Being this close to her and breathing in her scent has made my brain stop functioning normally. Her soft hands run over my broad shoulders and down my arms, her lips are kissing and sucking my chest. I groan and squeeze her ass when she sucks my nipple into her mouth. "Angel." My breathing quickens when she drifts lower, licking my abs and following my happy trail with her tongue. She lowers to her knees in front of me. Fuck what a sight. One hand caresses me from root to tip, her other hand massages my balls. I growl deep in my throat when she licks the pearl drop of pre-cum from the tip of my cock. I brace both my hands against the tiles behind her, my head falls forward, warm water runs over my back and I watch her explore me. I take a hand from the tiles and run it over her head. She peers up and I look into her beautiful eyes, they're full of fear! What the fuck just happened?

"Angel, what's wrong?" I run my fingers down the side of her face.

"Please don't grip my head. I want to taste you, but I need you to not to touch my head."

I nod and feel anger swell within me. What the Fuck did that asshole do to her? Realization crashes over me. Fuck, he made her do this and held her head so she couldn't move away. I'd bet my fucking life on it. Fuck, maybe I shouldn't let her do this.

"Angel, darling, you don't have to do this."

"I want to, unless you don't want me to?" Her eyes are filled with uncertainty while she waits for me to reply. I know this isn't the right time to talk about what happened to her, with her on knees looking sexy as fuck with my cock in her hand, but I need her to know I will never force her to do anything she's not comfortable with.

"I'm happy for you to do what you want. I will never force you to do anything you don't want to." I caress the side of her face, then place my hand back on the wall and focus on the water running down my back to calm myself down. My breath whooshes out when Brooklyn slides her mouth over my length, wraps her tongue around and around and takes me to the back of her throat. Her head bobs up and down as she sucks me harder than I've ever been sucked.

She takes my entire length and I feel the tip of my cock hitting the back of her throat. Fuck, she doesn't have a gag reflex! I close my eyes and bathe in the pleasure of her mouth on my cock and her hand massaging my balls. "Fuck, Angel." She hums and the vibration ricochets through me. I feel the slight graze of her teeth on the underside of my cock and I hiss when I feel her nails digging into my ass, pulling me deeper. I flinch at the slight bites of pain simultaneously inflicted by her teeth and her nails. My balls draw up into my body and when I open my eyes, she's gazing up at me. Her cheeks are sucked in and she's watching me through her lashes. It is the hottest vision I have ever seen. Fuck! "I'm gonna cum, Angel," I choke out. I want to give her plenty of time to pull away before it's too late, but she doesn't stop. She increases her efforts, grips my ass with both hands and starts to suck harder and faster. Fuck, she's sexy. I can't stop myself and ribbons of cum explode down her throat. "Fuck!" I roar, throw my head back and my hips jerk back and forth. Jesus. Fucking. Christ. "Sexiest thing ever," I gasp. My heart is racing, I'm bent forward trying to catch my breath, sweat beads on my skin mixing with the water.

Looking down, I'm gifted with the sweetest smile as her tongue pokes out and licks a drop of me from her lip. I groan at the sight. Bending down I lift her up under the arms and slam my mouth down on hers, growling at the taste of myself on her. "My turn."

Placing her on her feet, I run my hands down her body, listening to the soft sounds escaping her mouth. I run my tongue down her neck and across the top of her breasts, cupping them in my hands. My thumbs caress the hard points of her nipples and she gasps. My nose traces her collar bone and opening my mouth, I grip the top of her swimsuit in my teeth and slowly drag it down, exposing her breasts, latching onto one and massaging the other. I love hearing her panting and begging for more. I switch breasts doing the same to the other, her whimpers and cries cause an instant erection. Grabbing the material of her swimsuit, I drag it down her body, revealing her curves. As I kiss a path to her belly, I lower to my knees until I'm at eye level with her pussy. Leaning forward, I breathe in her sweet aroma, my mouth waters. After sliding the swimsuit to the floor, I run my hands over the smooth skin of her legs, spread them and place one leg over my shoulder. I grab her ass with my other hand and leaning forward, I run my nose down her center.

"Dom, please. I'm begging you, babe." Angel moans as she arches and pushes harder to me.

I look into her gorgeous eyes and wink, that's what I've been waiting for. I run my tongue up her heat, groaning, licking her like my life depends on it. Moans and whimpers alert me she's getting closer. While I suck on her clit, I slide in a finger, then another, stretching her, curving my fingers to hit her g-spot. I'm humming into her sensitive flesh and I feel her muscles tense. The earthy moan which escapes her lips causes my cock to lengthen and become even harder. Fuck! I've just orgasmed, how the hell does she do this to me?

I release her and stand. A protesting whimper escapes her mouth at the loss, but I have something better in store for her. Lifting her by the ass, she wraps her legs around my back. I push her back into the tiles away from the spray of the water. The cold tiles mix with the warmth of her skin and I capture her gasp in an intoxicating kiss. Sliding into her warmth, all the way to the hilt, I groan at how tight she feels. Fuck, she is squeezing me so hard I swear I'll explode. I hold still for a moment attempting to regain control. Fuck, my woman is exquisite. When I open my eyes, I see Angels' are closed. I need her to look at me, I need that connection.

"Look at me, Angel." Her eyes snap open at the command in my voice. "I want you to look at me, while I take you."

She nods and I start to move, nice and slow at first, it's taking everything in me to take her this slow. But, I need her to believe I would never hurt her. "Mine," I growl.

"Yes yours, Dom. Only yours." She arches and her breasts press against my chest, her fingers twist in my hair.

"Faster, Babe. Please." The words leave her lips on a moan.

I bend forward and kiss her hard, pulling my hips back, I thrust harder, faster, pushing as deep as I can. "Fuck, *amore*. Fuck, come for me."

"Right there, Dom. Aaaah, fuuuuck!"

She screams as her eyes roll back in her head, squeezing me so tight her orgasm takes me at the same time. Thank fuck because I couldn't hold on much longer. Angel relaxes into my arms, we breathe deeply. Spent. Sated - for now.

"Angel, look at me." When her eyes met mine, I get lost for a minute in her deep pools of passion. "You, my sweet Angel are *la vita mia*. I can't live without you." Her hand cups my cheek and I lean into her soft touch.

"I need you in my life, you make me feel safe and cherished for the first time in my life. You also treat my daughter like a father should."

"I may not have helped create her, but she is mine, as you are."

"Yours." A beautiful smile lights up her whole face.

"Angel, I was serious this morning when I said I want to create a family with you, for you to have my baby. Please don't let it scare you away. I have tried to take things slow with you, but it's too hard. When you're in my arms, I want to show you how much I love you, how much I care. I need you like I need air. I know I don't deserve Evie and you, but I'm a selfish bastard and I can't bear the thought of letting you go."

"Don't let us go. Dominic. We're yours if you want us. I know you can do better than me, someone with more experience who can give your body what it needs…"

I place my fingers over her lips. "Let me take you to bed Angel, and I will show you how much I want you, and only you. I didn't know what my body needed until I met you."

Brooklyn

Lying in Dom's arms is what heaven must feel like. After an incredible day, followed by our shower, I didn't think things could get better. But, having him lay me down on the bed and showing me all the reasons he only wants me, topped the list. I'm exhausted, but happy. Dominic feathers his fingers up and down my arm and the sound of his heartbeat lulls me almost to sleep. I feel myself slowly drifting off when Dom speaks.

"Angel, why couldn't I run my hands through your hair while we were in the shower?" I'm instantly awake and not sure what to say. Should I tell him? I chew on my lip while I try and come up with something to say, but I guess he deserves the truth.

"Um..." I take a deep breath. "When Darren was angry with me, or he felt the need... he would force me to my knees and grab my hair so hard I thought it would come out at the roots. He said he had to control me because I didn't know what I was doing. Usually, when he finished, he would push me to the ground and force me to crawl into bed. If I'd upset him, I wouldn't make it to the bed he usually ... ... knocked me out and I spent the night on the floor." I finish softly and sniffle back the tears. Dom stops rubbing my arm and I feel his body tense. "I'm sorry, Dom. I shouldn't have said anything." I start to move to head to the bathroom, but Dom's grip tightens around me. He kisses the top of my head.

"You have nothing to be sorry for, my Angel. Fuck! You know I would *never* make you do anything you don't want to do, si?"

I nod, but Dom squeezes me again. "I know, Dom." I pause, how do I explain this to him? "Sometimes I get flashbacks of what has happened in the past. When I tell you not to do something, it's because I don't want to be reminded of what has been done to me before. I don't want it to ruin our time together." I shrug even though he can't see me in the dark.

Dom runs his hand up and down my arm again and I relax back into him. "Good girl. I like that you trust me," he whispers. "Angel, I need you to do something for me."

I tense, worried about what he is about to say.

"I need you to stop worrying about the past. I know it's hard, but when you do and you tense up. I feel like I'm doing something wrong, hurting you. I need you to talk to me. If I say something that upsets you, or do something you don't like, as I did in the shower when I grabbed your head, I need you to speak up so I can fix it. The last thing I want to do is hurt, or frighten, you."

He sounds so sincere, it hurts my heart to know I'm worrying him. "I don't want to be this way, and I'm trying hard to not let it affect me, but it's difficult sometimes."

"I know *il Mio Amore*, I can tell. I just wanted you to know for future reference. Never be afraid to talk to me."

"This morning when you said you would talk to me later, what did you mean?"

"I wanted to talk to you about my work, I can't tell you everything but what I can tell you I will."

Well that's fair enough I don't know a lot about the Mafia, but I do understand that less is best. "So you own *DESTINY*?"

"Si, and two other clubs. We also look after the docks in Newcastle, making sure shipments come in safely...."

Fuck, I cut Dom off. "You don't deal in drugs or people, do you?" I hold my hand over my mouth, I'm feeling sick. I don't think I could handle it if he does.

"No!!!" Dom speaks a little too loud and startles me. "Firstly, I despise drugs and anybody who takes them. As for people, do you mean human trafficking?"

I nod, forgetting he can't see me in the darkness. I clear my throat and speak. "Yes."

"No, Angel, I don't and never will. I'm not saying other families we deal with don't do it, but we don't. I promise you."

Okay. He doesn't like drugs and no human trafficking. I take a deep breath settling the nausea. Reaching to the bedside table, I flip on the night lamp and grab the bottle of water and take a sip. Dom rubs his hand over my back. I start feeling better. "Sorry," I whisper.

"Angel, like I said before, I can't tell you everything, but I will answer your questions if I can. I want you to understand, I will protect Evie and you, si? I know my being a Mafia boss is a lot to take in, and I'm sorry I can't explain more, but my line of work is dangerous and I have hurt people. I hope this won't affect anything between us, you have my word, I would never hurt you *il Mio Amore.* I need you to trust me, can you do that?" Dom pushes a tendril of hair behind my ear then slowly glides his fingers down my neck causing goose bumps to break out.

His beautiful eyes are pleading with me to understand and his eyebrows are drawn together with worry. How could I not trust this man? I told him last night, I did, but I guess after everything he has told me he has a right to feel insecure, I need to make it right. "I trust you, my darling." Leaning over, I kiss his lips and slide my tongue across the seam seeking entry. When he opens, I slide my tongue along his, moaning at his taste. He twists his hands slowly into my hair, guiding my head to the side for better access. His other hand glides up my stomach and cups my breast, pinching my nipple. I moan as my body comes alive with that one simple touch. He pushes my back to the mattress and takes control of the kiss. I raise my arms above my head and grab hold of the headboard, causing me to arch into his touch. Dom groans as he moves between my legs, his hands dance over my body, his cock teases my clit making me whimper for more. He sucks one hard nipple into his mouth as he enters me with the snap of his hips and one hard thrust. I scream out as pleasure, and a pinch of pain, run through my body.

Trust? You fucking bet I trust this man. With mine, and my daughter's, lives.

Dominic

Waking up wrapped around my Angel with my nose buried in her hair, every breath I take fills my lungs with her scent. Fuck, I will never get enough of this. Her. She has me so fucking hard it's becoming painful. After peppering her neck with small kisses, I look at the bedside clock to make sure we have time for what I want to do. We have one hour before Angel has to be up to start getting ready for work. I wriggle my hand down to her clit and start fingering the small bundle of nerves, slowly so as not to startle her awake. Pushing her back to the mattress, I slide between her legs and kiss a pathway from her breasts to her clit making small circles with my tongue. Small moans puff from her mouth and her eyes flutter open, two crystal blue orbs gaze back at me. After giving one last lick over her clit, I slide up her body, kissing her as I go. My arms support me as I hover above her, my lips crash down on hers as I thrust inside her tight heat. "Fuck, Angel." I thrust harder, my hips pistoning up and down, as she hums with ecstasy and arches her body into mine. Her hips lift and fall matching my pace and meeting my every thrust until she's letting go and screaming my name. I follow her over the edge with a roar. Wiping the sweat from my brow, I lean down and place a kiss on the softest lips I have ever tasted. "Morning, Angel." I roll to my side and pull her close.

"Morning, Babe." Brooklyn glances at the clock and sees it's now 6.15 am. "Wanna join me for a shower." Angel's voice is breathless and she wiggles her eyebrows up and down, before scooting from the bed and running into the bathroom, laughing. I hear the water turn on which gets my ass moving to follow her.

As I enter the bathroom, I stop at the counter and flick a switch, music blasts from the speakers in the ceiling filling the room.

"Oh, I love this song." Angel starts singing the lyrics to *Gangsta* by *Kehlani* and her voice floors me. Fuck, my woman can sing. I listen carefully and realize the words are about loving a gangster. How prophetic.

Stepping into the shower, I grab Angel around the waist and pull her toward me. Our long, deep kiss causes me to moan in the back of my throat. Fuck, I'm dying of thirst, but I know something that will help. I drop to my knees and commence devouring my Angel all over again.

⁕⁕⁕

Brooklyn

I push through the door into *Coffee Kat* after thanking Demetri for the ride. I'm still not sure if I'm comfortable with being followed around all the time, but it makes me feel safe at the same time. I know Dom is worried and trying to protect Evie and me. Evie has preschool today and she has a guard too. It's a lot to take in, I believe Dom is going overboard and I told him so over breakfast this morning......

"Angel, please let me protect you. I need to know my girls are safe." He gives me a heart stopping smile as he moves toward me and wraps his arms around my waist, making me melt. "I'll be there later and we'll go and pick up Evie together." How can I deny this man anything? He makes everything feel right. "Ok babe, but you don't have to come with me to get Evie, if you're busy I can go."

"I want to, Angel. I want to hear about what our Princess has been doing today."

And that, those words right there, make my heart flutter; knowing he's not doing it to make me happy, he actually wants to do it.

"Brooklyn! Earth to Brooklyn!"

I look up and do a double take when I see Kat at the counter fixing the desserts. But, that's not what gives me cause for concern, Kat's not dressed like her normal self. She's wearing calf length black pants and a white singlet shirt, her hair is tied up in a messy knot and she has barely any makeup on. My major concern?

There's no smile on her face. Oh, I hope Evie didn't give her any trouble.

"Morning Kat, is everything okay? You don't look like your normal self. Was Evie on her best behavior?"

Kat waves her hand dismissing my concerns. "Everything is fine and Evie was her usual fabulous self. And yes, she made it to preschool on time." My best friend is one of those people who, if you push too much, she'll shut down. It's best to bide your time and let her open up when she is ready.

I move to where she is standing and give her a big hug. "I'm here when you're ready to talk," I whisper in her ear.

"I know." She hugs me back. As we separate, I hear the doorbell go as the door is pushed open. We both turn at the sound and see Antonio stomp in. He's not looking so good himself. What. The. Hell. Is. Going. On?

Kat turns away and rushes to the kitchen. My stomach twists at the look of despair on Antonio's face when she turns away from him.

"Morning, Brooklyn. I just called in to check. Is Kat okay?"

"Is everything okay with you?" Instead of answering his question, I ask one of my own.

Antonio shrugs and runs a hand through his hair similar to the way Dom does, but he doesn't say anything.

"Would you like a coffee?" I offer.

"No thank you." He turns and walks out the door.

I'm not sure what has happened between them since yesterday, but I hope they sort it out. They are perfect for each other.

"Ok, Dollface, let's get to work." Kat walks back to the counter after the front door closes.

I notice how glassy her eyes are, I know she's been crying. Kat *never* cries, this is something serious and I need to find out what it is.

⁂

A couple of hours later, I still haven't managed to get anything out of Kat. I can see she's struggling with something and it's starting to worry me. Every time the door has chimed, Kat has turned toward it with a look of longing and then sadness. It breaks my heart knowing she's hurting and I can't do anything about it. What am I supposed to do when she won't talk to me, how can I help her? It doesn't help that Antonio hasn't come back, but I don't blame him after the way Kat fled from him. I could see he was hurt. I noticed earlier, he was sitting in his car watching through the glass windows. I have a feeling he must be guarding Kat and it must be torture to be here and not feel wanted. I may have to talk to Dom about it later and see if he knows what's going on between them.

Just before 3pm, Dom walks through the door. Even if I hadn't been looking straight at him, I would have known he was here. The air seems to thicken with his presence and he seems to take up the whole space, making it feel the size of a shoe box. Fuck, he's sexy as sin in a black suit. I run my tongue across my bottom lip salivating about what's underneath that suit.

He heads straight for me, leans down so our lips are a breath apart and whispers, "Angel," before his lips cover mine, sucking my bottom lip into his mouth and giving it a light nip. A hum wafts from the back of my throat at the sensation. When we part, I notice the hungry look in his eyes and it makes me want to jump into his arms right here.

"Hey, Babe." I lick my bottom lip, savoring the taste of him.

Dom's eyes lock onto the movement and his mouth curls into a smirk.

"Angel, you are even more breathtaking now than you were this morning."

I blush at his compliment, not sure what to say. "I'll grab my purse and we can go."

"Si."

After collecting Evie from school, we head back to Dom's place for dinner.

Evie chatters at a million miles an hour, she was so happy to see Dom at her school. After giving me a big hug and telling me how much she missed and loves me, she basically tackles Dom to the ground. I still worry that we may do something to piss him off, but so far he seems to enjoy the play as much as Evie.

I know I said I trust him, and I do, but sometimes it's hard to believe I have a man who loves me and wants to protect me. I have to try and forget the nightmares of my past and start living in the here and now, looking towards a future I never thought I would have.

Sitting and eating together as a family was wonderful, and the fact Dom cooked dinner just about blew me away. *"Angel, you have been on your feet all day. Relax and watch how Italian cooking is done."* And boy did I watch, but not the cooking. I have never seen anything so sexy in my life as Dom wearing an apron, his muscles flexing with every movement he made. I had to walk away, otherwise, I would have tried to have my way with him right there in front of Evie. I'm such a whore!

Fifteen

Dominic

Sitting at the desk in my office, I reflect on the past couple of days. Waking up to Brooklyn cuddled in my arms, making breakfast together and eating together at night. I didn't realize how much I had missed sitting down with someone and eating a meal. Putting Evie to bed and reading her a story has become one of my greatest joys. I never thought in a million years, a man like me would be able to have this. I have so many flaws, most people would say I'm not a nice person. I have done some bad shit, but when I lay down with Angel in my arms at night, my life seems full and nothing else matters. I have never needed anybody like I need her. With every little piece of her she shows, and gives me, of herself, I start to see the real Brooklyn. The woman she was meant to be, not the shy, scared woman I met a week ago. She's smart, strong and that mouth of hers is wicked! I can't seem to get enough of her, she is my new addiction.

Nothing has happened with that *cazzo*, Darren. Yet. I trust my men and I'm keeping a close eye on my girls until I find out his dead. Theo is still trying to find out why there is so little on him, I have a feeling when he does find something, it's not going to be good. The phone buzzes and cuts into my thoughts.

"Si," Johnny's number shows on the caller ID.

"Boss, shit has gone down in Sydney with the Chinese." Worry laces his voice.

"Like what?" Fuck! That's all I need now.

"Apparently, Joey got drunk and fucked one of their women." He pauses for a moment too long and I know there's more. "The *cazzo* bashed her brains in, Boss."

"*EGLI CAZZO CHE COSA?* (He fucking what?)" I slam my hand down on my desk "You find him, bring him to me. ADESSO! (now)"

"Si, Boss, the other problem was taken care of last night and you should hear about it soon," he says before hanging up.

Fuck, what a piece of shit Joey is. We should have dealt with him the other day. I need to call the men in for a meeting and make sure they stay on guard. Shit is about to hit the fan in a big way. I reach for the phone and hear glass smash as it hits the tiles in the kitchen. I catapult from my chair, round my desk and sprint to the kitchen. The first thing I see is Evie wrapped around Brooklyn, she looks terrified.

"Angel, what happened?" I rush to them and wrap my arms around Brooklyn's waist. She doesn't say I word but points to the wall behind my back. I turn my head in time to see a picture of Darren flashing on the television near a burned-out car. *Darren*

Jacobs found dead in a car fire, the news reporter says. I look back at Angel and notice tears running down her soft cheeks. I rub my thumb under her eyes and capture a lone tear as it rolls down her cheek. Leaning down, I kiss the top of her head. "Are you okay?"

"It's over, it's really over." She gazes at me, her crystal blue eyes bright with relief.

I nod. "Si Angel, it's over. Evie and you are safe and free." She relaxes against me and Evie wraps her tiny arms around my leg. I reach down, sweep her into my arms and sit her against my hip. She rests her head on my shoulder.

"Safe, we're finally safe." Brooklyn clings to my shirt and burrows her face in my chest.

I rub my free hand over her back as I hold her close. "You okay, Princess?" I kiss the top of Evie's blonde curls and she nods her head on my shoulder, then she pulls back and gives me a bright smile that leaves me breathless.

"Can I go swimming before dinner please, Dom?"

I chuckle and kiss her hair again, I guess this is a good sign and shows she's not traumatized. I wink at her before placing her down on the floor. "Go and get your swimmers on and I'll come out and watch you in the pool, si?"

"Si, that means yes, doesn't it?"

"Yes. it does."

"Then, si, you can come out to the pool and watch me." She giggles and bounces up and down before running up the stairs to her room.

I gather Brooklyn tighter into my arms and rock her back and forth a little. She lifts her chin and I gaze into her eyes. I lower my head and place a soft kiss on her lips. "You sure you're okay?"

"More than okay." She chews on her lip as she contemplates something.

"What's wrong, Angel?"

"Do... do we have to go home now?"

I grunt, not pleased with her question at all. "Angel, I thought I made this clear the other day. This is your home now. Unless..."

"Unless. what?"

"Unless you don't want it to be." Fuck, what will I do if she leaves me now? Darren is dead, she and Evie are safe, they can do whatever they want. I run my hand through my hair. I want to demand they stay here with me, but I won't force her if it's not what she wants. I would never make her do things she doesn't want to. I can be a nasty prick, but never to Evie and her. I only want the best for them.

"I want it to be Dom, I just want you to be sure."

"Angel, your clothes are in my closet. I have had someone come in and redecorate Evie's room and made it into a princess paradise for her." I chuckle when I remember Evie screaming with excitement and bouncing around like a little rabbit when she first saw it. "Of course I want you here with me. I can't stand to be away from you for even an hour. I worry though, I don't want my dominating ways to scare you off."

"Big man, I love your dominating ways and Evie and I would love to share your home with you for the rest of our lives. Well, mine anyway. Evie may want her own home eventually." Brooklyn leans up and kisses me, tears sparkle in her eyes.

"Evie may leave home when she's sixty."

Brooklyn laughs at my statement. "You're going to be one of those over-protective daddy's who gives every boy who's interested in her the third degree, aren't you?"

I laugh with her. "Probably." I pull her close. "This will be *our* home. I love the sound of that." She moans as I devour her mouth. Drawing back, I wipe her tears away again. "Why are you crying *il Mio Amore*?"

"They're happy tears, babe. You make us so happy Dom. Now kiss me again." I don't argue, I do what I'm told and kiss her until she is breathless and clinging to me for more. I will do anything she asks.

Fuck! She is my everything!

⁓⁓⁓⁓⁓⁓⁓⁓⁓ ❦❦ ⁓⁓⁓⁓⁓⁓⁓⁓⁓

Brooklyn

I strip off my clothes as I head into our bedroom. I begin replaying everything that has happened this past week and a half - meeting Dom and having him turn my world upside down in the best possible way. Then a couple of days ago, the news report and seeing the front page of the newspaper announcing Darren had been killed by a car bomb. I'm not too sure how I should feel about that.

I thought maybe I should be a little sad for Evie's sake, but I'm not. Even Evie, a five-year-old child with limited understanding, seemed as relieved as I was when she found out. It's comforting, knowing we don't have to look over our shoulder's every minute of every day. The nightmare we have been living is finally over.

I didn't ask Dominic if he had anything to do with it, and personally, I don't care. I don't dwell on the fact he is a Mob Boss, I believe we were meant to be. To those who don't know him as I do, he may be big and scary, but deep down, he's a wonderful man.

I love that he considers Evie as his daughter and he loves her, what more could I ask for?

He is my happy ever after. It just so happens that my prince charming comes with a little baggage himself, but who am I to judge him on the choices he has made in his life when he has shown us nothing but kindness and love? I know he would never let anything happen to Evie or me, he would lay his life on the line to protect us. I have to accept his men will be with Evie and me when he can't be there, it's a small price to pay when you fall in love with a powerful man like Dominic. Yes, he has hurt people and yes, he does things that are not legal, but I'm not worried. People may think I'm crazy to love someone like Dom, but I've been through hell and I have a chance to live a life with a man who loves me, a man who will worship the ground I walk on - I'm going to let him, and fuck what anyone else thinks.

I flip the taps of the shower on and step under the spray of hot water, it massages deep into my muscles. Tilting my head back and allowing the droplets to run through my hair, I think about my parents and the love they shared. The cold, rainy night which ripped me in two and changed my life forever, causing so much pain it was a struggle to breathe; invades my thoughts.

I wake with a start and look around my room trying to figure out what woke me. I hear the doorbell, that must have been it. I swipe my hand across my bedside table and grab my phone, its 1am. Who the fuck is at the door at this hour?

The doorbell rings again, I moan as I drag myself from the warmth of my bed and throw on a robe. I hurry down the stairs before the noise wakes Evie.

Rubbing the sleep from my eyes, I open the door to come face to face with two police officers.

"Miss Brooklyn Mackenzie?" the officer on the left asks.

"Y-Yes." I wrap my arms around my waist as an uneasy feeling washes over me.

"This is my partner Sargent Emma Jones and my name is Sargent Eric Hayes, may we come in?"

"Yes, yes of course." I step back so they can enter the house and close the door behind them. I lead them through to the living room as Darren comes through from his study.

"We're sorry to bother you so late, but there has been a break and enter at your parents' house. I'm very sorry to have to tell you, your parents have been killed," Sargent Hayes says.

"Wh-What d-d-do you mean?" I hug myself tighter, a chill runs through me and I begin shaking. "This must be a mistake, you're wrong. My parents were here a couple of nights ago having dinner. They're fine. You have the wrong people." Oh, God... Oh, God... this can't be happening.

"Thomas and Susan Mackenzie," Sargent Jones says gently.

"Yes, that's them."

"I'm sorry Miss Mackenzie, but they were your parents who were found murdered earlier this evening." Sargent Jones' tone softens.

"Fuck! Murdered? Oh God, this can't be happening. Please, I'm begging you, tell me this isn't right, please?" My legs weaken, my head is fuzzy and my stomach roils. I'm going to either throw up or pass out. "No... No... No... this can't be happening." I shake my head and begin pacing as Darren asks questions. I don't remember anything else that was said, but I do remember the feeling of my heart being ripped from my chest.

Weeks turned into months, with no leads or evidence pointing to why or who could have done this. I was left feeling

I jump as strong arms wrap around me and I'm pulled back into a warm hard chest. I relax when I feel tiny kisses on my shoulder.

"Shhh… it's just me." Dom whispers in my ear causing me to shiver.

"Why are you crying *il Mio Amore*?"

"I was remembering my parents; I miss them so much. I wish they had known you." I choke on a sob, turn and wrap my arms around his waist before burying my head into his hard chest.

"Will you tell me what happened to them, Angel?" Dom picks up my luffa from the shelf, squirts some body wash into it and runs it over my back. A moan slips free with how good it feels. The scent of coconut and vanilla wafts up my nose and relaxes me even more. I'm broken from the spell when Dom chuckles at my reaction. I lift my face and stare into his beautiful green eyes, thinking again how lucky I am to have this man in my life. I lean up on my tip toes and plant a soft kiss to his lips.

"Why are you so good to me?" He knows I'm changing the subject, but he doesn't call me on it.

"Well, *il Mio Amore*, the minute I gazed into your eyes and saw your smile, my world flipped on its head. I knew I would do anything to have you, to keep you happy. You brought me to my knees, and I don't want to get back up."

Tears spill from my eyes, this man is so sweet to me and I'm not sure what to say to that, I'm literally speechless. I lean up and plant another soft kiss before sucking his bottom lip into my mouth.

He groans at the contact. I run my hands up his hard-sculptured chest, breathing in his intoxicating scent. "Make love to me"

Fire burns in Dom's eye's as he bends down and kisses me with a hunger which makes my toes curl. He turns me around and places my hands flat against the wall. Soft nips and kisses travel down my neck and across my shoulder. I turn my head so he has better access and moan when his hand begins massaging my breasts. I whimper when he pinches the hard nub of my nipple, his other hand slides over my belly and latches onto my clit. I start to move so I can touch him.

"Keep your hands on the wall." Dominic's voice is husky with passion, commanding in my ear. My body comes alive, burning for what is to come. He slips a finger inside me and groans when he feels how wet I am for him. "Always ready for me, Angel." He sucks my earlobe into his mouth and a moan slips from me when he gives it a nip. Fuck, he knows exactly how and where to touch me.

"Oh god, Dom… please…" I whimper when his fingers are removed, then white hot lust shoots through my veins when his cock is pushed inside me and he starts to thrust. But, it's not enough, I need more. "Harder. I need it harder," I moan.

"Fuck, Angel." He grips my hips tighter and thrusts into me harder. "You just get better and better."

I arch and throw my head back against his shoulder on a moan. Hot water cascading over me mixes with the ecstasy of Dom's thrusts, heats my body until I teeter on the edge.

"Fuck, there! Right there." I squeeze my interior muscles and feel Dom's cock flinch hard.

Dom's grip on me tightens and I know he's close too. I lower my hand and tease my clit with a finger. My legs weaken and I moan loudly.

"Fuck." Dom groans and with another hard thrust, he sends me over the edge. Stars flash before my eyes and I feel Dom coming inside me. His shout echoes off the tiles.

We both collapse on the floor, wrapped in each other's arms, gasping for breath.

"Angel, when you squeeze me like that, how can I hang on?"

"Hmmm." My reply hums against his chest and I feel the vibration of his chuckle under my cheek. I'm completely worn out. I'm not sure how long we sit locked together, he strokes my back, I'm so comfortable I don't want to move.

"*il Mio Amore*, it's time for bed." Dom murmurs in my ear before standing with me in his arms and carrying me to bed.

Dominic

"Tell me something about you?" Brooklyn's head lays against my chest, her fingers trace lazy circles over my abs.

"When I was a young boy, not long after I started working for papa, my momma gave me a gold chain with a saint Christopher pendant and a crucifix on it. I never took it off. My momma used to tell me it would keep me protected and safe in the dark.

"What happened to it?" Brooklyn's fingers still and I place my hand over hers to encourage her to keep moving them. It felt nice and hopefully will calm me as I tell this story. Brooklyn takes the hint and starts moving her fingers again.

"I... I placed them with her when she... passed away, so they would protect her in the dark. I thought, since I'd failed her when she was alive, I wouldn't fail her in the afterlife." I feel a lump forming in my throat and cough to clear the obstruction. Tears threaten to fall so I squeeze my eyes closed. Fuck, I haven't cried since her funeral.

I regain some control and open my eyes to lock with her crystal blue orbs which instantly calm me. Brooklyn leans over and kisses me softly while wiping under my eyes with her thumbs. Fuck! Get it together Dom!

"I'm sorry, darling." She kisses me again. "How did she pass away?" There's something about her voice, so low and soothing. It cracks me wide open.

"It was the day I came home and found out what papa was doing. I didn't realize it at the time, but he had beaten my momma so bad in the past that this last time he had caused serious damage." Fuck, just thinking about it makes me want to kill him all over again.

"She had a brain bleed, by the time I talked her into going to the hospital a week later, it was too late. My momma had always suffered from headaches, so she didn't think much of it when she had one after the beating. The problem was, it lasted longer than normal and no pain killers were helping. When I finally got her to the hospital, they told me about the bleed and said there was nothing anybody could do because of the position it was in. I gave her my necklace to keep her safe in the dark." I close my eyes and see vivid pictures of my momma laying in the hospital bed, cords and monitors connected everywhere. She appeared so small and frail and I felt helpless. I open my eyes when I hear Brooklyn sniff and watch as silent tears run down her beautiful face.

"I'm so sorry Dom, I shouldn't have asked you to talk about such a sad time in your life."

I run my hand down her back and draw her closer. "Angel, I needed to tell you. If I expect you to tell me your secrets, I should tell you mine too. This was the saddest moment of my life and I wanted you to know about it."

Lying back down on my chest she starts running her fingers over me again, laying in silence for a moment. "My parents were amazing, always there for me whenever I needed them. I was so ashamed of the person I'd become and how I'd let my life get so bad. I wanted a love like theirs. They were true soul mates. My father would do anything for my mother, he worshiped the ground she walked on." Brooklyn sniffs back her tears. "Darren used to tell me I lived in a dreamland when it came to my parents. He said they only pretended to love me, but my mother had trapped him by having me, just like I'd trapped him. He would laugh and ask how could anyone love someone so needy and pathetic like me."

Fuck what a *stronzo*, another person I wouldn't mind killing again! "Angel...." Before I can say more, she speaks again.

"My parents never liked Darren, they insisted something wasn't quite right with him. But, they respected my decision and supported Evie and me. About six months ago, someone broke into their house and murdered them while they were sleeping. The house was trashed and the police suspected a robbery gone wrong. There had been a string of robberies in the area and the police believed it was connected. It was unfortunate my parents were home when it occurred. They never caught who was responsible, and there was never any evidence to point to who it was."

Fuck! I pull her harder against me and feel her trembling from the sobs running through her. I don't know what to say to ease her pain so, I hold her quietly and run my hand over her back. I coo soft murmurs in her ear until I feel her body relax into mine and her breathing evens out.

"I'm here Angel, I'm not going anywhere," I whisper.

"Hmmm."

Closing my eyes, I think about all we have shared over the past week and a half, it feels like we have known each other for a lifetime. She is mine, she is here and she is safe. I will make sure no one ever touches or hurts her again. I relax into her warm embrace and I let sleep take me.

Do you know that feeling you get when you feel like you are being watched? I open my eyes and Brooklyn snuggles into me deeper, moaning a little in her sleep. I look toward the bedside table and see Evie standing there in her *Frozen* nightie with a big smile on her face.

"Morning princess, did you have a good sleep?" I whisper so as not to disturb Brooklyn.

"Yes, it feels like I sleep on a cloud." Evie softly giggles and covers her mouth with her little hand.

"Do you want to help me make breakfast for momma?"

"Yes." Evie bounces up and down

"Okay, Princess. Give me a minute and then we'll head downstairs." I chuckle at her enthusiasm.

I struggle to untangle myself from Brooklyn's grip so I can get up without waking her. Evie giggles at my attempt. When I finally disentangle myself, and climb from the bed, I lean over and kiss Brooklyn on the head before padding to the bathroom.

When I walk back into the bedroom, I find Evie snuggled up on my side of the bed staring at Brooklyn. "What are you doing, Princess?"

"Watching momma sleep, she's so pretty." Evie pouts and plucks at her bottom lip as if deep in thought.

I sweep Evie into my arms and seat her on my hip before kissing her cheek. "Si, she is very pretty and so are you. Why the pout baby girl?" I ask as we head toward the stairs. Evie lays her head on my shoulder.

"Music?" I stare into her baby blues as we enter the living room, they are so much like her mommas. Evie nods her head so I turn the television on as we head toward the kitchen. After placing Evie down on the counter, I organize her a glass of milk. After handing it to her, I turn toward the coffee machine.

"Do you love my momma?"

"Si, very much." I nod and turn the coffee machine on.

"Do you love me?"

"Si, very much." I lean against the stove watching her, wondering what is going on in her little brain.

"Does that make us yours?"

"Si, it does."

"So if we're yours, then you must be ours?"

"Princess you are mine and I am yours, if you'll have me of course." I wink and she giggles. It has to be one of the best sounds in the world.

"Can I call you Daddy?" Evie's voice is barely a whisper. She looks everywhere but at me, twisting her fingers together and swinging her legs back and forth.

Her question knocks the wind out of me. I have wanted to be her daddy since the first time I met her, I would love nothing more.

"Princess, it would be my honor to be, and have you call me, daddy. I don't plan on leaving you and I would love you to be my daughter." I cross the kitchen and wrap her in my arms before kissing the top of her head.

"I love you, daddy," Evie whispers in my ear.

"I love you too, my Princess." My chest is tight, my throat clogged and tears prick at my eyes. I love this little girl deeply and would give her the world. We remain quiet, clutching at each other until Evie speaks, "I'm hungry."

I laugh and step back. "What do we want to cook for breakfast?"

"Pancakes!" Evie bounces up and down on her bottom. Her smile is so big, it lights up her entire face and her eyes sparkle.

Sixteen

Later that night...

Brooklyn

Today has been awesome, swimming, relaxing in the sun. I swear, I've gotten back ten years of my life since being with Dom. I know he's worried about a few things that are happening in Sydney concerning some very scary men, and he's worried about mine and Evie's safety a lot more than usual. I've tried to ease his concerns by reminding him, we're safe with him and his men.

It's Saturday night, and after putting Evie to bed, I had a relaxing bath. Now I'm in bed, tossing and turning while waiting for Dom to come to bed. It's poker night with the boys. He told me about their regular games over breakfast - pancakes he made with Evie, which were delicious. It's no big deal, he works hard and deserves to have man time where he can talk and relax with his friends. I still can't help wishing he was here with me, though.

Rolling over, I look at the clock beside the bed - 10pm. I wonder how much longer he'll be. I want to make love and feel his muscles flex under my touch. I squeeze my legs together; trying to relieve the constant ache in my pussy he causes these days. Only one thing can fix it, I need Dom. I wonder if I can tempt him to finish playing cards early and come and play with me. I giggle to myself when I notice the black baby doll lingerie Kat gave me to wear, *just in case*. I'm feeling kind of naughty, I know I should leave him be, and I know how much Dom hates his men seeing me in so little, but I want to see if I can tempt him into giving me what I want. Only one way to find out...

⚜

Dominic

Glancing around the poker table at the men, my attention settles on Antonio. He hasn't been himself the last couple of days, but with everything going on with the Chinese, I haven't had a chance to talk to him properly. I know something happened between Kat and him, but I haven't quite figured it out yet and he is being tight lipped about it all. Angel said something the other day about the way they both acted at the café and that she was worried because Kat wouldn't talk to her about whatever it was. I might pull him aside later and have a chat, see if I can do anything to help fix the situation.

"Boss." Antonio nods towards my hand

"Si sucsa." I look at my hand and place my bet, glancing at my watch, I take note of the time. "One more hand, gentlemen." I want to go and make sure Evie is peacefully sleeping and then crawl into bed and make love to my Angel. Ever since hearing the news about Darren's death, she has been a completely different person. I love seeing her this way, more confident, no worries, enjoying life as she should be. She still has nightmare's now and again, but at least I know, the demons she is fighting in her sleep have already been taken care of. It still guts me to see her upset and I do my best to comfort her in her sleep.

"Boss," Antonio says again.

Shit, concentrate Dom. Just as I'm about to place another bet, I look up at the sound of my office doors opening and Brooklyn is standing there in a short black, silk and lace nightie.

What. The. Fuck!

Just the sight of her has me turning instantly fucking hard. I scan her body from her blonde curly hair laying over one shoulder and curving around the side of her breast, to her pink painted toenails. After I pick my jaw up off the table, I look around to make sure my men are not staring at what is mine.

"Sorry I didn't mean to interrupt."

The way she bites her lip and smiles at me after she speaks, makes me think otherwise.

"I was wondering if I could borrow… *The Boss*"

She says *Boss* so seductively, I feel my cock turn to granite and I'm in danger of losing control.

"FUORI!" (GET OUT)

I don't take my eyes off her while my men leave the room, their heads and eyes lowered as they pass by my woman. Fuck! I could kill them all. I'm pissed and so fucking turned on.

"Angel." My voice is barely a croak. Fuck! Taking a deep breath, I try and rein in my anger. "What the fuck do you think you are doing?" I throw the cards I was holding onto the table. I'm far from calm, but fuck it.

"I'm sorry, Boss." Her voice is seductive as she glides toward me swinging her fucking hips. I suck in a deep breath at the way she says Boss again, it's like her voice has a direct line to my cock.

"Fuck," I growl as I push back the chair so I can stand. Before I can rise, Angel squeezes between me and the table and stands between my legs. Fuck, she smells good. I'm so mesmerized by my vixen running her hands over my chest and fondling my cock, I almost miss what she says next. With her lips a hair's breadth away from mine, she whispers,

"Play with me."

FUCK ME DEAD! I have created a sex siren for whom I have no resistance.

Brooklyn

Dom sucks in a huge breath between gritted teeth. His rough hands run up my legs causing goosebumps to break out across my skin.

"Fuck, Angel."

I knew Dom would be angry when I came in <u>dressed</u> the way I am. I saw the unmistakable tick in his jaw and didn't miss his glance around the table making sure none of his men were looking at me. But, I also knew he wouldn't stay mad at me and that's why I love him so much. As for his men, even though they didn't do anything wrong and they did their best not to look at me, he'll still be pissed they were even here. I sort of feel bad, but he won't stay mad and now I have him to myself for the rest of the night. Selfish, I know, but I can't get enough of him.

Dom lifts me onto the table and lays me back with one hand while the other slides under my nightie making me shiver. I arch my back into his touch wanting more and whimper when he releases me and steps back abruptly. What the Hell? I narrow my eyes and watch as a smirk curls his lips.

"I should spank your gorgeous ass, Angel."

My eyes lock with his and they mirror the smoldering passion I feel. Heat pools low in my belly. Fuck, why does the thought of Dom spanking me turn me on so much? Shouldn't it scare the shit out of me and make me want to run far, and fast? But, I want it. Fuck, I actually want it.

"Dom." My voice is breathless, full of passion.

"Fuck," Dom growls and slides his hands back over my body. The feel of his rough hands as they move with the silk of my nightie has me writhing and breathing heavy. He massages my breasts, bends down and kisses me hard and fast. As he pulls back, I hear a ripping sound and gasp as cool air hits my heated skin. He has torn my nightie straight down the middle. Fuck that was hot!

"Roll over." Dom voice is hoarse but commanding.

I'm quick to do as I'm told.

Dom's hands slide up the back of my legs until he reaches my ass. He cups my cheeks in his hands and squeezes. "Fuck I love your ass, Angel. Now, what have I said about walking around like this in front of other men?" He breathes into my ear before nipping the lobe. "You say stop, I stop. Okay? I will not hurt you."

I nod my head because I'm not sure I can find my voice to answer him right now.

"Angel." Dom nips my ear, making me whimper.

"Yes," I pant as his fingers slide between my legs and latch onto my clit.

"So wet, my Angel." He groans as he withdraws his fingers and sucks them into his mouth.

His fingers caress my back down to my ass again, he rubs his palm over my ass cheek in small circles. A loud slap startles me, it stings until he rubs small circles over the area. Heat spreads through my body and I feel fluid rush to my pussy. I push back into his hand and he groans at my bold move.

"Again?" Dom growls.

"Yes," I pant out. Two more slaps follow closely, my body is on fire and I feel like I'm going to explode at any moment.

He slaps me again, harder this time. I pull my knees under my body, arch my back and moan loudly. I feel liquid drip down my thighs.

"Fuck Angel, you present yourself to me like this. I can't take it; I need you now."

Before I can even register what is happening, I feel the head of his hard cock pushing against my throbbing clit. I need him in me now. I don't wait for my lover, I push back, taking him all the way in and moan loudly as Dom grips my hips and pistons his steel hard cock into my wet cavern.

He groans with pleasure as he pushes deeper. "Fuuuuck."

I feel a sting in my ass when Dom smacks it again, his soothing rubbing encourages the heat to spread deep into my pussy. "Oh, fuck." Pushing myself up onto my hands, I arch into him. He curls a hand through my hair and tugs my head back causing me to moan and arch even more.

"Fuck. You're. Fucking. Sexy." Dom grunts out the words between each thrust "So. Wet. So. Tight. Come for me. NOW!"

His hoarse voice washes over me, his deep groan in my ear is the last thing I hear before I take us both over the edge. Fuuuuuck!

⁂

Dominic

"Hey big man, a package arrived for you." Angel sashays into my office and rounds my desk, she's holding a square, brown box in her hands. Swiveling around in my chair so I'm facing her, I snag the box out of her hand and throw it onto the desk with a thud. My hands wrap around her waist and I pull her onto my lap. She squeals in surprise. I chuckle as I pull her tighter against me, place a hand to the back of her head, and take her lips in a long deep kiss. I love that she doesn't freeze up anymore when I touch her this way. Pulling back from the kiss, I lean forward and nuzzle behind her ear, breathing in her mouth-watering scent. Her unique scent still has the power to bring me to my knees and probably will until the day I die. Closing my eyes, I think about the last two months we have spent together. I have never felt more at peace than when she is in my arms.

"Darling, I have to get to work. Please don't start something we both don't have the time to finish, okay?" Angel whispers in my ear before sucking the lobe into her mouth. She runs her fingers through my hair and wiggles her ass on my already hard cock. Fuck! I ease her back and raise an eyebrow at her, she knows damn well what she's doing to me.

"Oh no, I know that look and it's not going to work on me this morning. I have to get to work and your men will be here any minute for your meeting."

I nip Angel's bottom lip with my teeth before sucking it into my mouth to sooth the sting. I hear the front door open and Antonio calls out as he enters the foyer. "You and that sexy mouth of yours jinxed us, Angel." She giggles as she climbs off my lap and runs her hands down her thighs slowly fixing her skirt. Fuck, she's a tease! I stand up to readjust my aching cock, it doesn't matter that we have already fucked twice this morning, as soon as she's in the room I'm instantly hard. Angel notices me trying to readjust myself and bursts into giggles.

"I'll see you at the café later." Angel leans forward and brushes her lips over mine.

"Si, I'll be there. I have to handle a few things first." I watch as she starts biting her lip and worry swims in her beautiful blue eyes. Everything has been quiet concerning the Chinese and I know she's worried, I hate that. I gather her back into my arms. "Angel, please don't worry. Nothing has happened, I just have to organize a few things with the dockyard."

"Okay, darling." She wraps her arms around my neck and kisses me softly, but I have other ideas. I hold her tighter and deepen the kiss. I can never get enough of her, it's as if she supplies the air I need to breathe. When we draw apart, we're both breathless, her lips are swollen. She fists my shirt in her hands and pulls me back to her, wanting more. We kiss briefly before she mumbles under her breath, "You don't fight fair." She turns and almost walks straight into Antonio.

She places her hand on his chest to steady herself. "Sorry, Antonio, your Boss is an asshole." Antonio chuckles and a deep laugh escapes me. It's not often Brooklyn swears, but when she does it's amusing.

"Ciao il Mio Amore, il vita mia," I call out before she leaves and closes the door.

I look toward Antonio who has a smirk on his face. It's the first time in a while I have seen any kind of happiness in him at all. I give him a once over and notice how much weight he has lost, he isn't looking at all well. I know Kat and him still aren't speaking except for the odd hello or goodbye. I have tried to talk to him about it to see if I can help in any way, but he assures me there is nothing I can fix or do to help. Brooklyn has also tried with Kat, but she closes up which ends the conversation.

"Boss?" Antonio shakes me from my thoughts. "Is everything set?"

"Si, I'll grab Brooklyn from the café as per usual and then we'll pick up Evie and come home, we'll go from there."

"Boss, you deserve those girls. I'm glad you're happy."

I nod. I'm not sure if I'll ever deserve Angel and Evie, but I'm not letting them go. They are mine. In this, and the next, life.

Antonio takes a seat, respecting my silence. He knows me well and would know exactly what I'm thinking. I sit down and glance at the clock, the rest of my men will be here soon.

"How are things between you and Kat?" I try again to see if he'll open up to me.

He drags a hand through his hair and shakes his head like he's frustrated. I think that's the end of it until he speaks.

"Fuck, I don't know. We were good, and then all of a sudden, we weren't. She's hiding something, and I'm not gonna stop until I find out what it is."

"Si, I know you will."

Brooklyn

I have a spring in my step as I enter the café, I can't remember the last time I was this happy. I have a beautiful daughter who is happy and settled, not to mention she is growing like a weed. I couldn't be prouder of her. I have a man who loves me and would bend over backward to make sure we are both happy and safe. I'm not saying things have been perfect because they haven't. Dominic and I disagree on things, but the difference is, I can speak my mind without fearing what might happen next.

This thing with the Chinese is still going on and it worries me, but it's not like I can do anything to help the situation. I trust Dominic when he says he will handle it. And yes, I still have to be guarded by Demetri when Dom's not with me, but I have accepted the fact it will never change as long as Dom is who he is. Demetri is a really nice guy and easy to talk to. God help the woman he ever sets his heart on because that boy oozes charm.

As for Kat and Antonio, only time will tell. Yes, it upsets me to see my best friend hurting and not being able to help, but Kat is stubborn and as far as I can tell, so is Antonio. Except for this morning, I haven't seen him too far away from Kat in the past two months. When I asked Dom about it, he confirmed my suspicion that he is the one guarding her. Apparently, he wouldn't hear of anyone else doing it.

"Morning Dollface, how are you this morning?" Kat strolls out of the kitchen wiping her hands on a tea towel.

"Morning Kat." I smile.

"We need to talk about tonight, are you nervous?" Kat tilts her head to one side.

I think about it for a minute before shaking my head. "No, not really. I mean, I am, but I think it will be okay."

"Dollface, it *will* be okay. You'll see he's not anything like Darren and this is something you guys have spoken about several times together. You *both* want it." I look at Kat when she pauses a bit too long, I notice she's staring out the window with a faraway look on her face and her eyes are filled with unshed tears. I'm instantly on alert and when I swing around to look out the window. I see Demetri by his car, but nothing else.

I turn to face my best friend. "Kat, please tell me what's wrong?" For some unexplained reason, I feel panicked.

"Uh…" Kat clears her throat before waving her hand around like she's shooing a fly away. "It's nothing, I'm so happy for you guys." Kat wipes the tears from her cheeks before stepping forward and giving me a quick hug. She draws back and places her hands on my shoulders, she has a soft smile on her face.

"Evie was bouncing off the walls this morning before I dropped her off with Gwen." I smile thinking about when I told her the news yesterday and what our plan was on how to tell Dom. *Daddy*, as she corrected me. Lucky for me, Aunty Kat picked her up for a sleep-over before Dom finished in his office last night. I don't think she would have been able to hold her tongue.

"Let's get started, being a Friday we are bound to get busy."

I grab my apron off a hook near the kitchen door and get to work stocking the cakes and slices into the glass cabinet.

Dominic

I nod at Demetri, who is sitting in his car, as I move toward the door of *Coffee Kat.* I turn to Sergio. "Let Demetri know what was discussed in the meeting this morning and then tell him he's' good to get going."

"Si, Boss. I'll be in the car for when you're ready to leave." Nodding my head, I push through the door and notice Brooklyn behind the counter. She's on a small ladder reaching for the top shelf.

I move silently around the counter and stop behind her. I admire her smooth, sexy tanned legs which lead up to her lush ass. My cock flinches with interest, I need to put a stop to this ogling before I become hard as a rock. I'm still suffering from having blue balls this morning and the ache is almost unbearable.

"What are you doing, Angel?"

She squeals in surprise, her foot slips and I catch her before she hits the floor. "You scared the crap out of me, Big Man." She slaps my chest but has a playful smile on her face.

I chuckle and lower her feet to the floor, but I don't release her. Instead, I pull her closer. She melts in my arms when my lips lower onto hers. "I missed you today."

"Missed you too, darling, but you can't creep up on me like that. I could have fallen and hurt myself."

"I'm sorry, sweetheart. I thought you would have heard the doorbell." Thinking about it, I didn't hear it either.

"It's broken, I have to get it fixed."

"Are you ready to go, I want to pick up my princess? I have a surprise waiting for you girls at home."

Brooklyn's face breaks into a huge smile that takes my breath away.

"Yeah, I'll grab my bag and we can leave."

Lowering my head, I give her a soft kiss before letting her go with a small smack to the ass.

She giggles as she hurries away.

Sergio parks the car in front of Mr. and Mrs. Peterson's house, I nod letting him know I'll get Brooklyn's door. I round the back of the car before opening the door and offering the lady my hand. I keep her small hand in mine as we walk up the front steps, but before Angel can knock, it swings open and Mr. Peterson is standing there with a smile on his face.

"Good evening, sweetheart, how was work?" He leans forward and gives Brooklyn a quick hug and kiss on the cheek before holding his hand toward me. "Mr. Grasso, good to see you again. You taking care of our girls?" His hand always grips tighter when he asks me that question.

It amuses me, and maybe someone else would get pissed about it, but I don't. I know he means well and he loves my girls as if they were his own. "Always, Mr. Peterson, and please call me Dominic." I release his hand and place it on Angel's lower back, guiding her into the house behind Harry. We are barely inside the house when I hear laughter coming from the kitchen.

"Mommy." Evie squeals and leaps into Brooklyn's arms. She almost knocks her to the ground before jumping down and climbing me like a tree. I laugh at her excitement.

"Precious girl, be careful with mommy, you don't want to hurt her," Gwen says as she smiles toward Brooklyn.

"Are you ready to go, Princess, I have a surprise waiting for us at home." I wink at her, she knows exactly what's going on.

She smiles at me and tries to wink, but ends up closing both eyes. I can't help but chuckle.

"Would you guys like to stay for coffee? You can sample the cupcakes Evie and I made together." Gwen flips the switch on the kettle to on.

I want to get going. "Oh, I'm sorry but..."

"We would love to." Brooklyn cuts me off. I try to attract her attention, but she is already deep in conversation with Gwen and either doesn't notice or chooses to ignore me.

Evie places her tiny hands on both sides of my face and turns my head back to face her. When I make eye contact, she has a pleading look in her eyes.

"It's okay, Princess, we have time for one coffee for momma and one glass of milk for you." I kiss her cheek before placing her on the ground. She goes to sit on Brooklyn's lap, but changes her mind, and hops up on Gwen's. Feeling a hand on my shoulder, I turn to find Harry standing next to me.

"It's a beautiful sight, isn't it?"

I look toward Brooklyn and can't help but smile.

"Si, it is sir." I nod.

"You're a loyal and honorable man, Mr. Grasso, and I know exactly who you are. I may be old, but I'm not stupid. If you hurt them in any way, you will face my wrath. Do you understand?"

I don't take threats kindly, but I understand where he is coming from and he means a lot to Brooklyn and Evie. I restrain the irritation I feel at his comment. "Si, I understand sir, but let me be clear. Those two girls are my life, if something happens to them you may as well put a knife through my heart because I would rather die than see them go through an ounce of pain."

"Good." He smiles and pats me on the back.

A knock sounds at the front door. "I'll get it." Gwen excuses herself.

I seat myself next to Brooklyn, and as soon as my ass hits the chair, Evie is in my lap. She told me, it's her favorite place to be if she's not sitting on Brooklyn's lap. I kiss her hair and stretch my arm across the back of Angel's chair, just as Kat and Antonio follow Gwen in. I'm instantly on alert. "*Fratello*, is everything okay?"

"Si, Boss. Katherine wanted to visit." Glancing at Kat, I notice she's not acting like her usual self. Strange, she hasn't come back with a smart comment at the use of her full name. She shrugs her shoulders and looks away.

"Coffee's up." Harry's words break the tension which has suddenly fallen over the room.

"Oh, the cupcakes." Gwen is behaving excitedly and clapping her hands.

Evie bounces up and down in my lap, I laugh at her enthusiasm. "Wait until you see them, daddy. They're so pretty." Evie sing-song, excited voice making me wonder if she really needs any more sugar.

Gwen places a tray of cupcakes in front of Evie and me, they have pink and blue icing on top with little flowers surrounding a letter of the alphabet. They are cute. "Good job, Princess." I kiss the top of Evie's head. I glance around when I realize, it's gone completely quiet.

Then Evie bursts into laughter. "Daddy, read what they say!" She points to the line of cupcakes in front of me, there are a lot of them. I study them closer.

Y-O-U A-R-E G-O-I-N-G T-O B-E A D-A-D-D-Y

I'm completely speechless. Fuck, I'm going to be a dad again? I gaze at Brooklyn, she's staring at me, biting her lip as worry swims in her eyes.

"I'm going to be a dad?" Somehow I manage to choke out the words as I look into her beautiful eyes.

She fidgets with her fingers in her lap and nods.

"Angel?"

"Yes." She lifts her head and whispers, her eyes locked on mine.

Wrapping my hand around the back her neck, I pull her into a deep kiss. I rest my forehead against hers and watch as tears stream down her cheeks. Someone clears their throat, breaking our moment. I look up and proudly announce what they already know.

"I'm going to be a daddy again!" Kat and Harry stare at me strangely, Gwen smiles brightly and Antonio chuckles.

"Again?" Kat rubs her forehead.

"Si, again. I already have Evie and now this little bambino."

Evie jumps off my lap and giggles as she removes her little apron. "Look what Aunty Kat and I made last night." She points to her shirt which reads - *I'm going to be a big sister*. She smiling and her eyes twinkle like stars.

"Do you think she's excited?" Brooklyn leans over and whispers in my ear, turning my head I brush my lips over hers.

"Thank you," I murmur against her lips.

Angel leans back and stares at me. "For what?"

I place my hand on her stomach. "For giving me this and for being mine."

"Dominic, you gave this to me along with so much more. You have made Evie and me whole again, babe." I lean forward and kiss her cheeks. I can't wait to get my girls home, take Angel to bed, and show her all night long how happy she has made me.

"I hope you're not tired Angel," I mumble into her lips before kissing her deeply.

When we draw apart, I watch as she realizes what I mean. She runs her tongue along her lip and I moan at the motion. Fuck, I need to take her home. Now!

I remain patient while we are congratulated, and protest when Brooklyn eats one of the cupcakes which ruins my message, but we finally say our goodbyes and I get to take my girl's home.

⁂

Brooklyn

I don't think I have ever seen Dominic so happy before. Talk about possessive over the cupcakes, it was like if someone ate one, then the message wouldn't be true. I reassured him it was true, but he was adamant, the cakes weren't to be touched. For fuck sake! I realized I couldn't reason with him, so I picked up, and ate the first one. I don't think I have ever seen a grown man pout that much and he's supposed to be a big powerful mob boss. It was kind of cute to witness that side of him.

Sitting in the back of the car on the way to Dom's, I mean *our* place, I rest my head against his shoulder watching the scenery go by. I place my hand on top of his arm which has been wrapped around my stomach in a possessive hold since we left the Petersons. I run my nails lightly over his arm. Closing my eyes, I relax into Dom's hold, I'm feeling content. Then, I hear the screech of tires and a loud bang. I'm jerked back into my seat, my head hits something hard and then nothing. I come to with a jolt and hear Evie screaming.

"Fuck, what happened?" I moan as I lift my hand to rub my aching head, a small bump has formed on the side of my temple. What the hell just happened?

"Brooklyn! Brooklyn, can you hear me? Open your eyes, Angel." When I open my eyes, I'm met with green orbs swimming in panic.

"Evie?" I reach forward and grip Dom's arms.

"She's okay, sweetheart. Kat's here and she's taking care of her. Antonio is calling an Ambulance."

I sink back into the seat, relieved Evie and Dom are okay. My head starts to spin, I feel light-headed and close my eyes.

"Brooklyn!"

Dom is shouting at me. I groan, why won't he let me sleep? I'm so tired.

"Angel, come on, *il Mio Amore.* Open your eyes."

I moan again and my eyes flutter open. Dominic's face is swimming in tears.

"You're bleeding, babe." I raise a shaky hand to his face and try to wipe the blood away, but I'm too weak. My hand crashes back to my lap.

"Don't close your eyes, Angel. Stay awake for me."

"I'm tired, so tired. Need to sleep."

"I know but you can't go to sleep."

"Where the fuck is that Ambulance?" Dom yells which causes my head to pound even more.

"Shhh, too loud."

"Sorry, beautiful."

"They just turned up, Boss," Antonio shouts.

I feel Dom's lips against my forehead and he whispers, "Thank, Christ" into my hair, before pulling away and speaking with Antonio.

"Don't leave me, Dom…" I murmur before closing my eyes again

"Never, Angel."

Seventeen

Dominic

I storm into my office after settling the girls into bed. My men stand to attention. "I want whoever did this brought to me now!" Am I angry? You fucking bet I am.

Antonio steps forward. "Boss, I have Theo searching the number plate Sergio recorded. He's at the hospital getting his arm fixed. The car that hit you was abandoned and it's been moved to the docks. Johnny and Michael are going over every inch of it as we speak. We will find who did this, I swear."

"Si." I pace back and forth before stopping in front of Theo. "When you have something, I don't care how inconsequential you think it is I know first! Capisce?"

"Si Boss, it may take..."

"NON ME NE FREGA UN CAZZO QUANTO TEMPO CI VUOLE!" (I DON'T GIVE A FUCK HOW LONG IT TAKES!)" I suck in a deep breath and try to rein in my anger so I don't disturb the girls upstairs. "You come to me immediately, understand?" My tone is menacing, deathly low. "That *stronzo* almost killed my family and I want him found!"

"On it, Boss." Theo focuses back on the computer in his lap.

I step over to the bar next to my desk and pour myself a generous amount of scotch into a crystal tumbler. I take a long drink and feel the familiar burn as it slides down my throat.

"How are your girls?" Antonio asks quietly as he steps up beside me.

I grip the glass in my hand tighter as I relive hearing Evie's screams seeing Angel not moving beside me in the back seat.

"Sleeping, thank God." I drag my fingers through my hair. The paramedics and my family doctor, who has just examined her, said, I have to wake Brooklyn every couple of hours in case she has a concussion. if she has a headache, I have medication to give her. As for Evie, she's fine just a little shaken up. Thankfully she was in her car seat, otherwise, it could have been much worse.

"And the baby?"

I take another sip allowing the scotch to sit in my mouth before I answer. "The baby is fine. The paramedics had a machine that lets them check the heart beat and they told me it was strong and steady." I try not to think about the *what ifs* because I don't think I could go on should anything have happened.

"Did Doc take a look at your head?"

I wave away his concern, I want to make sure he knows what I want. "Antonio, my head is of no concern. I need answers and I want the piece of shit found." I slam the glass down hard on the bar.

"We've got it, Boss. I'm going to take Katherine home and then head to the docks."

I nod and cross my office to the door, I want to be with my girls.

"Until you find this stronzo, you talk to Antonio." With those last words directed to my men, I head upstairs.

When I enter the bedroom, I find my girls snuggled up together. They are *la vita mia,* what the fuck would I do without them? My fingers dig into my scalp and I blow out the breath I feel like I've been holding all night. I pad to the bathroom and stand staring at myself in the mirror. I *cannot* fail them. I *will* protect them. I will find the *stronzo* who hurt my girls and I will tear him limb from limb. He almost took something from me, that I have sworn to protect until I take my last breath. *I WILL NOT FAIL THEM LIKE I DID MOMMA.* I grip the sink tightly, so tight I swear I hear the glass creak in protest. I lower my head and attempt to calm down. A tear slides over my cheek. "They're here. They're alive. They're safe." My soft voice reminds me.

"Daddy."

I turn to find Evie standing at the door with tears running down her face.

"I'm scared." She sniffs and wipes the back of her hand under her nose.

I open my arms. "Come here, Princess." She throws herself into my arms and I hold her tight to my chest. My heart breaks to see my daughter so upset. I take her to the bed and lay her down beside Angel, then climb in, lay on my side and pull her into my arms.

"I will protect you, Princess. Please don't be scared."

"I know you'll protect me, daddy. I'm scared for momma; will she be okay?"

"Yes, momma is going to be fine. How about you try and get some sleep."

Her soft lips touch my cheek in a kiss before she burrows into my chest. I barely hear her whisper, "goodnight daddy, I love you"

"I love you too, Princess."

I stretch one arm out and rest it on Angel's hip. Laying in the dark, holding my girls, I know I'm not going to sleep tonight. Touching them, and knowing they're still here, calms me. I think about the past couple of hours - being told I'm going to be a papa again and how excited Evie was to become a big sister is a moment I will remember forever. Then some *cazzo* tried to take that away from me. I need to find that piece of shit and make him pay.

Brooklyn

I groan when I attempt to roll over, fuck it hurts to move. My eyes flutter open, but I close to alleviate the pain in my head. My body tenses as I'm thrown back to the past, remembering far too many mornings waking up feeling this way. I gasp for breath inhaling and exhaling slowly. My heart thumps in my chest and I reach over blindly searching for my glass of water. I push myself up a little and take a slow sip. I search my memory for what must have happened to me. I recall telling Dom he's going to be a father and watching as a huge smile spread across his handsome face. Then, saying goodnight to Gwen and Harry and relaxing into Dom as Sergio drove us home.

Fuck! It comes flooding back. Some asshole drove into us! I remember Evie screaming, my head hitting something hard, Dom's panicked face, the sounds of an Ambulance and someone talking to me. I remember being carried up to bed, held in Dom's warm arms - safe, secure. Some stranger, a doctor I think, checked me over and asked a bunch of questions. For the rest of the night, I remember being woken up and Dom asking if I was okay.

"Angel baby, do you have a headache? I have some pain killers for you if you need them."

Slowly opening my eyes, I see Dom leaning over me and his worried eyes stare down at me. I try to smile to ease the worry on his face, but it hurts. Reaching up, I run my fingers lightly over the butterfly plaster that crisscrosses over his eyebrow. "Are you okay, big man?"

He chokes out a quiet laugh, gathers my hand and brings it to his lips. He kisses each fingertip before nipping my little finger, making me yelp and him smirk.

"Hey I'm hurt, don't start something we can't finish." I pout.

I watch as the playful look leaves his face and he focuses on the side of mine. "I'm sorry Angel, so fucking sorry, baby." He crouches beside me and bows his head.

I lift his head and place my palm on the side of his face. "Hey, it *wasn't* your fault. I'm fine. *We* are fine."

Dom stares at me, the sadness in his eyes almost breaks me. I need to change the subject. I hate that he's hurting over something he had no control over.

"Dom, please I'm fine, the baby is fine. I only have a slight headache, I swear."

"If that headache doesn't go away, I'm taking you to the hospital."

I agree only because I can see the fear in his eyes and I know he needs me to agree with him on this. I need to turn his mind onto something else and get that look off his face.

"Where's Evie?"

"Downstairs with Kat and Antonio fixing lunch."

"Lunch!" I turn my head glance at the clock on the bedside table for the time. Holy crap, it's just after 12pm!

"Si, I had to keep disturbing your sleep all night, so I thought I would let you sleep in."

A knock at the door interrupts us.

"Come in," Dom calls out.

Evie runs in carrying a single pink rose. "Mommy you're awake."

"Good morning Sweetpea, you don't have to knock." I look to Dom after I speak, he raises an eyebrow. Was I wrong to tell her that?

"Aunty Kat said I have to knock." She jumps up onto the bed, hands me the rose and snuggles in beside me.

I wrap my arms around her and kiss the top of her head. Thank God she's okay.

"Yeah Dollface, I didn't want us to walk in on anything." Kat enters carrying a tray "I didn't want a show 'n' tell today." She winks at me.

"Ooooh… I like show 'n' tell." Evie claps her hands together excitedly.

I bite my lip to keep from laughing but when I turn and see the expression on Dom's face, the battle is lost. Kat bursts into laughter with me.

He shakes his head and stands up to take the tray from Kat's hands. He mumbles something in Italian under his breath before placing the tray over my lap. I look at all the food they have put together, holy crap I won't eat all this. There are two chicken sandwiches, fresh fruit diced in a bowl, a yummy looking salad, cup of coffee and a glass of orange juice. On the side sits a beautiful little vase with a red and white rose placed inside.

"This all looks delicious, but I don't think I can eat everything."

"No mommy we get to share." Evie laughs at me.

"Thank God." I breathe out relieved as Dom and Kat laugh.

"Okay, *il Mio Amore,* I have some things I need to take care of in my office. I'll be back to check on you soon, be good."

"Okay, big man. Does this mean I'm stuck in this bed all day?" I no sooner speak than Kat gasps and I see her eyes widen.

"What? What's wrong?" I look around the room searching for I don't know what.

"Oh, I forgot something" She holds her hand out. "Evie come with me." She turns to Dom and I. "We'll be back in a minute."

They hurry from the room and I'm left wondering what the hell that was about. I look at Dom to see if he knows, but I can't read his face. Is he angry at me? Did I do something wrong? Is that look because I told Evie she didn't have to knock.

"Are you upset with me because I told Evie she didn't have to knock?"

"Angel, I'm not upset and I'm certainly not angry. I have no reason to be, of course, Evie doesn't have to knock. I am a little annoyed by the fact you think you need my permission to do or say something. This is your home now, you have the right to make decisions. You don't have to ask me, okay?" He leans over and places a soft kiss to my lips. Pulling back, he locks eyes with me, waiting for my reply.

"Okay, I'm sorry."

"You have nothing to apologize for *Il Mio Amore.*" When he bends over to kiss me again, I wrap my arms around his neck and deepen the kiss, it drags a groan from the back of his throat. I love the fact I can do that to him. We pull apart at the sound of laughing when the girls walk back into the room. When Dom places his forehead against mine, I notice the sparkle is back in his eyes.

"I'll be back soon, enjoy your time together." I'm gifted with a small kiss on the nose, he pats Evie on the head and strides from the room.

After we devour most of the food, I lay back against the headboard and rub my belly. If I eat anything else, I'm sure I'll explode.

Kat holds up a brown box. "Dominic had this dropped off so we had something to do until he finishes what he has to do today."

"What is it?" I study the brown box in her hands.

"A puzzle. He doesn't want you out of bed today so this is the best it's gonna get. I know it's probably not what you want to do, but deal with it." Kat grins and pokes her tongue out.

"Come on, Mommy pleaseeee…" Evie bats her eyelashes at me. Damn Kat for teaching her that move, I can never say no when she uses it on me.

"Okay, we can do it."

"Yessss." Evie fist pumps the air and bounces on the bed.

"Babydoll, you have to sit still if you want to do this." Kat pats the bed as she places the box in front of her, it's strange, there's no picture on the front. It's just a plain, brown box.

"Kat, I think Dom may have given you the wrong box, there's no picture on it. How are we supposed to know where the pieces fit?"

Kat opens the box and sure enough, there's a puzzle inside. "The pieces are big enough that we should be able to guess where they go. It doesn't look like there are that many, we should be able to work it out." Kat shrugs her shoulders.

I laugh at her thought process, and Evie has a bright smile on her face. They're up to something, I just know it. But, I'll play along. "Okay, so where do we start smarty pants?"

Kat pokes her tongue out again. "Let's start with the corners, they're always easy and then we'll do the sides."

Half an hour later we have three-quarters of the puzzle finished and I realize there are quite a few pieces missing. We have what looks like multiple colored roses laid out before us minus the parts in the middle. Well, that sucks! "What do we do now?" I hate it when I do a puzzle and find I can't finish because pieces have been lost.

"I'll go and see if Dom knows where the other pieces are." Kat jumps off the bed heads downstairs.

"I guess we wait here then," I say sarcastically to Kat's back.

"Mommy." Evie holds an envelope out to me.

"What's that, Sweetpea?"

Shrugging her shoulders, she passes it to me. "It was in the box."

Well that's odd. Taking the envelope, I feel tiny groves through the paper. What the hell? When I open the envelope, and turn it upside down, the missing puzzle pieces tumble into my lap. There's a small note folded in half. I unfold it and read, tears flow over my cheeks.

My Dearest Angel,

I was lost in the darkness before you came into my life,

One look into your eyes and I felt complete.

You and Evie are the missing pieces to my heart.

We fit together so well…

The way your small hand fits in mine,

To the way your head rests perfectly on my shoulder.

The way our hearts beat as one, as our bodies melt together.

My life is finally complete,

So, say you will be Mine forever,

And

Marry Me?

Tears stream down my face and I place my hand over my mouth as I read the last line.

I was so focused on the letter; I hadn't realized Dom had slipped back into the room and was now down on one knee beside the bed. In his fingers, he's holding a huge diamond ring. I cover my mouth with one hand as I gasp.

"Angel?" His voice is breathless and his eyes are locked on mine.

I start nodding my head, thinking I probably look like one of those bobble-head dolls you see on the dashboard of cars. But, in true Dom fashion, he raises an eyebrow and waits for my words.

"YES! Oh God, YES!" I squeal, Evie starts screaming and laughing. Quicker than I thought possible, Dom's lips are on mine sucking the air from my lungs. As he kisses me, he slips the ring onto my finger. The cool of the metal against my skin sends shivers down my spine as he deepens the kiss.

"PG people, Babydoll's in the room." Kat stands at the doorway laughing, Antonio is behind her chuckling.

Pulling back giggling, I rest my forehead against Dom's.

"I love you *il Mio Amore*." Dom lifts my hand and places a forever binding kiss where my ring sits.

"I love you too." I brush my lips over his.

"Mommy, let's finish the puzzle." Evie is clinging to Dom and kisses his cheek. "Pleaseeee?"

"Okay, why not?"

Gathering the remaining pieces from my lap, Evie and I place them into the puzzle. When we finish, I sit back trying to hold back more tears. I was right, it has colorful roses as a backdrop, with two candy hearts in the center, Evie's name is on one, mine is on the other and written in the space between the two hearts is -

"Il Mio Amore,

La Vita Mia.

Forever Mine"

I wonder if he will finally tell me what *La vita mia* means? I have asked a million times, but he always said, when it's the right time he will explain. I wonder if now is the right time? Before I can ask, he explains.

"My Love, My Life, Forever Mine."

"Oh, Dom." Tears of happiness trickle from my eyes.

"We did it, Daddy." Evie squeals and hugs Dom hard around the neck.

"Si, we did Princess." Dom chuckles and kisses Evie's cheek.

"Hold up a minute…" I knew it, they were in on it together. I lift my hands to get their attention, but before I can say anything, I pause when I get a glimpse at my ring. I bring it closer to my face, it's breathtaking. Three twisted bands wrap around each other and one of the bands is full of pink stones, set on top is a beautiful princess cut diamond. It's so sparkly, I'm transfixed.

"Do you like it mommy?"

"I do." I smile as I keep staring.

"Angel, the pink stones are rare pink diamonds, they represent our Princess here. The diamond in the center is a five karat princess cut stone."

"Five karats, are you serious? Holy Fuck, Dom."

"Mommy…" Evie chastises me.

"Sorry Sweetpea, but …." I don't know what to say, I'm absolutely speechless.

"Angel, you deserve this and so much more."

I'm not sure what to say, so I launch myself at him and like he always does, he catches me.

"Wait until tonight," I whisper in his ear.

Eighteen

Brooklyn

It's been just over a week since the accident, and just as long before Dom allowed me out of this damn bed, even though I've been fine for a couple of days now. Every time I ran my fingers over the bump on my head and tried to hide my discomfort, I saw the worry on Dom's face. I've reassured him a dozen times that I didn't have a headache and it was only slightly tender but it's as if my words went in one ear and out the other. Finally, I agreed to go to the hospital to double check everything was okay. The doctor assured us the scans were clear and I watched as relief washed over Dom's face. Maybe I should have been taken earlier so he didn't need to worry so much.

I decided I would show him just how good I was feeling when we arrived home. Evie was still with Gwen so we had the house to ourselves. I urged him to lay down on our bed and proceeded to trace every ridge and muscle on his sexy body with my tongue before taking his cock deep into my mouth. I sucked, licked and kissed until he was pushed to the edge and came close to losing control. Flipping me onto the bed, he thrust into me balls deep and sent me careening over the edge multiple times. As much as I love him for taking such good care of me, nothing beats having his body over mine and making me scream in pure ecstasy.

Sergio received a broken wrist from the accident, but he refuses to relax and take it easy until we find out exactly who it was that collided with us. Hopefully, in the next couple of days, they will have it figured out. The number plate came back as stolen so it wasn't any help, but Antonio managed to get the serial number off the car, quite an effort as he said it had been filed down. I'm not sure what magical trick he used, but in the end, he was successful.

At the moment, I'm waiting on Kat to turn up so we can head to the beach. Much pouting and whining has taken place and Dom finally caved and said we could go as long as Demetri was with us. Antonio and Dom have a meeting this morning and then they were going to run down the lead from the serial number.

My phone vibrates as I'm placing our towels in the beach bag. I smile at the message.....

Kat: Don't laugh I slept in, what are we doing today?

I shake my head, the girl is hopeless. I told her last night what we were doing. I type out my reply.....

Me: lol... I told you. We are going to the beach.

Kat: Which one? I'll meet you there

Me: Young Mariners pool, next to Newcastle Baths. Evie can swim there without waves.

I wait, but nothing comes back so I guess she's getting ready. After throwing my phone in the bag, I pack the rest of our stuff and go in search of Demetri to let him know, we are ready to go.

While Demetri drives toward the beach, I sit in the back seat of the *Lexus* with Evie. Looking through the window, I watch gray clouds rolling in, hopefully, they hold off for a bit longer.

"Mommy, can we build the biggest sandcastle today please?"

"Of course Sweetpea, anything you want."

"Ice cream?" She bats her beautiful baby blues at me.

"We're meeting daddy after we have a swim, so we can…"

I stop speaking when Demetri's phone rings. I place my finger over my lips, So Evie knows to be quiet. She nods her head and turns to look out the window.

"Si," Demetri answers. I hear Sergio's voice over the loud speaker. They speak in Italian, which is normal.

I tune out and run my fingers through Evie's hair, when she looks at me we start pulling funny faces at each other. She's giggling when Demetri turns into the carpark and as luck would have it we get a park straight away.

I lean forward, making sure everything is in the bag at my feet when I hear a car backfiring. At least that's what I thought it was until I jolt upright and see Demetri slumped forward over the steering wheel. "OH, GOD!" I scream and pull Evie close, holding her head into my chest so she doesn't see the blood sprayed across the windscreen. "DEMETRI!" I let out a blood-curdling shout, but nothing. "SERGIO!" I scream when my door is flung open and I'm dragged from the car by my hair. I scream and yell until my voice becomes hoarse, a gloved hand is wrapped around my throat. Sergio is yelling out to me through the speakers, but all I register is the fear in my daughter's eyes as silent tears roll down her face. I claw and fight, but my captor is far too strong. My mouth is covered with a sweet-smelling cloth, dizziness engulfs me and darkness descends.

The smell of mothballs and stale alcohol are the first things to penetrate my senses as I begin to regain consciousness. I wrinkle my nose, trying to ward off the smell as my stomach roils. The throbbing in my head is excruciating. What the hell happened to me? Fuck, where's Evie?

I try to move my hands, but they won't budge, something has them tied behind my back. I open my eyes but quickly close them again when I start to sway. Shit. Fuck. What's going on? I take a couple of deep breaths and slowly open my eyes again. I'm on a hard floor on my knees. I try to move my head to check out my surroundings, but something is attached to my neck holding me in place. When I try to slide my legs out from underneath, I hiss in pain as something cuts into my wrists. Shit! My hands are tied to my fucking feet!

I look around the dimly lit room the best I can without moving my head and notice a small lamp in the corner sitting on what looks like an old milk crate. I manage to turn my head slightly and wince at the pain, I hear a soft whimper followed by sobbing coming from the somewhere in the room. I squint in the dim light and attempt to focus in the direction the sounds came from. I cry out in anguish when I see a small cage, but it's not the cage that makes me cry, it's what's inside - Evie!

Sobs are ripped from my chest. Oh, God! Oh, God! I have to get to her! Fuck! What kind of monster would do this? I struggle frantically to free my hands, but whatever is binding them digs in deeper. I pull harder, the ties cut into my wrists and I feel blood pool in the palm of my hands. I breathe deep through the pain and keep attempting to get free, but the ties seem to get tighter. Shit! Shit! Shit! I'm breathing hard trying to work on getting free when I hear footsteps coming nearer to the closed door. I hear Evie whimper.

"Shhh…. Baby." I try to soothe Evie with the sound of my voice. "Pretend you're asleep and close your eyes, okay?"

"Okay mommy," she whispers back before curling herself into a ball and closing her eyes.

I turn my head toward the door when I hear it pushed open, ignoring the pain in my head with the quick motion. I suck in a breath, my heart slams against my chest wall and I shake in terror when I see who's standing there. Fuck, NO!

Dominic

Tapping my fingers on the table, I check the time. I'm starting to get impatient. What the hell is taking him so long? I check my watch again.

"Boss?" I glance at Antonio when he speaks, but I don't have a clue what he just said.

I'm not interested in what's going on. Demetri should have called by now, he was supposed to call when they got to the beach. My skin prickles and the hairs on the back of my neck stand on end. "Have you heard from Demetri?" I snap at Antonio.

He shakes his head.

"Call him, now!"

Antonio nods, grabs his phone and makes the call. I watch while waiting for Demetri to pick up and his voice to come through on the speaker. The phone rings out with no answer. My stomach knots and a light sweat breaks out over my body. Something is wrong, I have no doubt. They should have been at the beach by now and Demetri would have called.

Antonio would be able to read the worry on my face. "Boss, it could mean anything. Maybe he's getting Evie ice cream or something."

I rake my fingers over my scalp. No, something is wrong, my Angel needs me. I can feel it. "Call him again."

Before he gets the chance to hit redial, my phone starts ringing. I pull my phone from my pocket hoping to Christ it's Brooklyn.

"Boss." It's Sergio.

"Si?"

"Demetri's been shot, and Boss…. Brooklyn and Evie are missing."

I drop into a chair, it's like time stops and the realization of my worst nightmare has come true. I can literally feel the blood drain from my face. "What the fuck do you mean they're missing? Where the fuck are they?" I slam my palm down on the table in front of me, hard enough that our cups of water shake and one tips over. He pauses way too long. "SERGIO!" I shout into the phone. I get to my feet and rush to the car with Antonio at my back.

"I don't know, Boss." He starts swearing in Italian.

"Where are you now?" I climb into the car.

"At the Newcastle Baths car park."

"Wait there." I disconnect the call and tell Theo where we are going. I sit back and tear at my hair. Who the fuck could have done this? I only just received word, the Chinese are happy with the shipment of guns I sent them, along with my word that I would take care of Joey myself. It couldn't be them unless they want a war on their hands?

"Boss, what's happened?" Antonio has only pieces of what's happened.

"Someone has taken my girls. Demetri has been shot. Call the men, then call Doc and send him to the house." I swallow down on the lump which has formed in my throat. "Fuck! I let them down again, Antonio. The one thing I promised them was to protect and keep them safe and I have failed them again. FUCK! Theo, faster." I feel the car accelerate. "I need to find them, and whoever has them will pay."

"Boss, we *will* find them, we are going to get them back. Kat would kick my ass if we don't." His words are deadly serious.

He locks eyes with me, I know he's trying to calm me down, but nothing will work until I have my girls in my arms again. I see the worry in his eyes also. I know he has grown to care for them too, but they are my world. I can't lose them, I couldn't survive it if I did.

"We are going to find them." Antonio pats my shoulder.

"But, will they be alive when we do?" I murmur and a shiver runs down my spine as tears burn my eyes.

Nineteen

Brooklyn

"Darren," I murmur. "You're supposed to be dead."

Darren throws his head back and laughs like a madman, sending chills down my spine. He pulls a knife from behind his back and I suck in a deep breath. I realize how truly stuck I am as he stalks toward me like I'm his prey. Squatting in front of me, he runs his finger down the side of my face to my lip. I snap my teeth at him but he pulls back before I can catch. A sharp pain across my cheek as he backhands me causes me to cry out. I can't move and take the full force of the hit. My eyes water and my cheek throbs. I run my tongue along the split on my lip tasting the copper of blood.

Darren waves the knife back and forth in front of my face. I freeze as he runs the tip of the blade down my arm. I close my eyes, waiting for the knife to be thrust into me and for the searing pain which I know is to follow. But, he leans forward and I hear a snap as he cuts whatever was holding my hands and feet together. When I flex my fingers to get rid of the tingling, numbing feeling which had set in, I notice my ring is gone. The bastard has taken it. Tears burn my eyes. I raise my hands and finger the metal chain wrapped around my neck.

I swallow as some of the tension in the chain loosens and I'm able to take a deep breath, but it's short lived. Darren pulls on the chain to drag me to my feet. I gasp for air and attempt to pull the chain away, but it's no use, the chain tightens, cutting off my airway. Not having a choice, I struggle to my feet. I'm dizzy and my mouth tastes like cotton balls. I swallow thickly as I try to walk, but the room starts spinning and I stumble into the side wall.

"Move Bitch." Darren shoves me forward.

I try walking again and this time I'm stable enough to make it outside the door. As soon as I'm through, I'm pushed to all fours.

"Crawl Bitch," he demands and wrenches on the chain.

I gasp for breath and placing one hand in front of the other, I slowly make my way down the hallway. It feels like I crawl forever on the rough carpet, but is probably only mere seconds.

"I have a surprise for you, Bitch."

I whimper in fright, not sure what he means. A dank, musty smell assaults my nose and I want to throw up. I breathe rapidly in an effort to settle. He tugs on the chain and I follow him into another room. There is a dirty mattress in one corner surrounded by beer bottles, magazines, and old newspapers. He tugs my head upward and I gasp as I catch sight of a pair of bare feet dangling in front of me, slowly I raise my head further. I'm petrified of what I'll see next.

"Nooooo!" I scream at the sight of a shock of red hair hanging down. "KAT!!" I shout as gut-wrenching sobs wrack my body. Kat slowly lifts her head and groans in agony. Her lip is split and swollen, ugly bruises are forming on one side of her face. She's been stripped down to her bra and undies, there's a chain wrapped around her chest which loops over and under her arms and she's attached to a hook in the roof. GOD, PLEASE. Help us!

"Brooklyn, I'm… Sor-Sorry."

"No, you have nothing to be sorry for. I'm so sorry, Kat. I love you."

Darren crouches in front of me and waves a finger in my face. I would love to lean forward and bite it off but can't risk another beating. "This is your fault, Bitch. If you hadn't run away, none of this would have happened. You just couldn't behave, if you had just known your place everything would be fine." The chain tightens around my neck, I try and gain my footing as he raises it and attaches the metal to another hook in the ceiling. I wobble, standing on shaky legs. Once I'm on my feet he grabs my arms and pulls them behind my back. I whimper as he ties my bleeding and swollen wrists together again.

"Well, ladies, I hope you're both comfortable?" Darren speaks as if we're gathered here for a fucking tea party. "Now I have your attention; I'll show you your next big surprise." He flips on a light that blinds me, I close my eyes at the sudden brightness and when I open them I see Kat wide-eyed with silent tears cascading over her cheeks.

I'm almost too scared to look, but I follow her line of sight and suck in a breath as I see newspaper clippings stuck all over the walls. It's like some kind of shrine, pictures of women's bodies litter the walls with huge headlines in bold letters attached -

RAPED AND MURDERED

SERIAL RAPIST ON THE LOOSE

WOMAN'S BODY FOUND DUMPED

"No" I whimper when I see one I know so well -

ROBBERY GONE WRONG. COUPLE MURDERED

"No... No... NO!" I sob violently.

"Calm down, Dollface. Please, honey," Kat begs while crying uncontrollably herself.

Darren steps up beside me. "Ah, I see you noticed my most treasured piece. Don't worry, daddy went fast. Unfortunately, mommy dearest had a bit of fight in her, I showed her the error of her ways." He cackles like the deranged psychotic killer he is.

I can't breathe, my chest is tight and my heart seems to be refusing to beat.

"YOU SICK FUCK! WHAT IS WRONG WITH YOU? YOU ARE A PATHETIC EXCUSE FOR A MAN!" Kat wrestles with her chains.

Darren storms toward her and grabs the back of Kat's hair, he pulls it hard and lifts a knife up to press at her throat. Kat whimpers and I see droplets of blood as they appear around the edge of the knife.

"STOP! Please stop! I'll do anything you ask, just please stop." I need his attention on me; he needs to focus on me. It's my fault we're here, I can't allow anything to happen to Kat.

He releases Kat and looks me up and down, my stomach twists at the hard, vicious look on his face. "Oh, I know you will, but first, we'll have some fun.

He laughs maniacally as he looks between Kat and I. My knees shake as he gets closer to me and runs the tip of the knife up my leg. I tense when he cuts the dress from my body leaving me only in my swimmers. Violent tremors wrack my body as he circles the knife on my skin, I scream out at the sudden stab of pain in my thigh.

Tears roll down my face as try to breathe through the pain. "Fuck," I hiss out when he pulls the knife from my thigh, blood runs down my leg.

"Dear, dear, dear, Brooklyn, what a dirty mouth you've developed. It must be the bad influence from that dirty, fucking mobster your spreading your whore legs for."

Dominic, he should be here soon. I need to keep us alive long enough for him to find us. "When he finds us…"

Darren bursts into laughter. "I forgot how funny you are." He steps closer and speaks menacingly. Do you *really* think that Italian prick will find us? I hate to disappoint you, but nobody's coming for you. I've told you time and time again, nobody gives a fuck about you. *I* didn't even give a fuck about you." He begins pacing between Kat and I. "You were a means to an end. You were my first and *only* fuck up and you had to go get knocked-up didn't you? I guess at the end of the day you served a purpose with the head jobs you gave me."

"What the fuck are you on about you fucking asshole? You fucking raped her!" Kat screams at Darren.

I really wish Kat would keep quiet so she doesn't get hurt.

"Hmmm, that was necessary, unfortunately. I had to show her how naive she was, and still is. Her getting pregnant was never meant to happen and then when she refused to get rid of the thing. I was forced to make a choice. It worked out well actually because I needed to appear to be a family man to get a promotion so me and Matt could keep doing what we were doing."

"Matt?"

"Yeah Matt, my friend you came onto at the party. Well actually, he's my brother. We had to pretend to be friends, instead of family when we changed our names"

What the hell is he talking about? He had to change his name, and he has a brother? "What do you mean, you had to change your name?"

"I don't have the time to talk about all this now, but after our parents died we had to live with our grandma. When we were old enough we changed our names so we could get a decent job and keep doing what we were doing."

"I don't understand?" The only response we get is him smiling and waving his arm around the room as if it should be obvious. Then the smile is gone and he turns to face me again. He skims the tip of the blade over my other leg before pulling back and stabbing me in the side of my stomach. My eyes widen and a scream tears from me at the sudden pain.

"I'll make you suffer, for what you've done." He grunts as he pulls the knife from my body and I feel blood ooze from the wound.

I hear the clink of chains and Kat yells, "What did she do? Darren, look at me, what the fuck did she do? You're the one who threw a brick through her window and pushed her into Dom's arms. Tell me what she did wrong?"

He whips around and trails the knife down the center of her chest. "What the fuck are you talking about? What brick?"

My eyes widen and I notice Kat has the same look on her face. If he didn't throw the brick, who did?

"She had my brother killed!" He hisses in Kat's face.

"How did she kill your brother?" Kat asks, pretending she doesn't have a clue what he's talking about, but we both know how he died. *He* was the one who died in the car fire, it wasn't Darren.

"Your brother was in your car?" Kat asks, but Darren doesn't reply, he stares at the wall. "So you weren't stalking Brooklyn?"

"Oh, I was watching her, biding my time. Working out the right way to get at her, but then she met that Italian piece of trash which complicated things and I had to come up with other plans."

"But why, Darren? You never wanted me." I'm starting to fade out of consciousness.

"Because you decided to have that thing in the cage out there. While you were under my roof, everything was fine. Once you left, I couldn't risk you remembering what had happened that night and go to the police." He stalks toward me again. "You would have ruined everything Matt and I had going on. I couldn't allow that to happen."

"Tell me about this room, it must be important to you?" Kat is trying to get his attention on her and away from me.

I feel dizzy and my eyes droop closed until I feel a sharp sting across my cheek, they flash open again. "None of that, we still have things to do." I stare into the same cold dark eyes that have haunted my dreams.

"All these articles you have pinned up, Darren, they must mean something to you. Talk to me." Kat is persistent, I'll give her that.

"Ah Katherine, there's no need to be jealous. My attention will be on you soon enough; you have to wait your turn. You know, I've never had a redhead before." He turns to face her and runs the knife down her chest as he licks his lips. He whips his arm back and stabs her in the arm. "Arrgh,… You fucking piece of shit." Kat spits in his face.

"Mommeee," Evie screams out

Oh, no! Please… please… please… No!

"Ah, the little bitch is awake. I think I may keep her around a bit longer than planned."

Nausea grips me and my heart thunders in my chest, I'm terrified for my daughter. "Darren please let her go, she hasn't done anything wrong. PLEASE!" I scream at his retreating back.

"No, I might go and say hello to the little darling," he tosses over his shoulder.

"NOOoo!" I cry hard and squirm in an attempt to get free. It's no use, I can't save my daughter.

A loud bang vibrates through the room as a door flies open and Darren rushes back in followed by one very pissed off Mafia Boss. Dom raises his arm and fires, I watch as Darren crumples to the floor.

"Dominic, you c-c-came." His green eyes lock with mine. Rushing over, he lifts me from the hook and releases the chain around my neck, for the first time in what feels like forever I can breathe again. He lays me down, rips his shirt off and pushes it onto the wound in my side. I scream out in pain.

"I will always come, *il Mio Amore*. Always." His tears splash onto my face as he leans over me.

"Evie. Dominic get Evie." I lift my head to look around.

"Sergio" Dominic commands and the man takes off at a run.

I hear a low groan and see Kat being lifted down into Antonio's arms, he whispers to her as she breaks down in tears.

"Daddy!" Evie screams and I watch as she wriggles out of Sergio's arms and into Dominic's. "Daddy, I was so scared, but I knew you would come for us." She sobs against him.

"It's alright, Princess, I have you now." He kisses the top of her head and gazes at me with tear filled eyes.

I feel the life draining from me and brush my fingers down the side of Dom's face. "I love you, Dominic. Look after our girl." Tears run down my face, everything hurts, I'm dizzy and losing consciousness fast. I need to tell Evie I love her. I place my hand on her back. "I love you so much, Sweetpea, I'll be watching over you."

"BROOKLYN! Don't you leave me, I need you, *we* need you. Sergio take Evie now." Dom's voice is slipping into the distance.

"Mommy." Evie cries out, but I can't answer.

Darkness is beckoning me, but before I let it completely take over me, I hear Evie crying and feel the warmth of Dominic's body near mine. I hear his whispered words in my ear, telling me to fight, stay with him and how much he loves and needs me. I squeeze his hand with what strength I have left before I let go and float into the darkness.

Twenty

Dominic

I knew I'd shut off part of myself when I lost my momma, but I was still living my life the best way I knew how. I wouldn't allow anyone to get too close to me, worried someone wouldn't accept me for what I do, who I am. But, that changed the day my eyes landed on Brooklyn. It was like she was a bright, beautiful beacon in the night bringing me home. I wasted so many years thinking life was what it was and it wasn't going to get any better, especially for me. I didn't deserve the goodness that was her, but if I had known Brooklyn was out there sooner, I wouldn't have stopped until I had found her. She was all that was good and pure in my life and I've let her down. I failed my mother by not protecting her from a man I thought was a hero and now I've failed my girl's too. How will she ever forgive me? Maybe this is the penalty I have to pay for the life I've lead and the people I've hurt.

"Boss," Antonio speaks quietly from where he sits next to Kat in the waiting room.

I ignore him as I pace back and forth. Sergio stands in the doorway keeping guard. Kat has Evie sleeping in her arms. The doctor has checked them both thoroughly and stitched up Kat's arm. Evie has a few bumps and scrapes which have plasters applied.

I'm not sure how much time has passed but it feels like forever, before the doctor appears holding a clipboard in his hands. He looks tired.

"Mr. Grasso?"

I hurry to stand before him. "Si, how is she?"

"Miss Mackenzie has lost a lot of blood, but we have managed to stop the bleeding, and stitched up both wounds. Thankfully the knife didn't hit anything serious and she should make a full recovery."

I breathe for what feels like the first time in hours. My legs threaten to give way so I lower myself onto a chair and drop my head into my hands as I absorb the news. My Angel is fine and will recover. My breath whooshes out as another thought hits me. I raise my head and look at the doctor. "The bambino?" I feel the tears well in my eyes, my muscles tense as I wait for his reply.

"The baby is fine Mr. Grasso. Like I said before, the knife didn't hit anything serious. We have blood up to replace what she has lost and Brooklyn is currently being moved to a private room. When she is settled, the nurse at the desk will direct you where to go. She'll be sore and may tire easily for the next couple of days."

I nod and extend my hand to shake. "Thank you, Doctor."

"Mommy is ok?" Evie's sleepy little voice comes from beside me. Reaching over, I pick her up and set her on my lap. I breathe in her unique scent so much like her mommas, but there's still a hint of the stale, musty smell.

"Yes Princess, momma is fine and so is your little brother or sister."

"I want to see mommy." Evie sobs into the side of my neck. I run a soothing hand over her back and raise an eyebrow at the doctor. He stares at me for a moment until he realizes what I am silently asking.

"I'll go and check if she's ready for visitors."

"You do that." I don't mean to be terse, but my daughter needs to see her momma is okay with her own eyes.

Brooklyn

A constant beeping sound and the hum of a machine alongside me is like a fucking jackhammer in my head. Then, I feel the soft press of lips to my forehead and I moan.

"Angel." The familiar husky voice whispering in my ear, makes me smile and heat floods through my body as his warm breath tickles my neck. My eyes flutter open and I'm greeted with the same beautiful green eyes which captured my heart just a couple of short months ago. There was always something about his eyes, they have the ability to see straight into my soul.

"Big man." My voice is hoarse and I swallow at the dryness in my throat. Dom holds a cup of water with a straw toward me. Taking a welcoming sip, I clear my throat. "Thank you."

"Always." He leans over me and kisses my forehead.

"Where's Evie?"

"Antonio and Kat took her to get a drink once we knew you were okay. I wanted to speak with you alone." He sighs and runs a hand through his hair before settling on the side of the bed and gathering my hands in his. "Do you remember what happened?"

I watch my fingers twisting in the blanket covering my lap and nod. He places his hands over mine to stop the movement. I look up into his eyes, as tears roll down my face. "I'm sorry Dom, so s-s-sorry." I gaze out the window of my room.

"Shhh... Angel, please don't cry. Look at me, darling." When I make eye contact, he continues. "You have *nothing* to be sorry about. It's me who should be sorry, I fucked up. I didn't keep my promise, I failed you and our daughter." He bows his head and tears drip from his chin. My heart aches for him.

I squeeze his hands. "No, Dom, please. You didn't fail us. You couldn't have known, we all thought he was dead. This is not on you, *I* brought that monster into your life."

I wince when I scoot over a little, I try to hide the pain, but Dom notices and gives me a sad look. Patting the bed beside me, I whisper, "Hold me." In less than a second, he's beside me. He places his arm around my shoulders ever so gently and I snuggle against his hard chest. I moan at the contact, realizing how much I've missed him.

"Are you okay, Angel. Did I hurt you?"

"No big man, you didn't hurt me."

Bending down he kisses the top of my head.

Running my fingers lightly over his chest, I feel the shiver that runs through his body. "I love you Dom, so much. Please don't leave me. Please don't toss us away."

He places his fingers under my chin and lifts my head. "Angel, I promise from the bottom of my heart, I'm not going anywhere. I'm not letting you go. I can't. You have stolen my heart and without you, I couldn't survive. You make every day worth living. You give me a joy I didn't know existed. I love you with every fiber of my being."

"I'm sorry…"He places his fingers over my lips.

"Don't be sorry, my Angel. Just keep loving me and allow me to love you." He runs his fingers through my hair.

"Okay," I whisper as I breathe in his scent.

I must have drifted off because I wake up at the sound of the door opening and see Antonio, Kat and Evie enter the room. I can't, and don't want to, stop the tears from falling when I see they are both okay. They both smile brightly at me. Antonio lifts Evie onto the bed before sitting in a chair and pulling Kat onto his lap. I smile at Kat through my tears and she shrugs her shoulders.

"Mommy," Evie speaks softly as she crawls up beside me. "I missed you so much."

I pull her into my arms and kiss her head. "I'm here, Sweetpea. I'm not going anywhere, I promise." I hug her tight trying not to let the pain show on my face, I guess I don't do a good enough job though.

Dom pats Evie's back. "Gentle with momma, Princess."

Evie pulls back and wipes her hand under her nose. "I'm sorry, momma."

Before I can reassure her that I'm okay, the door opens again and a doctor walks in studying a chart in his hand.

"Oh, there's a full house in here." He smiles warmly at me, but when he looks toward Dom, the smile leaves his face.

Dom is scowling, he's jealous. I think I'm correct when I feel Dom's arm around me, pull me closer. It's caveman behavior, but I love it. It means I'm his and I know he is mine. I glance at Kat and she is trying hard not to laugh.

"Brooklyn, how are you feeling? My name is Dr. James Williams."

"I'm okay, a little sore but okay."

"You will be sore for a couple of weeks and you may tire easily. I came by to check in with you and give you something for the headache you must have, it's safe to take these while you're pregnant." I take the small cup containing pills which he offers. "I also wanted to have quick chat about something if that's okay with you?"

Dom straightens and I feel him tense. "Is everything okay, Doctor?"

"Yes, it's nothing to be alarmed about. I hope."

"What is it?" I'm starting to become worried.

"Would you like to talk in private?" The doctor glances around the room.

I follow his line of vision, this is my family, I have no issue with him speaking in front of everyone. I shake my head. "No, I want my family here."

Dr. Williams nods and glances at the chart in his hands before looking up again. "When you were brought in and we were informed you were pregnant, we gave you an ultrasound to check everything was okay with your child."

I nod my head, chewing my bottom lip as I wonder where he is going with this. "Is something wrong with our baby?" I grip Dom's hand and squeeze when I feel him tense up beside me.

"No, everything is fine. It's just, the ultrasound revealed something, I don't think you're aware of."

"Tell us now, Doc."

I watch as the Doctor swallows hard at the demand in Dom's voice. "I believe you're having twins."

My mouth drops open and my eyes widen, did he just say twins? "What?"

"We can't be one hundred percent sure this early in a pregnancy, and there are a number of other things it could be, but there's a good chance you are carrying twins. When the technician performed the ultrasound she heard a faint echo of a second heartbeat and detected what could be the start of a second child."

"Oh god, Dom… Twins!" I notice the sparkle in his eyes and the sexy smirk that starts to curl his lips.

"Thank you, Doctor." Dom dismisses the doctor while still not taking his eyes off me. When the door shuts, Dom slides his hand into my hair, pulls me closer and kisses me like a man who is completely and utterly in love.

"Twins. Two. Two babies. Two of them." I know I'm rambling.

Dom chuckles and winks at me.

"I'm going to have two brothers!" Evie squeals and bounces on the bed as she claps her hands. Kat scoops her up so she doesn't accidently jump on me.

"Brother's? Two. Two boys. Maybe two girls. Maybe one boy and one girl." I'm in shock.

Everyone bursts into laughter. Dom hugs me close and kisses my temple.

"Si, two, darling. That's usually what twins are."

I look at our daughter. "Brothers, Evie?"

"Si, brothers. Daddy said we're not allowed to have any more girls in the family, only boys. He said you and me are his girls and we're special."

I swing my head towards Dom, waiting for him to reply. When he doesn't, I raise my eyebrow, trying to pull off an intimidating look. I guess it doesn't work when he bites his lip to stop from laughing. *"Grande Uomo?"*

Dom gives me a surprised look when I call him 'Big Man' in Italian. "Angel, if we have any more girls, I'm likely to spend my later life in prison. I'm already going to be getting into trouble when Evie gets old enough to start dating. Do you think I'm going let any boy come near my girl?" He raises his eyebrows at me. "So, my Princess and I have decided, it has to be boys."

Kat and Antonio burst into laughter, setting me off. I stop and cry out when a sharp pain tears through my side.

"Okay, Angel, that's enough excitement for one day. Time for you to rest now, my darling."

"I want to go home to our bed?" I pout.

"I'll see what I can do after you rest here for a few days." Despite his words, I know he'll get me home as soon as he can regardless of what the doctors say.

I sink back against the pillows as Dom gets to his feet. Evie crawls back up the bed and snuggles into my chest. Kat stands and gives me a hug before whispering in my ear, "Congrats Dollface, love you so much."

"I love you too Kat, I'm so happy you're okay."

She steps back so Antonio can give me a hug and a small kiss on the cheek, he chuckles low when we hear Dom growl.

Antonio leans back and raises his hands in the air. "Boss, she's like a sister to me." Wrapping his arms around Kat, he bends and kisses her gently. "I have all I'll ever need right here."

"Awww," I say, that was so sweet.

"Shut ya face bitch," Kats laughs.

Dom chuckles as he looks at Antonio. "Si, I understand, but right now, I think it's time for my girls to get some rest and then we can all head home."

Kat and Antonio wish us goodnight and head out the door. Once the door closes, Dom plants a small kiss to my lips. "I'll be back soon. I'll go and take care of the paperwork."

"I love you, big man," I mumble as my eyes become heavy.

"Love you too, *il Mio Amore*. Now sleep." He kisses my forehead before doing the same to Evie and instructing her to watch over me.

Twenty-One

Dominic

I speak with the doctor and tell him to get the discharge papers done so I can take my girls home. He's not happy about it, but I agree to have Brooklyn checked daily while she's at home and bring her back if there is any concern.

I enter the room quietly and lower myself into a chair by the bed. I watch my girls sleeping. I can't get the image of Brooklyn in the filthy room, so pale and beaten, out of my mind. There was so much blood, my heart stopped when I thought I'd lost her. The thought of never hearing her laugh again just about broke me. I put my hand in my pocket and feel the weight of her ring. It needs to go back where it belongs. I take it from my pocket, reach over, take her small hand in mine and slip it back where it goes, planting a forever kiss to seal her fate.

"I thought he stole it from me," Angel whispers out

"I'm sorry, I didn't mean to wake you."

"You didn't."

I grunt, the sleepy look on her face tells me she's not speaking the truth. She smiles squeezes my hand in hers.

"Twins, Dom."

"Si, twins. I couldn't be a happier man." Having that bombshell dropped earlier blew my mind. Never in my life did I think I would be lucky enough to ever have a family. But, now I do I will lay my life on the line for them.

"I will protect my family. I will not fail you girls, or these precious babies, ever again." I reach over and place my hand on her belly, lowering my head to the bed. Brooklyn places one hand over mine and runs the other through my hair.

"You didn't fail us, Dom and I know you will always protect us. Where did you find my ring?"

I know she's changing the subject, but I go along with it "It was in the back seat of the Lexus, it must have come off when…" I trail off, not wanting to finish.

"Oh, God. How's Demetri?" She whispers so as not to disturb Evie.

"He's okay. Doc took care of him at the house, he's sore but okay. the bullet grazed his shoulder."

"How did you find us?"

"Well…" I breathe out I knew this conversation was coming. I just didn't expect it to be right now. "Sergio called and told me you girls were missing and Demetri had been shot. Antonio and I raced to the Newcastle baths to meet with him. When we got there, I checked the car. I found your bag which had your phone in it, I wasn't happy."

Brooklyn gives me a strange look so I explain. "I had Theo put a chip in your phone a couple of weeks ago so I could track you if something happened. I'm sorry, but I was worried and I wanted to know you were safe when I wasn't with you." I pause and wait for her to yell at me, but she doesn't.

"I understand," she says quietly.

Fuck! I thought there would be a fight on my hands about it. "You're not angry with me?"

She shakes her head "No Big Man, I'm not angry. I would have preferred you tell me about it, but I understand why you did it."

This is why I can't lose her, this beautiful woman gets me. She understands me. "It didn't matter because it was in the car so I couldn't track it anyway. I was lost, I didn't know who took my girls or where they took you. Sergio and Antonio rang every contact we had, but they came up empty. Antonio tried to call Kat, but her phone either rang out or kept going to voice mail. I thought maybe she was ignoring his calls so I grabbed your phone to call her When I opened it, your messages flashed on the screen. Antonio was looking over my shoulder at the screen. He had just finished telling me that Kat was supposed to meet you at home, she had gotten up early and left the house before he had to leave for our meeting. Knowing the two stories, everything clicked into place and we realized, Kat was being used to find you girls. We knew Kat had her phone so Antonio had Theo put a trace on it. Antonio got the program up on his phone and began tracking where she'd been taken, we knew you would be there too. We had a rough idea where you were, but needed to be sure. Kat's phone was either in a bad service area or it was going flat because we had to keep pulling over and waiting for the signal to come through again. Once we got into Sydney the signal was stronger and led us to where you used to live with your parents, that's when we knew who had you. That piece of shit actually took you to his old house next to your parent's place."

I close my eyes, not able to stand the tears coming from her eyes "I'm sorry I wasn't there soon enough, Angel. I'm sorry I didn't deal with him myself two months ago."

Brooklyn caresses my face and wipes away the tears. "It's not your fault. He was a psychopath. He murdered innocent people and k...k...killed my parents." Her voice cracks on a sob.

I lay on the bed and pull her into my arms, her head rests on my chest. FUCK! "I'm so sorry, Angel." I run my hand softly down her side making sure I don't hurt her. She cries and I hold her in my arms, thankful that she is still here with me. I whisper in her ear how much I love her until her breaths even out and she drifts off to sleep. I need to take my girls home where I can take care of them.

Brooklyn

After spending the night in a very uncomfortable bed, with monitors beeping and drips being checked, I'd had enough and wanted to go home. The doctor finally agreed and we spent the next three hours in the car traveling home. While Evie slept, I spent the time explaining everything that had happened yesterday to Dom. He had listened quietly, but I had noticed how much it affected him, from the clench of his hands to the tic in his jaw. When I explained, Darren had not been the one who threw the brick through the window, I saw the worry swimming in his eyes. I knew he wouldn't stop until he found who was responsible.

When we arrived home, I was carried bridal style to our bed and ordered not to get up. I protested and pouted, but Dom explained, the doctor had said I needed to rest because he worried about the stitches in my side tearing. Reluctantly, I agreed. I didn't want to worry Dom and I had two babies to take care of. So here I am, snuggled up in my blankets with a sleeping Evie beside me. Dom is downstairs in his office taking care of some business and making a couple of phone calls. I start to drift off to sleep, determined not to think about the last day and a half. We're home and safe.

⸎❧❦❧⸎

My stomach growls, waking me and letting me know I need to eat. Evie is still sound asleep so I wriggle to the other side of the bed and push myself up on shaky legs, ignoring the shooting pains in my side. I reach for the walking stick the doctor insisted I use for the next couple of weeks. I need food and I really don't want to bother Dom. I know he's busy trying to work out who threw the brick and there's still the matter of the car that ran into us.

I leave the bedroom and take the steps one at a time so as not to lose my balance and fall. I hear a woman's voice coming from the living room. *Who the fuck is that?*

"She stole you from me," she cries out. "You were mine, and she took you away from me."

"I was never yours," Dom snarls. "Put the gun down. Now!"

I freeze when I hear a gun is involved. What the fuck is going on? And, where have I heard that voice before?

"Tell me how you got in here?" Dom asks more calmly.

I descend the stairs as quick as I can, ignoring the pain shooting through my side. I try to make as little noise as possible. Once on the ground floor, I breathe through the pain and peek around the corner of the door. Dom is standing near one of the chairs and has a hard look on his handsome face. There's a woman standing in front of him, her back is to me. She has long black hair, and sure enough, her hand is raised pointing a gun straight at Dom's chest. SHIT! What am I supposed to do now? I glance to the other side of the foyer toward Dom's office and wonder if I can make it in there without being seen. I place the walking stick on the floor softly, so as not to make a sound and tiptoe toward the office door, wincing in pain when I put weight on my leg. Am I really going to do this? Yes, I am I can't shy away, I need to be strong and protect my man.

<hr>

Dominic

God, it feels good having my girls home again. Leaving them in bed to rest was hard because all I wanted to do was lay down and hold them, but with what Angel told me on the way home about Darren, I knew I had to try and figure this shit out. I need to protect my family.

Hearing a noise in the kitchen I glance at the clock and see it's after 7pm. Shit, I didn't realize how late it had gotten, Angel and Evie must be starving. Pushing back from my desk, I head towards the kitchen to make dinner. I don't want Brooklyn out of bed. As I cross into the living room to switch on some music, I stop dead. Fuck, what the hell is she doing here?

"Good evening Dominic," she purrs. Her voice is like nails on a chalkboard.

"How the fuck did you get in here?"

"Did you miss me, baby?"

"Janet, how the fuck did you get in here?" I fold my arms over my chest letting her know I'm damn angry.

"Joey." She shrugs like breaking into my home is no big deal.

She struts toward me like she's on parade on a catwalk. I don't want her anywhere near me so I cross the living room and stand near one of the armchairs opposite her.

"You need to leave. Now!"

"I'm not going anywhere." Her voice is cold, menacing.

"Why are you here?"

"I came here because that little bitch of yours was too stupid to understand, you are mine. I need to get rid of her so we can be together."

"I'm not yours and never will be." I shake my head, has this bitch completely lost her mind?

"She stole you from me," she cries out. "You were mine and she took you away from me."

She pulls a gun and points it straight at my chest. Fuck! "I was never yours." I need to try and calm this shit down. "Put the gun down, now!" I need to get her talking so I can work out a way to get the gun away from her. "Tell me how you got in here?" How did I not notice how crazy this bitch was?

"I thought for sure the brick would have done the job, but when it didn't work, I got Joey to run you off the road. The stupid dickhead was high and fucked it up, so I took matters into my own hands and stole his keys. I knew one of them would get me in here, so I could show you what you were missing by being with that slut and her brat of a child."

I nod my head for her to go on because I don't trust myself to speak or move right now. I want to rip her apart for saying shit about my girls.

"It should be me, Dom? You were supposed to be mine. I have waited long enough, so if *I* can't have you, then neither can that stupid bitch." She raises the gun in her shaking hand as tears roll down her face.

BANG! BANG! BANG!

WHAT THE FUCK! I watch as Janet's eyes widen and watch as blood seeps through her shirt. The gun falls from her hand, she falls to her knees and clutches at her chest to stop the blood. It's no use and she crumples to the floor. Dead.

I look up expecting one of my men to be standing near, but it's my Angel.

"She tried to take what's mine." Angel shrugs her shoulders.

"Fuck, Angel"

"What? I told you, you're mine and *no-one* takes what is mine."

"You look sexy as fuck holding my gun." I'm lost for words, my Angel saved my life. I expect her to realize what she has just done and fall apart, but she doesn't. She gazes into my eyes with a look of lust and defiance. This woman blows my fucking mind. I look her over and that's when I notice the blood on her pajama pants. "Shit, Angel you're bleeding." I rush to her side, sweep her into my arms take the steps two at a time heading for our bedroom.

"I'm okay, Big Man."

After placing her on the bed, I bend and kiss her forehead

"I'll call Doc, and then call my men to come and clean up the mess downstairs."

"Daddy, what was that banging noise?" I look to Brooklyn wondering what the hell to tell her but she speaks first.

"Daddy was testing some fireworks he bought, for when we get married. I'm sorry they woke you."

I glance at Brooklyn then at Evie thinking there is no way in hell she'll believe that. I know she's only five, but she has the intelligence of an eight-year-old. Yeah, yeah, I know, I'm biased.

"Ok mommy." She sits up and rubs her eyes. "I'm hungry."

Well fuck me, she believed it. Now I have to get my hands on some fireworks.

"Why don't you stay with momma, and I'll bring food up."

I don't want her coming downstairs and seeing blood everywhere. My Princess has already seen enough shit in her life, and I will spend forever protecting her from anymore.

"Okay, daddy. Ice cream too please, daddy?" She bats those damn eyelashes at me, and I can't say no.

"Si, but will you have a sandwich first?"

Worrying her little lip with her teeth, she's quiet for a moment as if deep in thought. "Okay, I guess I can eat a sandwich." She pouts just like her mother.

Chuckling, I look toward Angel and notice she's watching us closely. "Are you okay?"

"Never better Big Man. Can I have some ice cream too, please?" She bats her eyelashes as well, making me laugh. Like mother, like daughter. I'm fucked.

"Si, but a sandwich first for you too?" Brooklyn looks toward Evie and pouts, then they both look at me with big puppy dog eyes. My heart beat a little bit faster, and my breath freeze in my chest. Fuck! Me, a Mafia Boss reduced to jelly by two girls.

"Jesus Christ!" I leave the room and hear the pair of them start giggling. I smile to myself as I make my way down the stairs. Pulling the phone from my pocket, I send Antonio and Doc a quick text. I'll have to organize my men to find Joey. I'll get Antonio onto that when he gets here, we may not find him straight away but he can't hide forever.

I have to be the luckiest *stronzo* alive. I have the love of a beautiful woman who sooner, rather than later *will* become my wife. A beautiful daughter who stole my heart the moment she smiled at me and not one, but very possibly two precious babies on the way. What more could I ask for? I never believed in fairy-tales and love at first sight, I thought it was all bullshit, but looking into those crystal blue eyes, brought me to my knees and changed my life forever. I wouldn't have it any other way.

Brooklyn

I lay back on my pillow, hold Evie closer and run my fingers through her silky soft hair, my other hand rests on my belly. I reflect on what happened downstairs. I probably should feel bad about pulling the trigger and taking somebody's life, but I don't. I heard her confess to throwing the brick through the window and organizing the car crash. She tried to kill my daughter, the children in my belly, and the one man who has shown me what true happiness and love really are. A man who wants to give me the fairy-tale I was told of as a child. There was no way in hell I was going to let that bitch take it all away from me. So, no I don't feel bad, I finally found the strength and the courage to protect what was mine.

Dominic is the best thing that has ever happened to Evie and me, and though he says he doesn't deserve us, I will spend the rest of my life proving him wrong. I know he will love us completely and protect us with his life. I'm not weak anymore and I have Dominic to thank for that.

With all the shit I've been through in the past few years, most people would probably run scared from a man like Dominic.

A man who walks in and turns your world upside down. But, when you go through what I have, being beaten and broken so badly you are driven into a deep dark hole that you never believe you can crawl out of, not knowing whether you will survive the next time something happens. You realize, a man like Dom is a man you think you will only ever read about in books.

When a man like Dom does come into your life, a man who offers you the world and promises to keep you safe in the dark, then a person like me will jump at the chance to have a love like I never knew existed. To many, he may not be the white knight riding in on a horse to save the day, or a Prince planting a small kiss on your lips to wake you from an eternity of sleep so you can ride off into the sunset together. All they see is a dangerous man, a man who has the power to hurt you. They don't see his struggles or that he has had to fight his own demons to get to where he is now. A man who believes he's a failure because he couldn't protect his mother from a monster he once thought was a hero.

Yet, with all that he struggles with, he is still willing to fight your demons so you can sleep peacefully at night. He will build you back up when you get knocked down. I will take him as he, faults and all because the Dominic I fell in love with is not just a Mob Boss, he's a man of honor and loyalty who everybody else can only dream about finding.

I will be forever his missing piece and he will be forever Mine.

Epilogue

6 months later...

Brooklyn

I stare at myself in the full-length mirror in our bedroom, I can't believe how big I have grown. I run my hands over my belly thinking how truly lucky I am and shiver when I feel him come up behind me. He pulls me back against his hard chest and I melt all over. At first, I worried the connection we had would fade over time, but every day it grows stronger. I turn in his arms and stare into those captivating emerald eyes that reflect how much he loves me.

"If you keep looking at me like that I will bend you over the end of the bed and take what is mine." Dom nips my ear before sucking it into his mouth, soothing the sting and making me moan, as I feel a sensation of pure lust run through my body.

Unfortunately, Dom smacks my ass and takes a step back with a cocky smile on his face. There will be no satisfaction from him this time. Bastard, he knows exactly how his words affect me. Especially with all these pregnancy hormones running wild through me. It feels like my body is on fire all the time and I can't get enough of the big man.

"Don't pout, Mrs. Grasso, we have to go pick up Evie and take her for ice cream."

I love it when he calls me Mrs. Grasso, it makes me feel like I belong and that I'm loved. I look him up and down. I swear the man gets sexier every day. He's dressed in a pair of black suit pants that fit him perfectly in all the right places, he has a white singlet vest on, and hanging around his neck, the gold necklace with a St Christopher pendant and Cross which I gave him as a wedding present. He never takes it off and he constantly tells me, apart from Evie and I, it's the best gift he's ever received.

Our wedding was such a magical day and I will never forget it. Maybe one day I'll tell you all about it but right now I'm pissed! I want his hard body over mine making me scream. God, damn it! But, like Dom, I miss my Sweetpea, and can't wait for her hugs and kisses. She spent the night at Gwen and Harry's so I could rest before I bring these babies into the world. Right. Rest? Not much of that happened with us here alone.

Yes, that's right, I said babies as in plural. We received confirmation a while back that we are indeed having twins. Dom has been even more protective than ever before. He reads every piece of information about twin pregnancies that he can lay his hands on and tries to follow most of it to the letter. I don't get upset, I know it comes from a good place and he only wants us healthy and safe. I smile knowing he really is the sweetest man I have ever met.

"What's that smile for *il Mio Amore*?" He steps toward me and rubs both his hands over my belly. We decided we wouldn't find out what we are having. Dom said it didn't matter because he already knows I'm going to give him sons. He talks to my belly every night telling them how he will teach them to be big and strong so they can help him protect their sister from future boys who will never deserve her. Like I said before, he is the sweetest man. And I am lucky enough to call him Mine.

"Um, I'm thinking about hugs and kisses from Evie and ice cream."

He cocks his head to the side as if waiting for more and I try not to laugh but a giggle slips free.

"And?" I cock an eyebrow when he smirks at me.

"Oh, and how sweet you are, like a little puppy." I laugh when the smirk drops and a stern expression takes over his face.

With a growl of desire, he scoops me up and places me on the bed. He hovers over me, careful not to place his weight on my belly. Leaning forward, he growls in my ear and I shiver. "I'll show you how *sweet* I can be and then we'll go and get my princess." He nips my ear, sending shocks of electricity zapping through my body, running his hand through my hair, he grips it at the back of my neck and kisses me hard waiting for me to grant him access. His other hand slides over my swollen belly, heat pools low in my belly as he cups me in the possessive way I love so much. He massages my throbbing clit with the palm of his hand. "Mine, Angel!"

"Yours. Forever Yours, Big Man."

THE END

Katherine

The day Antonio walked into my Café, I knew things were about to change. He had a presence about him that commanded attention. I could see the shadows in his eyes of things I could never understand. He was a force to be reckoned with, taking what he wanted, when he wanted. He was big, strong and had eyes the color of the finest chocolate. Everything he made me feel, scared the hell out of me.

When he opened his mouth I wasn't sure if I wanted to slap him or kiss him, he made every nerve in my body come alive. But, I have a secret. I didn't want to let him go, but it's better this way. I have let enough people down in my life so I tried to distance myself and push him away. I never thought I could love or trust any man after my father left, but Antonio was here to prove me wrong and he wasn't going to back down.

Kitten: Antonio was determined to take me to my knees and crack me wide open.

Antonio

Katherine was the kind of woman you could only ever dream about in your wildest fantasies. A woman who screamed sex kitten with every sway of her hips and she had the attitude to go with it. Her hair resembles fire as hot as lava, her eyes are as clear and as blue as the sky on a perfect summers day. And, her body, I swear has a direct line to my cock.

She pushed me away, but I don't go down that easy. I didn't get to where I am today without fighting tooth and nail for it. In my mind and my heart, Katherine was mine, and no matter how long it took me, I was going to make her see she belonged with me like I already belonged to her. I know she is hiding something, I can see it in her eyes every time she looks at me. I don't care what I have to do, or how long it takes, I will find out what it is that keeps her running scared. My kitten isn't the only one with secrets.

Antonio: Katherine brought me to my knees and I was going to take her down with me.

If you have enjoyed reading my book, please leave a review on Amazon.

Kay.